# BEYOND THE GOODNIGHT TRAIL

ROY V. GASTON

For the grand-kiddoes: Isaac, Amari, Mia, Mason and Nick Jr.

Once again, I owe a tremendous debt of gratitude to my tireless editor, Debra Gaston Brigman. Thanks for keeping me inside the lines, on the page and off.

# JIM CLEMENTS

I also want to express a huge and very special thanks to my new friend Jim Clements, the wonderfully talented artist and fellow lover of the West who generously allowed me the use of his painting, "Long Drive Ahead," for my cover.

Jim's painting perfectly captures the trail-weary determination, toughness, grit and guts - with a touch of tenderness and humanity - of both my character, Pete Horse, and the West as I imagine it. Everyone should treat themselves to a trip to the Old West by visiting Jim's page: www.jimclementsart.com I guarantee you'll feel better for doing so.

Thank you, Jim, for the use of your painting, and capturing the spirit of the West and sharing it with the rest of us.

> "To me, painting represents ultimate freedom - so it's just natural that the wide-open spaces, rich history and independent people of the American West translate so well to canvas. My desire is to honor the spirit of the West in each painting I do."
>
> Jim Clements

Jim's work has won many awards over the years and has been featured in numerous publications including the El Dorado Times, the Wichita Eagle, USA Today, Florida Today, Art Calendar magazine, American Art Collector, Southwest Art, Bridle and Bit, Rodeo Attitude, Derby Now magazine, the Topeka Capital-Journal and Better Horses magazine.

The National Day of the Cowboy Organization based in Fort Worth, TX, selected Jim's painting titled "Simple Things" as the image for its prestigious Cowboy Keeper Award, given annually to individuals or organizations that have made a substantial contribution to the preservation of the West.

Over the years, his work also has been selected for exhibition in many national shows including: the National Cowboy Symposium & Celebration, Lubbock, TX; the Annual Stampede Western Invitational

Art Exhibit, Greeley, CO; the Annual American Plains Artists Juried Exhibit, held in various galleries throughout the West; Kansas Academy of Oil Painters exhibits; the National Small Oil Painting Exhibition, Wichita, KS; American Royal Western Art Show, Kansas City, MO; Birger Sandzen Memorial Gallery, Lindsborg, KS; Art on the Llano Estacado, Lubbock. TX; Windows to the West, Estes Park, CO and Spirit of the West Festival, Sioux Falls, SD.

His paintings are in the permanent collection of The Coutts Memorial Art Museum in El Dorado, KS. He was also the solo artist at a show in the Woolaroc Museum in Bartlesville, OK.

Jim counts actors Barry Corbin (Lonesome Dove, Urban Cowboy, Conagher) and Robert Fuller (Laramie, Wagon Train, Emergency!) among his collectors. His work has also been praised by popular singer Michael Martin Murphy (Wildfire, What's Forever For, Long Line of Love) as "A true master painter of the American West."

Jim's home and studio are located on the prairie in the Flint Hills region of south central Kansas.

Jim Clements

P.O. Box 402
El Dorado, Kansas 67042
Ph: 316.655.1248
Website: www.jimclementsart.com
E-mail: jim@jimclementsart.com

"I won't be wronged. I won't be insulted. I won't be laid a-hand on. I don't do these things to other people, and I require the same from them."

John Bernard Books, "The Shootist"

# Contents

# ONE

# TEXAS PANHANDLE
# NEAR THE PEASE RIVER
## DEC. 18, 1860

Chief Peta Nocona's Comanche village spread out along the creek two hundred yards below us, partially hidden by a grove of bare-limbed cottonwoods. After five days of hard riding across West Texas we had cut the trail of Nocona's raiding party and followed it here, to where the freshwater stream of Mule Creek flows into Pease River. It was called the Rio de Los Lingos, the River of Tongues, for the many languages spoken by those who had met here for centuries to barter horses and women and cattle and children.

"A tad airish, ain't it, amigo?" Charlie Goodnight said. We were in heavy buffalo robes, stretched out on our bellies at the top of a brush-covered sand hill.

"A might," I said. It was time for sunup, but the roiling mass of storm clouds kept the sky black as a coal mine. The front winds of the coming Texas blue norther whipped sand and grit into our faces and the temperature had dropped twenty degrees in the last hour. The cold rain and sleet was just now hitting us.

"I don't see sign of any lookouts," said Charlie. "The Comanche must figure the storm kept us holed up somewhere east. Or turned back completely."

We had ridden 125 blustering, bitter-cold miles across the ravine-scarred mesquite prairies of Texas, from Parker County to this camp high in the Texas Panhandle canyons. Texans rarely pursued this deep into the heart of Comancheria. The rough country of the Caprock

Escarpment was a nature-made fortress for the raiders, but the brutality of Nocona's latest assault demanded retribution.

At least 23 people had been killed and mutilated by the Comanche in their rampage across Texas. Dozens more were slashed, outraged and tortured. Not dead, at least not fast or merciful. Women and children had been stolen, along with hundreds of horses and plunder. The horrors inflicted on the female victims had sickened and enraged the toughest of us. It was as bad as any of the savagery I had seen in my three decades on the frontier. The victims were friends and neighbors. Good, peaceful people, and barely a man with us was not kin to one or more of them.

"I don't see much but squaws and old folks down there. Sure ain't no five hunnert like some told," said Charlie. He'd only been with the Rangers for two years, but Charlie knew this part of Texas better than any other white man I knew. He was a cool head and steady hand.

"I know it," I said. "But Sul's so all-fired determined to attack him some Indians it ain't gonna matter."

A dozen tipis were beside the icy creek where the red cliffs of the canyon blocked the roaring wind. Small cook fires flickered inside the lodges, creating an orange glow like a field of fire-flies. Outside in the murky light, squaws in buffalo robes loaded pack-mules with heavy loads of hide-wrapped buffalo meat. Fifty yards past the southernmost tipi, a herd of a hundred or so Indian ponies grazed.

Hidden by the black clouds, Captain Sul Ross and a company of sixty Texas Rangers and soldiers from Ft. Belknap waited in the ravine a hundred yards back. They were a capable bunch, but they weren't exactly the Rangers of Captain Jack Hays, the bold and fearless warrior leader I'd ridden with in my youth.

"That's them, I take it," said Captain Ross after he joined us under the brittle sage bushes. He propped himself up on his elbows to peer down into the valley. A handful of others crouched just behind him.

"Some of them anyway," I said. "The big group split up into half a dozen small ones. Like we expected. Like always."

"No sign of alarm from the camp?" asked Ross.

"No, they have no idea we're here," I said.

"Complete surprise," said Ross. "Excellent. They never expected us to follow them all the way home."

"Only problem is, I've seen few warriors amongst them," said Charlie. "Squaws packing their winter meat and old men going about their morning necessary is all that's down there."

"I'm not sure how you can make that judgment in this poor visibility," snapped Ross.

"Plenty of light to see them folks," I said.

"That's not your concern. Governor Sam Houston himself has decreed all Indians seen on this side of Red River are open enemies of Texas. Our horses are played out, and, as you said, it looks like they're packing to move," said Captain Ross. "Am I not correct on those points?"

"You are," I said.

"Let's get after them before they spot us. We'll not have another opportunity like this," said Ross. "Sgt. Spangler, take your twenty men and form a line on those sand hills beyond the creek. If they get across there, they will scatter and disappear."

"We best hold back a bit when he sounds the charge," Charlie said as we rode back to the column. "Those boys are awful eager to blaze them pistols hot. I'd prefer not being in front of all that flying lead."

Each Ranger carried a rifle and at least two 44 caliber Colt six-shooters with spare, loaded cylinders. The soldiers carried about the same. Ross had made it clear we were going in under a black flag. There would be no quarter.

"I'm with you," I said. "They're ready to boil over. I don't think Ross could stop them now even if he wanted to. I sure understand avenging dead kin. I just don't think them down there is the responsible party."

The roaring wind covered the noise of our approach as Captain Ross led the column slowly around the hills and onto the flat river bottom. We formed a mounted line of battle in a thicket of mesquite a hundred yards from the camp. An Indian boy at the edge of the camp saw us and shouted the alarm. It was too late.

"Charge!" screamed Ross. The Rangers howled and thundered toward the camp, galloping full out and blasting their six-shooters. The squaws shrieked and ran for cover. Tent flaps flew open and Comanches sprang out, eyes wild in shock.

Bullets, arrows, Indians, and cavalrymen flew in all directions. The few warriors who tried to make a stand were shot to pieces by the onslaught of galloping Rangers. Soldiers charged the tipis, six-guns blowing holes through the animal skin covering. Panicked mules bucked and kicked through the camp, scattering cooking fires and kettles. Bursts of sparks and red-hot embers set tipis afire. Death struggles spun through the flickering orange light. Riderless Indian ponies stampeded through the camp and wounded Indians were trampled under charging cavalry horses. The wind spread the flame and whipped it higher. Gunfire roared over the storm as the Rangers and cavalrymen shot down fleeing Comanches.

In front of me a squaw slung a kettle of hot soup into the face of a charging horse. The horse went wild and pitched the rider. The next trooper shot a hole in the woman's head and galloped on. A charging cavalry horse slammed into a stumbling old Indian, sending him rolling through a campfire.

A dozen figures in flapping blankets and buffalo robes ran for the river and the safety of the wooded canyons on the other side. As the Indians plunged into the icy water, Spangler's men stepped out of cover and unleashed a volley.

A blanket-shrouded Comanche leapt out from behind a burning tipi with an old musket rifle aimed at the back of a mounted Ranger. I fired twice. The Indian screamed and fell backwards onto a half-burned tipi. I trotted my horse forward a few paces and looked at the downed Comanche. The face behind the dirt and blood was that of a young girl. The heavy red blanket had fallen open and ugly pink bubbles leaked out of the hole in her chest. Her lips moved as if to speak but no sound came out. She didn't look at me, just lay there, eyes somewhere in the sky.

I was contemplating whether to finish her suffering when a movement snapped my eyes away. I met the glare of a young Indian boy, ten feet away, younger even than the girl. He was unarmed, but coiled and ready to spring. His light-colored eyes burned with fury as they moved from mine to the pistol I aimed squarely at his bare chest. Before I could squeeze the trigger, three mounted Comanches rushed past, leaning low into their horses' flowing manes. Right behind came two whooping Rangers.

One Ranger's horse crashed to the ground with an arrow in its ear. The rider skidded across a campfire, sending up a shower of sparks. He cursed and rolled out of the fire, hot ash falling from his buffalo robe.

"Come on, let's get after 'em," Charlie shouted and pointed at the fleeing Comanches. I looked for the unhorsed Ranger, saw he was already swinging up onto a loose Indian pony. The boy was gone.

We galloped after the Indians who split up when they reached a long, flat valley. The Rangers pursued the ones that went left. Charlie and I chased the one that veered right and we gained ground quickly as the rider struggled with a heavy bundle. I realized it was a woman with an infant just as Charlie closed in from the other side, unable to see the child.

"Charlie, don't shoot! Don't shoot! She's got a baby," I shouted. I was surprised he heard me above the wind, but he holstered his pistol and spurred to catch up to the fleeing Comanche woman.

At a full gallop we pulled abreast of her and pinned her between us. Charlie grabbed the horse's bridle while I grabbed for the rider. She swung and clawed at my face but lost her balance and plummeted down between the galloping horses. She twisted as she fell, landing hard on her back, but keeping the child hugged safely to her chest.

Charlie hopped down off his horse while I scanned the ridge for any returning Comanche. The woman lay silently on her back, staring at the black sky with wide, terrified eyes as she squeezed the baby tighter. We pulled her to her feet and she didn't resist.

"Americano! Americano!" she suddenly sobbed out. With tears rolling down her face she looked Charlie in the eye, opened her deerskin blouse and exposed her pale breast. Charlie stared hard at her deeply tanned face, darkened even more by dirt and blood and grease from handling the buffalo meat. There was no denying that breast was of a lighter complexion.

"This here is a white woman," said Charlie. "Indians do not have blue eyes."

"Me Cincee Ann, Me Cincee Ann," the woman shouted, slapping her chest with one hand and holding the whimpering child with the other.

"Not just any white woman," I said. "I do believe that is Cynthia Ann Parker. You have rescued the most famous white captive in all Indian country."

"Well, I'll be," said Charlie.

We put Cynthia Ann and the baby on her horse and returned to the smoldering fires and anguish of the few Comanche survivors. Dead Indian bodies sprawled between the charred tipis. The ground was littered with buffalo robes and pieces of lodge cover, blankets, bowls, and moccasins. We had captured some women, children, and ancient white-haired men. They huddled together in misery as cavalrymen gathered souvenirs. At Spangler's cut-off, Indian bodies bobbed face down in pink water. Bright red blotches stained the ice.

Charlie and I left Cynthia Ann with Captain Ross and rode down river to a side canyon that blocked the storm. We built a small fire and seared a big buffalo steak we had pulled out of a Comanche cook fire.

"What did you see back there that's got you so dumpish?" asked Charlie.

"Other than the kilt women and kids?"

"Yep, beside them. This ain't the first fight you been in where people got killed that wasn't supposed to."

"I don't know," I said. "Myself maybe. Maybe nothing."

"What do you mean?"

"Did I ever tell you about when General Jesup's men raided our village in Florida, and shot my people down like dogs? When I was about the age of that boy back there?"

"What boy?"

"Never mind. I've just soured on this whole mess, Charlie," I said. "I've staved this off a long as I can. I just can't do this anymore. I don't know, if by God's rights, whether it's Comanches or Texans or Americans or even Mexicans are entitled to this land. Or none of them. I'll let someone else puzzle that out. I took my personal vengeance long ago. It don't seem right anymore. My daughter and my farm are in Ohio, and I need to get back to 'em. I can't do nothing like this again."

"I reckon you're right, but when they finally start their shooting war back east, they'll need soldiers," said Charlie. "They'll empty every fort in the West. Someone's gotta stay here and keep these settlers safe."

"I venture it's going to be rough on everybody, but I just can't stomach it no more," I said. "I just want to do some farming, raise some horses. If a shooting war breaks out, I'll have to throw in. I hope it don't come to that, but it ain't right, people owning people. I should know. I was owned once myself."

"But it was your pa what owned you, and he set you free before you was growed."

"He did," I said. "I have no memory of my days in bondage. But all them other people, they ain't free, and ain't about to be."

"Yes, sir," said Charlie. "I agree with you there, but, well, I'm a Texan, and I'm duty bound. I got no dog in this fight, but I can't hold with Yankees coming in here and taking over. I'll protect my home from interlopers, Comanche or Yankee. If you join up, I sure hope you don't come this way. I'd hate to have to shoot you."

"That ain't likely," I said. "I figure the fighting will stay well to the east."

# ALONG THE CROSS TIMBERS
## APRIL 1866

"Charlie's a good man to ride the river with. You'll learn a lot from him, as long as you ignore his churlish manner. He generally don't mean anything by it," I said. "If he does, they'll be no mistaking it."

Andy and I were riding south from Oklahoma Territory, headed toward Fort Belknap, Texas. Charlie Goodnight had asked me to scout for a big cattle drive from Belknap up into northern New Mexico Territory.

"I reckon I will," said Andy. "I'm just eager for life off the reservation. I ain't meant to be no plow jockey. This Goodnight fellow, he was a Texas Ranger when you was?"

"We scouted a few trails together."

"He rode with Devil Jack Hays, too, killing Comanche?"

"No, Devil Jack was 20 years ago. Charlie didn't join the Rangers until shortly before the War," I said. "Charlie's a good deal younger than me."

"I was hoping to meet me a great Comanche killer," said Andy. "I'm hoping to get a shot at a few out here."

"He's dispatched his fair share. You shouldn't be so eager to fight a Comanche, or you'll likely have a short, unhappy life," I said. "It can't be made right, what happened to your ma. That was a long time ago. You just got to forget about it."

"Have you? What happened to your mother and sisters?"

"No, I ain't forgot. But I know it's frivolous to be thinking it could be made right."

Andy was as close to family as I had. He was my size, small and lean.

Like me, his long black hair was tied in a thick braid down his back. We had the same dark skin and, with our 25-year age difference, we looked enough alike to be father and son.

We were both Black Seminole, both born as slaves. By years, Andy was still a boy, just seventeen. But three years ago his mother had been stolen by Comanche. He'd been riding as a border guard, protecting our people from slavers, ever since.

There wasn't much call for border guards on the reservation now with the War over and slavery abolished. The situation had been different when I'd first arrived twenty-five years ago, along with a thousand other Black Seminole forced from our home in Florida. We'd been marched across the country to desolate Oklahoma with 100,000 Creek, Cherokee, Seminole, Choctaw, and Chickasaw. We were the Five Civilized Tribes, uprooted by Andrew Jackson's Indian Removal Act and exiled on a journey known as the Trail of Tears.

As Black Seminoles, we were escaped slaves or descended from them. My brother, John Horse, was the man who'd negotiated our surrender with General Jesup. Jesup had promised our emancipation in the new Indian Territory if we laid down our weapons. Of course, that had been a lie. The shame of being duped in that agreement had haunted John ever since.

The acreage allotted for our Black Seminole settlement was actually on Creek land, and the Creeks were very different from the Seminole. The Creeks and Cherokees, both much larger tribes than the Seminoles, had been the earliest tribes exiled to the west under the Removal Act. Unlike the Seminole who had fought ferociously, and very nearly to the last man, the Creeks and Cherokees had barely resisted the Americans. Instead, they had negotiated for cash payments to give up their fertile Georgia territory after gold had been discovered there. For their compliance, the Creeks and Cherokee had received better land, and positions of authority over the other tribes in Oklahoma. Many of the Creek were slave owners themselves, and viewed us as property, either theirs to take, or somebody else's to be returned for a reward. Slavers raided the Black Seminole settlements. At first the slavers were Creeks or whites, but wild Comanche soon followed. There were substantial bounties to be paid for any escaped slave they returned to bondage, and free blacks were snatched up to be sold in Mexico. By the time I reached Oklahoma, I had been manumitted twice, once by my father and once by Colonel Jesup. But our freedom depended on the gun, which never lied, and not the pen, which often did.

"You act like I ain't shot it out with no bad men," Andy said.

"You ain't shot it out with no men as bad as a Comanche war party, that's all I'm saying," I said. "Just don't be all cocky and overconfident, make some dumb mistake. That pretty hair of yours will be adorning an Indian pony bridle."

The boy had guts all day and was a solid hand but chasing a few half-drunk Creek slavers or Army deserters off the reservation wasn't the same as a painted-up war party charging at full frenzy. I knew how he felt. I had once burned with the same hatred of the Comanche.

I was barely twenty when I left the reservation in '42, chasing Eagle Claw. That blood-thirsty savage and his band had just committed a rampage through Oklahoma, killing twenty Seminole and Black Seminole and taking several captives. The captives included my mother and sisters. I set out to take my vengeance at the same time Jack Hays and his Ranger Company showed up in Oklahoma. They were also chasing Eagle Claw and his band, after his similar rampage through Texas.

Since we were chasing the same man, I had practically begged Jack Hays to let me join his Ranger company. Jack couldn't hire me outright as a Ranger, but he did buy fifteen of the horses I'd been ranching. He also paid me a wage to scout. After I signed on with Jack never again was I asked about my manumission papers

It took more than a year for the Rangers to catch up with Eagle Claw's band, after a slight detour of a few months to fight the invading Mexican army. We finally jumped the Comanches at Walker's Creek after they had joined Yellow Wolf's large war party. Fifteen Rangers fought two hundred Comanche, and we whipped them soundly. Captain Jack had armed each of us with five-shot Colt Paterson revolvers. We had one for every pocket and two more around the saddle horn. The Comanche didn't know what hit them. We'd killed nearly fifty Indians at the loss of only one Ranger killed and four bad hurt.

Eagle Claw escaped, and my search for him continued for several years after. Sometimes I rode with Captain Jack; sometimes not. Besides being a fearless warrior, Jack was also a highly sought-after surveyor and was often called away for work. He made a handsome living with that trade in between fighting Comanches, bandits, and Mexicans. By 1850, Jack had his fill of Comanche and moved out to San Francisco to become sheriff.

Mine had been a life of adventure which the boy envied. He ignored my warnings that it was also a life fraught with danger and fear and burying friends. And that the main reason I was alive was almost entirely due to the poor marksmanship of my enemies.

I had gone east after the Pease River incident and made a life. When the War came, I joined the Union Army. I'd been a sergeant in the U.S. 6th Artillery, Colored, defending Fort Pillow, when Gen. Nathan Bedford Forrest sent his cavalry in. I'd taken a bullet to the skull in the slaughter and looked so dead they didn't finish killing me. My brother John paid for a private ambulance to bring me all the way out here to Oklahoma Territory to recuperate.

Six months later, I was healed enough to ride as a border guard against Creek slavers. I soon made fast friends with Andy, who was already guarding our people. After the War, we'd hired on a few times to guide Federal Marshals from Fort Smith across Indian Territory. We'd tracked some half-way tough outlaws and exchanged a few long-range shots with Comanche or Creek raiders. Young as he was, I trusted Andy in a tight predicament.

I'd gotten Charlie's letter back in March, telling me of his grand plan to drive a herd of several thousand wild longhorn cattle six hundred miles, from Central Texas into northern New Mexico, to feed eight thousand starving Navajo at the Bosque Redondo reservation there. His planned route crossed prairie, desert, and hostile Comanche hunting grounds. When Andy found out what I was contemplating he was determined to ride along. He would not take no for an answer.

We were riding light, staying near the edge of the Cross Timbers. The Timbers was a twenty-mile wide strip of dense blackjack and post oak that stretched from the Red River in Oklahoma south to the Brazos, splitting Texas about evenly in half. We stayed close enough to get to the cover of the trees in a hurry, but far enough away not to get jumped from someone hiding in them.

We carried spare guns, ammo, and a little food and grain on two spare mounts. I'd killed an antelope that morning, to go with the hard-tack crackers and cans of beans in our saddlebags. We took our time, as I wanted the horses to get as fat as they could before we started the cattle drive. Our mounts were hot blooded, deep chested, Anglo-Arabian geldings that could run like the wind and keep it up for miles. They'd leave any Indian pony in the dust, and I knew this because they already had. I rode the flaxen-maned silver dapple. The others were bays. I'd raised them on my little ranch, and they had the blood of the best racehorses in the Oklahoma territory.

We rested often in the meadows bright with bluebonnets, orange Indian paintbrush and pink primrose. Streams were plentiful with bass and blue gill; game and graze for the horses was abundant. We spent about half of every third day with fishing lines tied to long sticks soaking in cool pools in the creeks. I figured we should pamper ourselves now since over the next couple months such opportunities would be rare.

"Hold up," I said to Andy. I pulled my binoculars out of my saddle bags and watched the line of specks cresting a distant hill. We were riding right down the Comanche War Trail and my eyes were always on the horizon. It wasn't time for their fall raids yet, but we always needed to be wary.

"Twelve riders, fifteen, coming fast. Get to the trees," I said.

"Trouble?"

"Not if they don't see us," I said. The trees were half a mile to the east, and these riders were a good five miles away. They were pushing lathered-up horses and looking over their shoulders. In these parts, people didn't run their horses into the ground without reason.

We reached the trees and walked the horses back a hundred feet into the cool darkness of the forest. After we hobbled the horses in a patch of shaded sweet grass, we laid our rifles and ammunition out behind a log and waited. It was unlikely they'd spot us, but we could handle a siege if it was called for. Each of us had two 15 round 44 caliber Henry lever action repeating rifles, one carried in our saddle scabbards, another on a spare mount. We also each had five 44 Caliber Colt 1860 Single-action Army pistols. One on our hip, two on pommel holsters, and two more in the saddle bags. The bags also held six extra loaded cylinders apiece, ready to switch out.

That was the Hays way. Always carry all the pistols you can. When I rode with Jack, each Ranger was armed with enough Colt revolvers to fire twenty shots before needing to reload. Central Texas had been cleared of hostiles for a good many years that way.

An hour later the group passed our hiding place, walking their drooping horses now. With binoculars I could see every detail. They looked about done for, red eyed and flagging. I worried they might stop right in front of us, but they continued on a few hundred yards to a finger of trees where the stream formed a small pool.

I'd never met him, but I knew the man in front. Luther Walsh, with his plumed Hardee hat pinned with a Jeff Davis eagle. Walsh, depending on who you asked, was variously a dashing Rebel cavalry colonel, a fire-breathing radical secessionist, a wealthy slave planter or a wanted outlaw and murdering bandit. He still wore his cadet gray officer's shell jacket with the two yellow stars of a lieutenant colonel on the collar. Gold braided Austrian knots covered his sleeves from wrist to elbow, and black dragoon boots rose over his knees.

"That's the Luther Walsh gang," I said. "Good thing we came over here."

"They have a problem with you?"

"No, not personally, but those boys are true believers in the way things was before the War," I said. "They're the ones been burning Freedmen's homes, along with assorted destruction and disruptions waged against the Yankee government in Texas."

It was a rough looking group in odds and ends of tattered and sun-bleached Confederate jackets or yellow-striped cavalry trousers. They wore black knee-flap boots and battered kepi's, or wide brimmed slouch hats pulled down low over their eyes. The outlaws carried smooth handled tied-down Colts worn cavalry style and bandoleers of rifle cartridges crisscrossed on their chests.

There were many defeated Rebels at the end of the War, but these men did not look defeated. Trail-worn and hungry looking, no doubt, but still itching for a fight. Rugged, expert horsemen, absolutely fearless in battle. All were heavy with trail dust, unshaven for days or with long unkempt beards down to their chests. There were a couple Indians in cast-off army coats and black, flat-brimmed hats. They were Creeks that had ridden with Colonel Stand Watie's Cherokee Confederate Cavalry, probably some of the ones who used to hunt slaves on the Seminole Reservation. All of them had pistols or long guns sticking out of every possible holder.

Texas had a lot of trouble right then. Charlie had explained it in his letter, but I knew it anyway. The War had ended just about exactly a year ago and Texas was full of resentful young veterans with few jobs. They nurtured a seething resentment against their Yankee occupiers and Freedmen. There had been few battles in Texas during the war, but 70,000 Texans fought for the South. Walsh, Cullen Baker, and a few other Confederate officers weren't taking the loss well and were trying to start a guerrilla war against the Northern invaders. The outlaw gangs were still fairly small, but recruitment was relentless.

"Well, still, we can't hide from every dust cloud or we'll never get there. We've come across people almost every day," said Andy. The outlaws sat cross-legged in the shade and smoked, letting their horses graze and water freely.

"We don't hide from everybody. Just the ones I think look dangerous. These looked dangerous and they are. Lots of folks look dangerous in these days," I said. "One day you'll see the wisdom in my ways. We're in no hurry. That's why we left plenty early."

The gang made a fire, ate, and moved on with two hours or so of daylight left. They were apparently concerned enough about whoever it was chasing them that they didn't want to risk a fire after dark.

"We might as well make camp here," I said. It was a good place to hold up if we had to, with the creek nearby. "These trees will hide the campfire."

17

I sliced a couple tenderloins from the young pronghorn and stuck them on a skewer over the fire while Andy rummaged through a pannier and pulled out the skillet, a can of tomatoes, an onion, and some Tabasco sauce.

"What are you going to do with all that money you'll make on the drive?" I said, once the juice from the seared steaks was dripping and sizzling in the fire and the aroma had filled our little hideout in the trees.

"Maybe I'll become a big rancher," Andy said, breaking some branches and tossing them in the fire.

"Hell, son, I've seen you get discombobulated trying to get that cantankerous old milk cow of yours in the pen," I said, stretching out on my bedroll and laying my head on my saddle. "Wait until you've been two months with 2,500 of them."

We sat on our horses on a gentle, bluebonnet covered ridge overlooking a green valley where men on horseback rode slowly through the herd of Texas longhorn cattle. Like most men that made their living in a saddle, Charlie was a small man with a rawhide toughness that thrived in the adversity of harsh Texas weather and Indian fighting. He wore a wide-brimmed gray Stetson and had deep crow's feet around his eyes in skin the sun had burned a deep copper.

"This is mighty impressive," I said, after Charlie laid out a few more details of the planned drive. "And ambitious. I didn't even know you owned a herd of cows."

"As much as any man owns them. Half and half with Mr. Oliver Loving," said Charlie. "I had a hundred and eighty head when I left with the Rangers after the War began. Thousands of longhorn cattle were left to roam free all over Texas. With natural increase, there's hundreds and hundreds of thousands of them. Millions, probably by now. All over West Texas. Wild and free and unbranded. Who can say what unbranded critter belongs to him? Texas is broke, but by God, we've got longhorns by the millions."

"Huzzah for Texas," I said.

"I appreciate you coming all this way to help me out," continued Charlie. "I reckon I'm going to have to spend most of my time bossing 2,500 head of cantankerous range cattle and 20 head of ornery cowboy. Mr. Loving will be running the show, but you probably won't see much of him. He's riding ahead to New Mexico, for the business end of it. I'll be dealing with the day to day. Bose is my segundo. Bose and me, I expect we'll have our hands full. There's others that could scout that would be more than fair, I suppose, but I need better than more than fair. We really need a good scout. Someone that really knows the Comanche."

"You're a good scout. You know the Comanche. Bose, too. I wouldn't want Bose to think I was stepping on his toes," I said. Charlie had been surly and peevish during our years trailing together, and that was before he took on the burdens of ownership and logistics. Bose Ikard, a slave up until a year ago, was Charlie's ranch foreman. Bose was a strong, quiet man with a gentle manner, and he was slow to anger. He would be a good buffer between Charlie and the boys, to smooth down whatever Charlie left raw. I suspected that would be a full-time job.

"He don't think that. If it was you that was here, and I knew Bose was available to help get this big job done, I'd ask him to join up. Just like I asked you. I need everybody to get 'er done. It can't be a matter of personal pride on an undertaking of this size. Bose is rock solid, but he don't really know the Comanche near as well as you," Charlie said. "As for me, most of the Comanche now won't even speak to a white man. Nothing. That surely ain't news to you."

"You remember it ain't always been real cordial between me and them," I said.

"Hell, the Comanche ain't cordial to nobody for long," he said.

"Be good to see Bose again," I said. "Ain't seen him since before the War."

"He's out with a crew along the river bottom, bringing in some cows we missed. Be back in a couple days."

Charlie's ranch sat in the middle of a wide grassy valley. The house was two good-sized log cabins under one roof, one a cook shed. There was a 12-foot dog trot walkway between them. A wide shaded porch ran around three sides of the cabins and the dusty front yard was busy with black and white checkered Dominicker chickens.

There was a little pond, chicken coops and a hog pen. On the far side of a large barn was a livery stable and network of pole corrals. Two blacksmiths were busy on forge and anvil. One burly man banged a heavy hammer, and the other dunked a yellow hot horseshoe in hissing water. At the stable, a couple old timers were tacking shoes on horses, and cowboys were busy in two branding pens. Two drowsy, glass-eyed Catahoula Leopard Dogs laid in the shade of the porch and occasionally gazed at the action.

The cook was Gunther Espinar, a white-haired man who had ridden with the Rangers in another life. He'd gotten himself fairly well boogered-up over the years from horse falls and Indian fights, and now served as Charlie's cocinero, medic, minister and emergency wrangler. Espinar had learned to cook from his mama, who'd been a Mexican Blackbird from down in Acuña, and his German daddy, who'd roamed for years as a beaver trapping mountain man. After Gunther Sr. retired from rough living, he married the Blackbird and they ran a cantina and whore house in San Antonio. Young Gunther tended the beans and tortillas and became a notorious hellion. His blade had tasted the blood of many a man before he turned to slicing rib eyes and pork chops. Now, behind the house, he kept a little garden of yellow roses inside a white picket fence covered with honey suckle vines. Most days Espinar would be outside his cook shed, white with flour and preparing meals for all those hard-working cowboys.

"You got a good man on your horses?" I said, looking out at several hundred horses in the green pasture.

"The best. Ray Benson's the wrangler. We've got no shortage of volunteers to un-rooster the mustangs. A couple of these California vaqueros is the best. They'd rather break broncos than deal with them ornery longhorns day after day. They knock most of the sparks out of them, and then the cowboys smooth out the last unbroke edges to their personal liking," said Charlie. "Cutting in and out of wild, boogly-eyed longhorns all day is no place to be riding a half broke horse."

"How big a string you bringing?"

"Everybody brings eight or ten or so. A cattle drive this size will wear a horse down quick.

"Spares for me and Andy to get a few?"

"Sure, plenty of good ones," Charlie said. "Ray's been building a real nice herd for ten years now. Mustangs heavy with quarter horse blood. Mostly five-year-old geldings for the drive. Smart and fast, and just enough wild left in 'em to skip out of the way of a rantankerous bull."

My horses weren't going to be working nearly as hard as the cow ponies, but I wasn't going to ruin my Arabians by overtiring them on a two-month trek over some mighty rough ground. I would take my silver dapple Arabian-cross as a runner, and picked out two bays, a buckskin, and a roan for work.

"Those cowboys sure look young," I said. Charlie had introduced me around to the eighteen cowboys going on the drive, and a few more who would work Charlie's ranch during his absence. Other than two grizzled hands who looked as weathered as a Texas canyon, they were mostly in their teens. I knew the old-timers, Braswell Beene and Orly Higgins, slightly. There were the vaqueros from California, about ten cowboys from south Texas, and four who'd been field hands on a cotton plantation. They all seemed earnest and hardworking.

"They is," said Charlie. "But they're more than middling and they've got sand. I've had plenty cowhands come and go over the past three years, and I'd say these here is about the best Texas has to offer. Don't go quoting me on that, though. It'll go to their heads and they'll get lazy and careless."

"Of course not," I said.

"They're workers, and don't shy from a challenge. Some ain't ever had no real job before, wasn't legally allowed to have no wage paying job, anyhow. They're tickled pink by the prospect, and backbreaking labor ain't a new thing to any of them. Most has never owned their own hoss before, and we got some fellers that ain't never worn shoes. They remain ambivalent about the manly footwear needed for cowboy work."

"They'll understand the need soon enough," I said, watching the cowboys working hard, roping, branding, making 'em steers.

"They'll be some Johnny Rebs riding with us," Charlie said.

"I've noticed," I said. A couple of the cowboys wore pieces of Confederate uniform.

"Is that going to be a problem?"

"Not unless they make it one," I said.

"Good," said Charlie. "I didn't expect that there would be. My crew has got along grand so far."

"They appear to be top hands," I said. "Andy seems to have fit in right away. Glad you hired him on."

"If he couldn't handle his weight, I wouldn't reckon you would have brought him," Charlie said.

"He's a daisy," I said.

"Who's the belvedere?" I said of the swank-looking, red-cheeked fellow loping toward us from across the valley. He rode a fine-looking English hunting horse and wore a green and gold tartan plaid hunting jacket and matching beanie. Tan jodhpur breeches were tucked into gleaming black stovepipe boots. One of the cowboys was riding along, staying just behind.

"He's a scribe and adventurer from back east. Harrington Pierpont, with the New York Tribune," said Charlie. "Horace Greeley's newspaper."

"Is that right?" I said.

"The scribe is Mr. Loving's idea. He thinks it would be a good idea to let him tag along. Good publicity. Seems Mr. Greeley is an ardent admirer of Colonel James Henry Carleton, the commander at Ft. Sumner and the Bosque Redondo. They plan a big story about the great Indian fighter who forced the Apache and Navajo onto the Reservation but is now battling to feed his longtime enemies. Carleton cleaning up the corruption in the Indian Agency is the big showpiece to the story, apparently. Never mind Carleton's blind eye that allowed it to happen.

There's some thought, perhaps, of running him for president down the line."

"Good lord, another general with political aspirations," I said. "The last words an Indian hears before his village is massacred."

"You ain't wrong, but this Pierpont fellow asserts Carleton is a changed man. Has really thrown himself into getting these Navajo real help," said Charlie. "Or so the scribe says."

"Seems like it would be a chore, having him around," I said.

"Wouldn't have been my choice, but we had agreed at the outset that Mr. Loving was to handle most of the business end of it," Charlie said. "And I guess he figured it would be good business if we got a good write up."

"Could be," I said.

"I guess it don't cost anything but the aggravation and the beans to feed him," Charlie said.

"Is them fox hunting clothes he's wearing?"

"That's what the man says. He likes to go out on a hunt of the mornings," Charlie said. "I send a cowboy with him so he don't get lost.

"He find any foxes?"

"Not likely in that get up," Charlie said. "I think Texas foxes is a bit more wily than them in New York."

"Can he stay on a horse, as far as we're going?"

"He said he could, and I made it clear I'd leave him if he couldn't," Charlie said.

"He won't make it far on that kidney pad he's sitting on," I said.

"No, I'll send Espinar in town to get him a real saddle before we leave. And some range clothes," Charlie said. "That get-up could make him the subject of derision down the line."

"What's he like?"

"He can be a little grating, but he's not so bad," Charlie said. "I actually met him a few years ago. He came out here and interviewed me about Cynthia Ann. You'd already gone back east. He was doing one of them White Squaw stories."

"Him and a thousand others," I said. "That poor woman. I wish we'd never caught up to her."

"I know it, podnuh, I know it," Charlie said. "But what the hell can ya do?"

"How do you do?" Pierpont said after Charlie had introduced us. "It is an honor to ride with the men that rescued the White Squaw. I'd certainly like to hear some of your adventures. I know they are prodigious."

"I don't reckon I'll do much talking for publication," I said. "You want to set a spell and have a friendly chat, I ain't opposed. But I don't think I want my words in a newspaper. And there's some things I won't want to talk much about. I fought and chased and killed the Comanche for many years. I wish't now I hadn't."

"As it suits you, Mr. Horse," he said. "You have my word. But could I ask about the Comanche taking your mother and sister? Your search for them?"

"I wish they hadn't done that, neither," I said. "Now I've spent half a lifetime killing Comanche. A whole bunch of them, but my people's still gone."

"That's an interesting perspective," said the reporter.

"Maybe it is" I said, "But you ain't the one with dead Indians troubling your sleep."

"Aren't you going out to fight them now?"

"Maybe. I hope not. I used to hunt them. There's a difference between hunting or fighting if you're boxed in," I said. "Now I'm just trying to lead a bunch of cows across the prairie."

"Wouldn't you agree that Mr. Goodnight has conceived an intrepid, even unprecedented, venture?" Pierpont said.

"I'd probably use smaller words, but, sure," I said.

"How did you put all this together?" said Pierpont to Charlie.

"Mr. Loving's the one got us the contract to sell beef at Ft. Sumner. It's an emergency, and the government will pay top dollar," said Charlie. "These cattle ain't worth but maybe $2 here in Texas, but even at five cents a pound, average maybe 1,000 pounds, that's $50 a head at the Bosque Redondo. That's fair profit. And there's reservations all across the West in much the same shape. Them and the soldiers watching over them need to be fed. Government beef contracts gonna make men rich."

"They already have, just the wrong people," Pierpont said. "That's why Mr. Greeley wants this story done. Those unscrupulous, avaricious Indian agents have gotten rich shorting reservation Indians and selling beef to miners and ranchers. Colonel Carleton has run an extensive investigation into such chicanery, to find out who's diverting the cattle meant to feed the Indians."

"Well, mister, I guarantee you nobody's diverting these cows. Not without a whole lot of lead flying," Charlie said.

"Is it true Carleton's going to run for president?" I said.

"I don't know. Mr. Greeley thinks he'd be a good man. He wants me to find out if that's true," Pierpont said. "Mr. Greeley is a passionate supporter of Carleton's cause, but few people pass Horace's somewhat puritanical standards."

"And you?" I said.

"I'll write the story as it is, not as someone back east wants it to be," said Pierpont. "I believe the suffering of those people needs to stop. That will be the focus of my story. Whether it's about successes, or the continued mire of corruption, my story will reflect the truth."

"Fair enough," I said.

"These cattle bear little resemblance to the ones back east," Pierpont said as we watched the meadow full of bawling, sharp-boned longhorns. They were big, gangly beasts with dagger-pointed horns that, on some of the biggest bulls, stretched seven feet across. There were some smaller heifers and a few big 1,500-pound breeding bulls, but most were around eight hundred to a thousand pounds. Unlike the nearly uniform coloring of the thick muscled white-faced beef cattle in the east, the longhorns came in all manner of color and design. There were solid and speckled browns and blacks and reds and yellows, along with grullas, slate duns, mulberry blue brindles and a dozen more.

"Well, sir, these cows ain't nothing like those cows in any respect. They ain't no tame cows. They're wild as antelope in the open and mean as a sore-teated mama grizzly if cornered. Some of these scarred-up old range bulls will charge you from a hundred yards away and run you for a mile. So, stay alert, Mr. Pierpont, stay alert," said Charlie. "They'll lure you into the brush and slice your horse like a Barbary pirate with them horns. I've seen 'em hook a horse in the flank and then tromp all over horse and cowboy both. Most cows seek the safety of the herd, but these are too dumb, stubborn, or just plain ornery. Or mean and looking for a fight."

All day five or six cowboys rode slow circles through the grazing cattle. Andy had joined the cowboys chasing the last few wild cattle out of the wooded river bottoms along the Brazos and into Charlie's valley.

"This drive won't work if we can't get these wild longhorns accustomed to any degree of captivity. Get 'em used to horseback cowboys pushing them around a little," said Charlie. "Otherwise, it'll be like herding cats. Danged old mean cats at that."

"I certainly hope you can get the beef to the Navajo," said Pierpont. "It's an audacious endeavor."

"I'm just trying to get rich. The hazards is great," said Charlie. "I had an entire herd taken by Comanche last year. Cost me a substantial bit of money and time. I don't expect I'll allow that to happen a second time."

"Looks like we got company," I said, when I saw three riders come into view, loping our way.

"That's Bose and a couple hands coming back from the river," Charlie said. "But they are coming hard."

"Well, howdy Pete. Charlie said you'd be getting in soon," said Bose Ikard after they'd reined up. "Always good to see you, too bad you might have landed in a mess of trouble."

"Trouble?" I said.

"Charlie, there's been more killings," Bose said. "At Judge Jeffers place."

"Judge Jeffers? Another judge?" said Charlie. "That sure ain't good. What's the full toll this time?"

"Eight."

"Comanche?"

"Nah, it ain't Comanche," said Bose. "'Bout halfway meant to look like it was Comanche, but it ain't. Luther Walsh, I figure."

"Let's go have a look-see," said Charlie, urging his horse to an easy lope. "You fellers can get caught up as we ride."

The Jeffers' place was in ruin. The house was reduced to a chimney and some crumbling, blackened half-walls. The barn was down except for a few charred pillars and beams. The livestock that hadn't been run off had been slaughtered.

The bodies were scattered outside the black skeleton of the barn. Most were naked, scalped, sliced open and burned. The women had clearly been violated. A man had been strapped in a rocking chair under the cross beams of the barn. His face was strapped in place to look at the bodies, and his eyelids were gone.

A handful of men in range clothes walked around the ruins, poking sticks through the piles of ashes. I recognized the two tough-looking, bushy-mustached black men leaning on the rails of the corral. Britton Johnson and Bass Reeves.

Bass was about 30, a towering 6'2" and 200 pounds of corded muscle. He wore two Colt six-shooters tied-down butt forward for a cross-draw and a bowie knife in a belt of Indian Beads. Britt was shorter, darker, and thicker. He had a smaller mustache but the same look of menace. These were hard men.

"Howdy, Pete," said Britt. "You look like you're doing well."

"Howdy Bass. Good to see you Britt, I heard you found your wife and little ones," I said. "I sure was glad to hear that."

I introduced Charlie and Bose to Bass, but they already knew Britt. Most people knew Britt, knew of Britt, or claimed to have ridden a trail with him. Most of those last were liars, as Britt was mighty choosy about who he parded up with. Two years ago, a couple hundred Kiowa and Comanche had descended upon a line of homesteads along Elm Creek, northwest of Fort Belknap. The raiders burned ranches and drove off hundreds of horses and cattle. They killed fourteen people, including Britt's son, and carried off a dozen more, including Britt's wife and two daughters.

Britt was still legally in bondage at the time, working as the foreman of the Moses Johnson ranch and raising his own horses and cattle on a little plot of land. After the raid, Moses gave Britt his freedom and a bag of gold to buy his family's freedom. For the next year and a half, Britt traveled throughout Comancheria looking for his family. He got along with the Indians, and even lived with one band of Penateka for several months. Eventually, he was able to ransom the release of nine white captives and his own wife and daughters. During his search, he had passed through our Seminole reservation twice following trails. He met Bass there. Bass had been living amongst us and riding as a border guard for the past two years after escaping his own slave master.

"What are you doing out this way?' I asked Britt.

"We're looking for a little girl the Comanche took," Britt said. "Heard about this here. Thought this might be the work of Comanche, but it ain't,"

"All by your lonesome?"

"He's got me," said Bass.

"A faint heart never filled no flush," said Britt. "I don't need no gaggle of men that ain't used to living rough slowing me down and complaining."

"You come all the way out here from Arkansas to retrieve that girl?" I said to Bass.

"I was riding guard on some freight wagons from Ft. Smith to Belknap when I seen Britt," said Bass. "Sounded like an interesting adventure."

"What's the girl look like?" Charlie said.

"Light skinned colored gal, about a half and half, since both folks is half and half," he said. "She around 17 years old now. Got took off the cotton plantation in Gillespie County a few years before the War started."

"Why are you just now coming after her?" Charlie said.

"After this raid where the girl got took, the massa got tired of getting his expensive slaves stoled by rampaging redskins. It wasn't the first time, apparently, but it would be the last time. He sold the ranch and horses to a German and the colored folks to a trader headed to the Galveston slave markets," Britt said. "Her mama went to Georgia, and her daddy ended up getting sold somewhere's else, running away, joining the Union army, and getting killed outside Richmond. Her mama had long since given up any hope of seeing her baby girl again. She had no freedom to search for her before the war was over, nor knew of anyone who could help."

"But she's back, the mama?"

"Moved in near me in Parker County. I'm living there now, started me a freight business of my own," said Britt.

"Her mama got money to pay you to find her girl?"

"No, she ain't," said Britt. "Some things just need done."

"That's how I feel on it," said Bass.

"You know these dead people here?" Britt said to Charlie.

"That's Judge Jeffers," said Charlie, pointing at the flayed, ghastly-staring corpse in the barn door.

"He doesn't have any eye lids," Pierpont said, looking at the body of the judge strapped tightly in the chair. The flesh of his legs had been completely blackened by fire. "He's got his eyes all right. But no eye lids."

"You're looking a little queasy there, Mr. Pierpont," I said.

"I've never seen such horror," he said, and sat down on the chopping stump.

"And set a fire under his chair," Bass said. "They cooked him while they forced him to watch his family get cut to pieces. That's a hard way to go."

"Oh, my lord," said Pierpont. "That's horrible."

"Looks like that's their tongues nailed on the barn door there," said Britt as Pierpont staggered off behind a wagon and heaved.

"That fella have a finical stomach?" asked Bass.

"Appears so," Charlie said. "Wouldn't expect that from a big city scribe, that muck and all."

"A pig don't recognize its own stink," I said.

"Them sons a bitches," Bose kept muttering as they covered the women's bodies with blankets from an oaken chest that hadn't burned. Shiny green flies and dragonflies and yellow jackets droned and dove at our heads. The buzzards had taken flight and circled overhead. "Them folks there is Fred and Sarah and their childrens ovah there. They was the caretakers that worked the Judge's farm. Fred and his people have lived in this county all their lives. Those was good people."

"The Judge's guards never did him much good," Bass said, looking down at two dead men that still had on their Yankee uniform shirts. Their throats had been cut, and they'd endured a hundred knife gashes below the waist. Two more dead soldiers were laid out near the corral.

"Look here," said one of the men, wiping off the ash and debris that covered a small steel safe. It was empty, with the door hanging open.

"Indians don't take cash out of safes," Britt said.

"Got to be Luther Walsh," said Charlie. "He's the boldest of them right now. This would be the second Freedmen's Bureau judge he murdered. He's trying to stir up as much trouble as possible, to cause another insurrection."

"But murdering judges?"

"I don't like the Yankees, but I sure don't hold with Walsh and the like. They hate to their core the Freedmen's Bureau, thinking coloreds is getting preferential treatment," said Charlie. "They want to burn this reconstruction government and end the Federal occupation. They won't never sign no Oath of Allegiance nor Loyalty Oath nor no oaths what so matter. The way some folks see it Luther Walsh is striking big blows against the Yankee invaders."

"Could be him, I suppose," I said. "But I seen him ten days ago or so. They were a hundred miles from here and headed toward Indian Territory. In a hurry."

"A lot can happen in ten days," said Bass.

"Yes, but the way they were riding their horses almost to death, someone was chasing them. It appeared the last thing they were thinking about was a return visit," I said. "I ain't saying he didn't do, just that it's odd. I don't know who they were running from, but they sure enough were running from somebody."

# FT. BELKNAP, TEXAS
## MAY 1866

"If you ain't doing anything tomorrow, Espinar is taking the wagon to get our supplies for the trip," Charlie said. "I'd like you and Bose to take a few men and go with him."

"I work for you. You're the one determines whether I'm doing anything tomorrow or not," I said.

"I know. But we go back a long time. I feel a little odd bossing you around," said Charlie.

" I'm taking your money, Charlie, that means you're my boss," I said. "If I wasn't comfortable with it like that, I wouldn't have come."

"Fair enough," he said.

"If I ever round me up a herd of jackalope or whatnot and I ask you to ramrod it, I'll be ordering you around from sunup to dusky dark," I said.

"Deal," he said. "So about them supplies?"

"Sure. A wagon needs an armed escort?" I said.

"A wagon load of supplies meant to feed twenty cowboys for two months will feed twenty outlaws for two months just as well," Charlie said. "That would be some mighty attractive plunder for the bandit gangs and Indians in the area. After what happened at the judge's ranch, hard telling what we might run in to."

"I expect so," I said.

"And take that reporter with you and get him some working clothes," Charlie said. "Dang fool, wearing a suit out here."

"That reporter? Not Mr. Pierpont no more?"

"Ah, he's all right. Just a little annoying sometimes, follering me around when I'm trying to get some work done," Charlie said.

"Hunh, never would have expected you to get irritable, Charlie," I said.

♧

We took Pierpont to the mercantile of Old Solomon, a long-time friend of Charlie, Bose, and Espinar. The store was a large, long white-washed adobe building filled with the smells of harness oil, leather, tobacco and spices.

"You want the new stuff, or some that's trail broke?" asked Solomon, fingers toying with his long white beard.

"New, of course," sniffed Pierpont.

"That's your call," I said. "But personally, I'd suggest that a long trail drive ain't the place to be breaking new duds in."

"That's a fact," said Bose. "Lots of folks decide this life ain't for them and sell all their goods before heading back east. You'll want some gently used equipage."

The first order of business was some mule-hide boots, and Solomon had just the right size in a pair of black ones with two inches of heel and a shaft to the knees. After that we found him a wide-brimmed, beaver-pelt Stetson.

"This heel's going to take some getting used to," Pierpont said, clomping around in the boots. He was fidgeting the hat around at the same time. "Sure are tight. And this hat feels as foreign as celestial China."

"I reckon so," I said. "The heel keeps you from getting hung up in a stirrup. They'll stretch out. And you'll grow mighty fond of what little shade that hat can provide, once you see there ain't a tree in a hundred miles."

"These boots here was hand made for a young cowboy," said Solomon. "But that was before the young fellow fell in with low companions and a love of saloon life. His poor choices resulted in a shootout that took the life of two innocent and respected citizens of town. While awaiting his hanging, the boy could see all the unmarked graves on the cemetery there. He got so maudlin he sold the boots so he could buy himself a marker and some daisies."

"Well, that's tragic," said Pierpont.

"No shortage of gunmen, bandits and hard cases since the war," said Bose. "And them that fancies themselves as such. Some of them don't get to wear the gun fighting costumes long."

"Yes, sir," said Solomon. "He died with his boots on. But they was removed promptly thereafter. And oiled"

"Is that so?" said Pierpont.

"Yes, sir, right there where the jail used to be before it burnt to the ground," said Solomon. "His winder looked out right at the bone yard."

"And the hat?"

"Same unfortunate feller. The sheriff sold the boy's hat to pay for the prisoner's meals," said Solomon.

Since I was pretty sure there had never been a city jail in Fort Belknap, I doubted that story was a hundred percent true. However, if the shopkeeper wanted to peddle stories to the man who peddled stories, I wasn't about to ruin his fun. I'm sure it sold more boots than a tale of a young knucklehead splitting his head open from falling off a horse or dying of fever.

"How are you with firearms?" I said to Pierpont, pointing at a pair of Colts behind the glass counter.

"I've hunted deer and moose and bear," he said.

"How are you with firearms when a screeching Comanche is charging across the prairie at you?"

"I've never had the pleasure," Pierpont said.

"Well, the pleasure part could be debated," I said. "But if you don't live past the first one, you'll never enjoy a second. That's fact. Nobody's good with a gun with a Comanche bearing down on them. But with a couple of these you can at least put enough bullets in the air that you might hit something. Or at least dissuade them."

"I might be better with the rifle," he said.

"Maybe," I said. "The idea's the same, though. Just fling as much lead as you can."

"You think it's likely we'll have Indian trouble?"

"It's not a matter of likely. It's a matter of you best be prepared either way," I said. "Failing your debut ain't an option."

Charlie and Mr. Loving armed all the cowboys with the same firearms. The Henry rifle and the Colt revolvers were the best made, and used the same 44 ammunition. I selected Pierpont's weapons as Solomon piled pants, chaps, slicker and a good double-rigged Texas saddle on the counter. After we finished outfitting him, we set off to find the supply wagon.

"Sure is a lot of used equipment," said Pierpont as a he wobbled out the door in his new boots, arms laden with gear.

"The cowboy life ain't for everybody," I said.

With Pierpont in his new gently used range clothes, Bose and I sauntered on over to the warehouse where Espinar was loading the supply wagon. Like everything else on this journey, Charlie had put a great deal of planning into constructing the rolling kitchen. He and Espinar had put steel axles on an old Studebaker army ambulance and reinforced the floor and walls. On the high sideboards they had built all manner of partitions, cupboard shelves, and cabinets. Skillets, pans, and five-gallon coffee pots hung from the iron bows holding the canvas tarp. Outside boxes held Dutch ovens, axes, and some blacksmithing tools. An extra wagon wheel hung on one side, and a large water barrel on the other. The wagon was crammed with hundred-pound burlap sacks of flour, salt pork, beans, onions, and salt. There were cones of white sugar and a keg of sourdough starter. The owner of the trading post had just wheeled out a dolly loaded with 100-pound crates of Arbuckles' Ariosa Coffee.

"Looks like you got plenty of coffee," I said, taking in a big whiff of coffee beans. "Nothing beats that smell."

"Charlie said not to scrimp on the coffee," said Espinar. "Won't get no work out of those cowboys without it, and it's my job to keep them upright and awake in the saddle. And we're bringing an extra hundred pounds to barter with the Indians. Even the Comanche will come to the trading blanket for coffee, and this flour and sugar. Twists of tobacco and good knives for the men. This pretty bright cloth for their lady friends will find us favor among the Indians."

"Sounds like Christmas for Comanche," I said.

"Rather have them drinking our coffee than stealing our cows or lifting our hair," Espinar said.

"I agree. It's always better to try and dicker," I said.

"And here we go with the last item. Don't forget this here," said the warehouse man wheeling out another dolly.

"Well, I'll be. Therapeutic biffy paper. Charlie sure thinks of everything," I said. The bold lettering on the bright blue packages said Gayetty's Medicated Therapeutic Paper.

"Only the best for his boys," said Bose. "You'll appreciate it even more after a week of eating Espinar's chili beans. Or have over-indulged in the alkaline Pecos River waters and experienced its powerful purgative power. It will soothe your piles. Charlie claims cowboys work better when their fundament ain't aflame. There's probably some merit to what he says."

"Well, I for one appreciate it," I said. "I reckon Charlie's the only rancher keeps Gayetty's in the privy."

"Onliest I ever seen," said Espinar. "And it's a danged nice privy to boot."

"Yep, real comfy. A three holer," I said. "You don't see many of them. That's dang near nice enough to make the Queen of England come by for a squat."

"Charlie's mighty considerate of his hands," Espinar said. "He just likes to act chuffy all the time."

"Since you worked so hard watching me load that wagon, I suppose the least I can do is buy a couple rounds of cool cervezas," said Espinar once the warehouse boys had finished loading the wagon. "Rudy brews a half decent beer, and he has a deep cellar dug where he keeps it cool. His whiskey's fair."

"Beer will do me," I said. As we walked down the dusty street, Bass Reeves and Britt Johnson were coming out of the livery.

"Well, howdy Tex," Bass said to Pierpont.

"Thought you boys were out chasing Comanche," I said.

"We just got back to town after a week looking for Big Hand's camp, supposed to be about fifty miles north of here. But no luck," Britt said. "Thought we'd reprovision and treat ourselves to a bed for a couple days before riding back out."

"Where are you headed this time?" I said.

"West, toward the Pecos," Britt said. "Horsehead Crossing supposed to be mighty busy with Comanche comings and goings for so early in the season. Thought we might find word of her there. That's where you're headed, ain't it?'

"It is," I said. "What's the toll so far?"

"Nothing really. Just lots of sightings of Indians roaming about. They've stole a few horses, but they haven't done any serious raiding yet," Britt said. "Running off some livestock, but not in great numbers. And no murdered settlers."

We continued on into the saloon. It was a quiet place, clean, with no visible bullet holes in the walls or ceiling. About half of the tables were occupied with ranch hands and workmen and freighters and frontiersmen of various colors and complexion. Everybody was engaged in friendly conversation. We found a table and pulled chairs up. Bass and I slid ours back to the wall.

"Do you fellows mind if I ask you a few questions?" asked Pierpont, after we'd had a couple rounds and relaxed a bit.

"We ain't working, so I suppose a few would be alright," said Bose. "What is it you want to know?"

"I sure would like to talk to you both about your adventures with the Comanche," he said.

"They wasn't adventures for one thing. They was mostly damned hard mean things that needed done 'cause some other mean hard thing had been done," Britt said. "I don't usually take much pleasure in recounting it.

"Yes, yes, you're right," said Pierpont. "There's another thing, since I have you all here together. The slavery. If I could understand what it was like. I'd like to write that story."

"Mr. Pierpont, if there was ever anything that couldn't be understood if you never know'd it yourself, it is being a slave," said Bass. "You'd have to be a mighty skilled wordsmith to tell that story, especially second hand."

"Well, that's what I meant. You could explain it, in your own words," Pierpont said.

"Well, I don't know that I can explain it, and even if I could, I don't believe you could ever explain it. Make you feel what it's really like. You either is one, or you ain't one. In your world, you look out on the horizon and wonder what's out there, kinda like what you're doing now," said Britt. "Most folks in bondage know there ain't much point in looking past the gate. Don't have to be no chain around your neck."

"Us here at this table, though, had different lives than most of them. We had a certain freedom, but we was still owned. Being owned, it wears on a man, regardless of a liberty or two," said Bass.

"How did you all meet if you were slaves?" Pierpont said. "Bass, how did you end up on Seminole land?"

"I was on the run," said Bass, more talkative than I knew him to be, but he had a couple shots in him. "During the War, my owner's son George got appointed as some kind of Major. George was a real mollycoddled nitwit, and he brought me along as his body servant, they called it. Plenty Reb officers did that. I'm not really sure why George went, since he avoided danger like a cat avoids water. He was drunk most of the time, and he'd get awful mean. This one night in Arkansas, George was swoggle-eyed stupid drunk and playing poker. He decided he would bet me against this other officer's $200 raise. I'd seen mean old George pull that trick before. He bet an old Negro, Titus, back on the plantation. He lost, and then claimed in the morning he didn't do no such thing. Then he claimed, even if he did it, he was clearly too drunk to think straight. The resolution him and the other planter came to was that George whupped poor old Titus for leaving, and the new man whupped him for going back."

"That's horrendous," said Pierpont.

"When I seen Massa Reeves had a hole-in-the-middle eight-high straight, I'd had enough. Proclamated 'mancipated or no, I whupped him from one end of camp to the other. Then I jumped on his hoss and lit out for Indian Country. Them other officers was shooting at me but they was laughing too hard and reckon I was in Oklahoma before their hangovers cleared. I freed us both that night. Me from bondage, and George from some misperceptions on the nature of our relationship."

"Small price for a valuable lesson," I said.

"When I first got to Oklahoma Territory, I lived with the Cherokee and did some police work for them," said Bass. "Then I found out them and the lowdown Creeks was stealing the Black Seminoles as slaves. That didn't set with me, so I joined the Seminoles instead, and that's where I met Pete. Since the War, we've joined up scouting into the Indian Territory for the U.S. Marshals from the Federal Court."

During my scouts with Bass we couldn't hire on with the Marshals officially because we were colored. Instead, they paid us as scouts and we shared some hefty dead-or-alive bounties. Bass was building a formidable reputation as a hunter of bad men by then. He was lethal with his firearms and unflinching in battle. He knew several Indian languages and could live as rough as any man. I'd been with him when we got jumped by a pack of Creek raiders. We bedded down three of them and turned the rest over to the Army for a nice reward. On a solitary scout, Bass had a surprise encounter with six members of the murderous Ralph Stone gang. He prevailed, bringing all six of them back for the bounty. Ralph and three others were belly down across their horses. There were plenty of bad men with prices on their heads to be chased, and the job had its interesting points. I didn't know Britt as well as Bass, but any man who goes off on his own stick into Comanche country is a man to be respected.

After another round, the conversation became more about slave life in general and I listened to the stories from Bose and Bass and Britt. Bose was a slave all the way up until the last shot was fired in the war. I had known him before the war, when I was riding with the Rangers and he was a ranch hand and Indian fighter. Sometimes his owner, Dr. Ikard, rented him out as a scout for whoever might be hunting Comanches. During the War, Charlie Goodnight, Dr. Ikard, Bose and a hardcore few formed the Texas Frontier Regiment of Parker County. They spent long days in the saddle and many nights on the hard ground, chasing Comanche from one raid after another and battling almost constantly. Still in bondage, Bose stood side by side with his master in fighting off Comanches and protecting their homes. The only difference was that for Dr. Ikard home was a ten-room colonnaded Georgian and for Bose it was a two-room, clapboard shanty.

Unlike those men, for the few years I'd been a slave I'd never even realized it. To the contrary, my birthplace, wild Florida, had been a refuge for escaped slaves since the Spanish abolished the practice 150 years before. I'd never felt the lash nor shackles nor hunger nor fear. I had no more idea what that was like than I knew the pain of childbirth. Like most Black Seminole families, mine lived alongside a Seminole Village. I lived like other Indian boys. My early years couldn't have been more free, playing in the fields and hunting and fishing.

My mother was born to a woman fresh off the middle passage from Senegambia. My father was a handsome Spaniard and Seminole businessman who kept my mother as his slave and mistress. She was treated with tenderness and my sisters, my brother John and I were treated as sons and daughters, not slaves. We were not subjected to any slavery laws, and our father insisted that we were to be educated in the European methods. Before meeting my father, my mother had worked in the master's house, and had been educated as a requirement. She was a voracious reader of books, historical accounts, mostly.

One day, when I was about twelve, my father called me, John, my mother, and my sisters into the parlor of the house he'd built us. He gave my mother some documents, and said we were manumitted. There was some weeping, and he and my mother spent the next few days mostly in the master bedroom.

I watched him get in the carriage that took him to a ship. He sailed back to Spain and that was the last I saw of him. We loaded a wagon and moved to a nice little cabin deeper into the Everglades. We lived right there as free people until Zachary Taylor put us on the Trail of

Tears, bound for the Oklahoma territory.

The saloon was busy, no noise but the low hum of a couple dozen conversations. Things got quiet when in through the batwing doors came a buster of a man with the build of a gladiator and the swagger of Goliath. He had a mane of thick, flaxen hair and a Biblical beard of shocking silver. Half a dozen loud, laughing gunslicks tromped in behind him.

"Well, I'll be," said Bose, watching the men.

"Who's that?" I said.

"Porter Higbee in the flesh," he said. "Ain't that him, Mr. Pierpont?"

"It is," said Pierpont.

I watched them closely as they took a long table in the rear and the senorita hustled a tray of drinks to them. Most of the customers watched them but tried to hide it. Those closest to the Higbee table either scooted away or left the saloon.

"He's a friend of yours?" I said to Pierpont. Porter Higbee was a notorious killer and intimidator who put fear in men's hearts wherever he rode. His wrath was legendary and ferocious. He'd been the fanatically loyal disciple and bodyguard of the Mormon prophet Joseph Smith, up until Smith was murdered by a mob in a Carthage, Illinois jail. In the years since, he'd been rumored to have committed several atrocities.

"No, he is not. He is a brute. But since Mr. Greeley and the Tribune have been following Col. Carleton's career for many years, I'm familiar with Higbee. Carleton, you are no doubt cognizant, is the man who led the investigation into Higbee's actions at the Mountain Meadow Massacre," said Pierpont. "His career and Carleton's are intertwined. I know a good deal about him. And his gruesome acts."

"Why isn't he in prison, or already faced a firing squad for what he did at Mountain Meadow?" I said. "Carleton must not be so all-fired great at investigating. Maybe he ain't quite the man for president Horace Greeley wants."

"I believe Col. Carleton did an exemplary job in collecting evidence and preparing a prosecution against Higbee. He was thwarted and resisted by Brigham Young and the Mormon Church. Witnesses were menaced, threatened with ex-communication. A few were even murdered," said Pierpont. "Still, Carleton persevered."

"So, again, why hasn't Porter been hung?" I said. "Bunch of women and little ones killed, too, I heard. That's been near ten years ago. '57 wasn't it?"

"Yes, '57, but with all the resistance and cover-ups Col. Carleton faced, it was a lengthy process," said Pierpont. "His investigation wasn't concluded until 1861, and once the War started, the government forgot about Higbee and the militant Mormons to focus on the secessionists. Mr. Greeley's sources told him the Government has re-opened the investigation into Porter. They do have writs and warrants prepared, and men coming after him. Not only for past crimes, either. Washington believes Higbee is up to something big."

"Is that right?" Bass said. "They're coming to arrest him? Who all's a coming? I'd sure like a piece of that reward."

"I probably shouldn't have spoken on the matter," said Pierpont. "If Higbee finds out federal agents are coming after him there could be war. That is the fear Washington has. They fear that the big thing Porter is planning is some kind of sectarian armed revolt. But, please, that must remain here at the table. Mr. Greeley's sources spoke to him with an understanding it remain secret for the time being."

"Your secret is safe with us. I just hope the government is serious about it," I said. "I can't believe he is boldly walking free."

"It's not due to any failures on Col. Carleton's account, I can assure you," said Pierpont.

"So, you know the facts of the matter, Mr. Pierpont?" asked Bass. "The Mormons really dressed like Paiutes? And then gunned them poor folks down?"

The waitress came over and Pierpont went silent, eyes flashing toward Porter Higbee. Once she walked away, he let out the breath he'd been holding.

"Don't you worry none, Mr. Pierpont," said Bass. "Ain't nobody going to bother you while you're with us. Especially not no woman killer. You just go on with your story."

"Yes, those are the facts," said Pierpont. "At that time, Brigham Young was trying to create a Mormon state in the Utah Territory. The Federal Government, worried about a Mormon insurrection, sent troops into Utah. Tempers were running hot both sides. Mormons had a great distrust of outsiders after what all had happened in Missouri and Illinois. The Fancher party, a wagon train of 150 settlers from Arkansas, was passing across southern Utah on their way to California. In a valley called Mountain Meadow they were attacked and massacred, supposedly by Paiute Indians. However, it soon leaked out that it was the Mormon Iron County Territorial Militia, disguised as Paiutes and led by Porter Higbee, who had done the deed. That's when the Army sent Carleton to investigate."

"Dressed up like Indians, hunh?" said Bose. "Ain't that as low down as it gets?"

"Yes. Carleton discovered that the Iron County men, all the while dressed as Paiute warriors, besieged the wagon train for five days. The suffering was severe. The wagon train was without water and desperate when Higbee came up with his terrible deception. Dressed in their regular clothes, Porter took a group into the wagon camp under a white flag. Porter told the Fancher people he'd negotiated a truce with the Paiutes. He guaranteed safe passage as long as the farmers turned over their guns until they were out of Indian territory. He told the Fancher party that the guns offended the natives. It's doubtful the ruse would have worked if not for the fact the train was suffering so without water. However, they agreed to the terms and loaded back into their wagons. Porter led them into a narrow valley where he gave the order to a hundred militia men to fire on the travelers. All of them, 150 men, women, children, were shot down, defenseless. The bodies were mutilated to make it look like an Indian attack. The only survivors on the train were the tiny children they thought were too small to remember. Those were adopted by the Mormons."

"But why?' said Bass.

"I heard the people in the Mountain Meadow wagons were the same clan that murdered Joseph Smith, and that's why they got kilt," said Britt.

"An absolute falsehood," said Pierpont. "What Carleton found out was that it was Porter Higbee likely started that rumor, then had his agents inflame it."

"To what purpose?" said Bass. "Just cause they feared strangers?"

"A great deal of valuable plunder disappeared off those wagons," Pierpont said. "Gold. The people on that train were affluent. They brought their lives' savings from Arkansas. They had many excellent pure-bred horses. Hundreds of cattle, dairy and beef. Much of that reportedly ended up in the possession of Brigham Young and high church elders. But not before Porter pocketed some gold and picked the cream of the livestock."

"So that's the story, hunh?" said Bass. "Maybe I should shoot him right here and take that reward."

"Let's hold off until we find that little gal," said Britt.

"So they're finally coming to get him for that?" I said.

"That. And several more reasons. After things cooled off, many church members realized the horror of what happened. There was a lot of guilt, shame, and finger pointing. Or maybe just plain old fear of exposure. People blamed Porter," said Pierpont. "Since he was almost definitely acting on Brigham Young's order, to some degree or another, Young tried to protect him. The church covered it up, but rumors persisted that people were disgusted enough to go to the Federal authorities. Finally, Young and the church elders were forced to step in. Porter and his top men were banished to the Utah frontier with a wink and a whispered promise of redemption and reinstatement. But then Bear River happened. After that is when he snapped."

"How's that?" I said.

"Porter and his clan were sent to Cache Valley, southeast Washington Territory," said Pierpont. "They opened a new settlement near the Bear River, right in the middle of traditional Shoshone hunting ground. Mormon dogma has a peculiar idea that involves bringing Indians to Jesus. Joseph Smith claimed Indians were the Lamanites, the Biblical Lost Tribe of Israel, children of Aaron or something or the other. The Book of Mormon says the purpose of the Saints is converting Indians to Christianity to bring on the rapture. Porter's twist seems to be to simply annihilate them if they put up a fuss. After the Shoshone in the area rebuked Porter's missionaries, Porter and his militia led an Army column to the Shoshone camp along the Bear River. They killed about 400 Shoshone."

"When was that?" I said.

"Bear River was in '63. And after the word of that massacre hit the newspapers, the Church members really screamed about Higbee's crimes. Brigham Young had no choice but to ex-communicate him, completely and permanently. Otherwise he would have had a revolt on his hands," said Pierpont. "Porter was furious. He and his brother Purnell broke off from the Mormons and took a few hundred followers with them. Porter, naturally, became the patriarch of the sect. He proclaimed himself the true prophet and calls himself the Lord's Avenging Angel. He has sworn a terrible retribution. He calls for death, the blood atonement, against Brigham Young and those that forced him out. He says they are enemies of the true church, perverting the religion's canons and covenants. Porter's sect follows much of the same dogma of the Mormon church. Except that he preaches Young is the anti-Christ, a usurper and apostate that will go to Hell for his treachery. Porter says the Mormon elders are the illegitimate sons of the whores of Babylon. Or something to that effect. He even now claims it was Young who had Joseph Smith murdered."

"Well, at least he don't hold a grudge," said Bass.

"Yes, quite," said Pierpont. "Porter is a strikingly charismatic leader. A fire-breathing prophet-warrior building a religious warrior society. Joseph Smith once promised Porter no harm would ever come to him as long as he never cut his hair. That's why he's out there looking like Samson."

"I'd like to put that to the test," said Bass.

"Let's not go getting sidetracked. We told Miz Tucker we'd bring Coralee home to her and that's what I aim to do," said Britt. "But I would like a slice of that bounty. We'd need to do some real strategizing to do 'er."

"Who all's that with him?" I said.

"Them young ones are Furman Haight, Eldon Jukes and Reuben Higbee. The two mean-eyed older ones standing at the bar are Joab Higbee and Hezekiah Haight. Gid and Ezra Smoot are brothers," Bose said. "Not sure the names of the others, but there's twenty or more others been loitering around town the last couple weeks."

"Reuben is Porter's favorite son," said Pierpont. "Ezra and Gid Smoot are the boy's protectors, assigned by Porter himself. Ezra, more so than any others."

"Can't believe the law's not hot on them," I said, watching the powerful looking Ezra Smoot bull his way along the bar, pushing people out of his way that hadn't even been in it. "What are they doing here in Belknap?"

"No one's sure. Has some folks worried. But, apparently, he ain't wanted for any crimes in Texas. And even if he is, ain't no one to enforce any state writs against him," Bose said. "As for any Federal charges against him, ain't but twenty soldiers in the fort. Porter's got several times that many."

We'd had another round when a young cowboy, tall and dark, walked through the swinging door. He had a thick Van Dyke beard and ringlets of black hair over his collar. He shot a hard glance our way.

"Who is that boy?" I said

"Clay Allison," said Bose. "He's one of Charlie's hands. He'll be on the drive. Why, you seen him before?"

"No, just looks near enough like somebody to give me a start," I said.

"Nathan Bedford Forrest, the Wizard of the Saddle?"

"Yes," I said. "Danged if he ain't the spitting image of him."

"You know Forrest?"

"Not personal," I said. "But I've seen pictures, and I seen plenty of his work. I survived his charge at Ft. Pillow."

"Well, you might have seen Clay then. He rode with Forrest in the War, and idolizes him," Bose said. "He knows he kind of favors him, so he keeps his hair and beard that way."

"Must believe in the cause then," I said. "Seems like that could provoke some trouble."

"Not usually, but it all depends on which Clay you get. He does have a terrible bad temper. His moods and all, like two people," Bose said. "They say he came to Texas after he killed a Freedmen's Bureau man who was foreclosing on the family in Tennessee. He hates anything Yankee, and the Freedmen's Bureau with fire. But that ain't uncommon in these parts. Hard to put a trail crew together if you only hire them that advocates Federal intervention. I avoid him, but Charlie's been good to him. The boy generally shows his gratitude for that and keeps his opinions to himself. Most times he's tolerable. Just awful moody."

The cowboy's dark eyes flashed as they swept the room, coming back to me and Bose for a long moment. He gave a tiny, mean eyed smile, tipped his hat, then sauntered on over to the bar beside a cluster of tough looking young men, most in some piece of Confederate uniform.

"Personally, I think he's not worth spit," said Espinar. "But sometimes he ain't all bad."

"He going to be steady enough for a cattle drive like you're undertaking?" I said. "Surprised Charlie tolerates much surliness in others."

"Charlie found a soft spot for him and just figures it's his raising and this might do him some good," said Bose. "His daddy was a Hell fire and damnation preacher who had some real strong opinions about sin and punishment. Seems the former was everywhere, therefore the latter had to be frequently and enthusiastically administered. Somewhere along the line, they say he was snake-bit and down for days, sick with a deathly high fever. His folks thought he was done for, but he made it. From then on, he started with the slobbering paroxysms and mad dog fits. Of course, that just made the thumpings get worse."

"Ain't no excuse for it," said Espinar. "It's best just to steer way clear of him, and don't ever bring up the War. He'll try to soon enough anyway. He rode with Forrest on his second enlistment. On his first one, he got discharged 'cause of them fits he'd have. He'd thrash around, or jump on someone and start pounding on them. He pulled a gun and threatened an officer for not pursuing Yanks with enough vigor. He was drummed out, but he re-enlisted with Forrest, where lack of enthusiasm for killing

Yankees was never a concern."

"I can attest," I said. "I'll be wary."

"Clay is something when he's on one of his furious binges," said Bose. "He'll be the hardest working cowboy in Texas, no matter the job. Sometimes he'll work 24-36 hours straight, two full days, non-stop. I've seen Charlie put him to work digging holes, just so he can burn that energy out. If he don't get it out, that's when he starts getting snorty and looking for trouble. And there's times he gets headaches that lay him out still as a dead man, for two days sometimes, just moaning and covering his eyes."

"He don't socialize much with us, which is fine with me," Espinar said. "He don't like the fact Charlie leaves Bose in charge when he ain't around. That really sticks in is craw."

"Charlie don't mind him consorting with the bad guys?"

"He does, but he says a man should be free to choose his companions," Bose said. "Since freedom of association ain't something I've always had in my life up to now myself, I ain't one to interfere with it."

"Fair enough," I said.

"Out here, we ride for the brand. That's what we do," Bose said. "We're the senior men, and we got to set an example. There's plenty of young hotheads like Allison out here, and they're always going to be pushing us. We got to show these young ones that pulling out a pistol at every offense ain't the answer. But I always got my eye on him."

"And I got both mine on him," said Espinar.

"Charlie ain't one to hold a man's past against him, and him and Mr. Loving welcomes Rebs, Yanks, and conscientious objectors. Just as long as the latter will do the work and don't object to killing Comanche should the situation arise," said Bose. "But he won't tolerate fighting. No cards nor liquor. He entrusted us to uphold his rules, and that's just what I plan to do."

"I don't reckon Clay will last the trip, but I ain't trying to be the one that brings about his downfall," said Espinar.

"Well, Mr. Pierpont, I reckon you best get down to the remuda and pick you out three or four," said Charlie the next morning at breakfast.

"From the remuda? I brought two fine riding horses with me," said Pierpont.

"Yes, sir," said Charlie. "But those big horses you brought wouldn't last two weeks on the trail, and you'd soon be riding one of those mustangs anyway."

"Mr. Horse brought something other than mustangs," said Pierpont.

"Yes, and that Arabian blood in them makes all the difference. A horse bred to survive the wild deserts of Persia will thrive out here. Those big bruisers of yours, no chance. None what so matter. What are those, a draft thoroughbred cross?"

"Yes, a thoroughbred and Irish Draught cross," said Pierpont. "And they are fine fox hunters, and that is also in rough country."

"Woods and dale ain't exactly rough territory, Mr. Pierpont," said Charlie. "And how long do fox hunts last? The horse might do fine as far as the Concho, but in two days past he'd be wheezing so hard you'd think a train was coming. He'd overheat and his legs would give out."

"I believe my horses are strong enough to tolerate it," said Pierpont. "They are well-blooded mounts."

"Yes, sir. Mighty expensive horses to lose to the pride of being right. These mustangs have some of that hot Arabian blood in them, too. From those Conquistador horses. They're feisty, and they stay in fighting shape. Even where the grass is lush, they won't eat more than five or six pounds a day," I said. "They're smart like that. Mustangs know fat, slow ponies are a wolf's favorite meal. So that's the pace we'll be moving at, so the horses can get six pounds a day. That big horse of yours would need three times that. He'd never make it."

"I never expected to be riding mustangs," said Pierpont.

"We can bring you some of these tame saddle mares if you'd like. The kids from town come out and ride them from time to time," Charlie said. "But they're pushing twenty years old and would likely not outrun a Comanche pony for long."

"That's not what I meant," said Pierpont. "I'm a top-rated equestrian in Pennsylvania."

"A which?"

"A horseman, sir," said Pierpont.

"Oh, all right, that's good," Charlie said. "Cause I was gonna say, there ain't much water out here for swim racing."

"Try as you might, you won't get my goat, sir," said Pierpont.

"Never saddled a goat," said Charlie. "But let's get you fixed up with a cayuse."

"They have been broke to ride?" said Pierpont.

"Sure, they'se cavvy-broke, as good as any you see these cowboys riding," said Charlie. "But they ain't been rode much. You'll need to put a few miles on them before we head out, get them accustomed to the bit and rider."

"I see," said Pierpont, looking a little skeptical.

"I'll tell you what, pick out three or four and I'll get one of these youngsters to knock the sparks out of them for you," Charlie said. "Bose, go fetch one of them Juarez brothers, would you? They're the good ones in getting animals trail ready."

"No, sir," Pierpont said. "The agreement was I wouldn't be a hindrance of any kind to you, or need special treatment. If the horses have been broken, I can ride as well as anyone."

"Just try to stay on, Mr. Pierpont, it ain't a contest," said Charlie.

# TWO

# THE GOODNIGHT-LOVING TRAIL
## JUNE 6, 1866

That evening all the young cowboys, lank, fearless and double-tough, gathered at the plank benches in the yard. Espinar had labored all day and the tables were heaped with platters of fried chicken, mashed potatoes and roastineers. He'd warned the cowboys ahead of time he'd cut their livers out if their heathen eating manners damaged his new red checked tablecloths or porcelain serving platters. From what I witnessed over the next several minutes, I hoped they were considerably more adept with their shooting irons than they were with their eating irons. Otherwise we'd have some dead cowboys and toes shot off along the trail.

"Listen up, boys, let's go over the plan one last time," said Charlie, standing on his porch after most of the chicken and fixin's had been consumed. "We're pushing the cows to Bosque Redondo Indian Reservation in Ft. Sumner, New Mexico. We'll start out southwest, down the old Butterfield Trail, and we should have plenty of graze and water all the way to the Clear Fork of the Brazos. That's where the hard part begins. It's close to a hundred waterless miles from the Brazos to Horsehead Crossing on the Pecos. That's six or seven days across the Llano Estacado shrub desert, and it's going to be mighty rough on everybody, cows, horses, and cowboys. The hardest miles you'll ever cross. If we make it across there, then we'll turn up the Pecos and follow it all the way to Fort Sumner. If you got concerns, express them now. This ain't for the faint of heart nor those prone to saddle sores. Gonna need an iron ass for this ride."

"An iron belly too, if Espinar is doing all the cooking," said a cowboy.

"Maybe I'll do the cooking for everybody but you," Espinar said.

"Insulting the cook right when you're about to light off for a two-month cattle drive is about the dumbest thing a fellow can do," said Charlie. "Any more of that and I'll question your mental fitness for this outfit. I reckon I make my meaning clear."

"Yes, sir," said the cowboy. "I reckon you do."

"You really figure it'll take two months?"

"Reckon about a six-hundred-mile trip, and I figure we'll make 12 to 15 miles a day. The cattle need to keep their weight on, so they'll be plenty of grazing stops. That's about two full months on the trail," said Charlie. "Since this trail's never been broke before, we can't know what really to expect other than Injuns, rustlers, stampedes, thunderstorms, a sore back and a calloused behind. It'll take real grit, gents, to get this done."

"You think we'll run into many Comanche?" said one cowboy. "We're crossing right through their territory."

"I imagine we'll run into them. It's too early in the summer for many Comanches to be out raiding. But I'd be surprised if they let us drive these cattle straight through their homeland without trying to steal at least a few," said Charlie. "No matter if we have 18 cowboys, or 180. September is the time for their peak bloodthirstiness. That's when the weather cools and their ponies are fat and healthy. Good grazing for buffalo and other game. I like our chances this early, though."

"Now, listen," said Bose. "Like Charlie said, its early. The Indians we see will be peaceful, so don't go shooting at any of them unless you're told."

"How do you know they'll be peaceful?"

"'Cause if they ain't, you won't see them until there is no misunderstanding their intent," said Bose. "Just don't go wandering off from the herd. We'll have time to explore a little, scout around sometimes. Just you don't never wander off by yourself."

"Carelessness like that will just get you killed, or some of us killed trying to save you," said Charlie. "I brung extra cowboys, not to do no saving, but to replace any idjits that wander off and get themselves in a difficulty. We ain't in the saving business, so take your prayer books with you."

"Amen," said Espinar.

"We hope to avoid the Comanche as much as possible, which is why the route loops so far south," said Charlie. "It adds a lot of distance that way, but hopefully subtracts a few hostiles. Two months from now, they could be taking scalps and drinking cactus juice and acting like a pack of rabid lobo wolves. But our chances stand pretty fair this early."

"Hell," said Braswell, one of the older cowboys, a muscular man of about thirty. "In two months of working two thousand rattle-headed longhorns, I might be taking scalps and acting like a lobo wolf, too. Tell 'em to bring it on."

"You ain't wrong, Braz. Now listen here, all of you, because I won't be repeating this," said Charlie. "I run this show, and if I ain't around, I'll leave Bose or Pete in charge. If you're going to have a problem taking orders from a colored fellow, now would be the time to grab your saddle and light out. No matter who I leave in charge, it'll be the same. Pete or Bose, or Espinar or Ray or Braz. The first person that squawks will draw pay and a fond farewell. No matter how deep in Indian Country we are."

Charlie looked at me and Bose to see if we had anything to say but we shrugged so he continued.

"We got cowboys of every color here. What I won't have is no sour-faced, pouting-ass cowboys harboring ill will or resentments. I won't tolerate no fractiousness in the camp, neither. They'll be discomforts, and they'll be plenty of them. If you're the complaining kind, this ain't the place for you. If there's ever a disagreement that leads to loudness or a take down by the ears, there better be a good reason, and whatever that reason is, it best be settled before the dust is."

Charlie waited several seconds, meeting every man's eyes, looking for sign of any contrarians or shiftiness.

"I won't have drunkards, card cheats or braggarts disrupting my crew. Braggarts most of all. I'll tolerate minimal goddamn cussing," said Charlie. "And the best way to avoid any of that is just not have any alcohol nor cards in camp, thereby removing all temptation."

"Braggarts is a boresome lot," said Bose.

"Nothing gets my ears bleeding after a day of herding dumb cows more than a bunch of blusteration. One fool or another lying about some sword waving cavalry raid or gunning down some desperado in a flash of blazing six guns," said Charlie. "We're overrun with icy veined killers. They're more common than prairie chickens anymore. If they was as tough as they let on, we'd a won the war."

"As I've made clear, I don't mind a man that's had a scrape with the law, but we don't need to be hearing about it," continued Charlie. "If a man's on the cuidado for honest, and trying to avoid trouble for his past mistakes, he won't be sharing his escapades with a bunch of loose-lipped cowpokes. And that's the way I expect it."

"That's about right," Bose said.

"I don't mind war stories," Charlie said. "As long as they ain't of the bloody shirt waving kind, or meant to inflame the patriotic passions of a wearer of the opposite uniform. This war business is over, and if there's any that don't think so, just gather your gear and move on. No zealots of no sort, not religious, patriotic, nor other. Any questions on that?"

When there were none, Charlie continued.

"No matter what a person's station was before the war, it is now cowboy in my employ. That's the way he will be treated, and that is the way he'll be expected to act," said Charlie. "Only color I see is that red trail dust and them gold coins I keep counting in my head."

"Sounds fair," Ray said, and most of the others nodded along.

"Just that one exception. Now, on the subject of zealotry, I will allow a few kind words spoken on Texas from time to time," said Charlie.

"Huzza! Huzza for Texas!" shouted three or four cowboys.

"There is none else like her below heaven," crooned a cowboy to laughter.

"The first few days will be rough, I won't lie," said Charlie. "We'll push the cattle hard, getting them as far from their home ground as possible. Far enough they can't smell home. We'll need them good and worn out when we bed down the first few nights. They'll be an unruly bunch when we first hit the trail. They'll try to run on you. After they get trail broke some, we can slow it down, and let them drift."

"In God's honest fact, the secret of trailing cattle is let 'em think the idea is their own," said Bose. "Normally, you'll not get far trying to force longhorn cows to do something they don't want to do."

"Now, one last thing. I don't want you boys spending too much time with Mr. Pierpont, the scrivener here. He's a fine feller and all, but I don't want you cavorting and cutting capers, thinking you'll effectuate some daring exploit or another and get your name in a New York newspaper," said Charlie. "There's a bunch more dead reckless cowboys than there is whose exploits is remembered for long. If they're talking about you and you're already dead, that's cold comfort for your mama. And if you lose my cows over some dunder-headed stunt, you'll wish you was dead."

"Ain't that what you did, when you was riding roughshod with the Rangers?" said a cowboy. "Getting big write-ups?"

"Son, when I was in the Rangers, I couldn't even read a newspaper," said Charlie.

"Ain't he here to write up your exploits now?"

"No, he ain't. He's here to write about a general and the miserable suffering redskins we're feeding these cows to," Charlie said. "I ain't expecting to see my name pop up in no newspapers. Just so we're clear on that."

'Head 'em up! Move 'em out!' Charlie shouted the next sunup. The cowboys jumped into action, whooping and hollering and twirling their ropes behind the cows. The yip yipping cowboys kept the herd moving at a fast walk all day, kicking up a tremendous, suffocating cloud of dust and flies to go with the rumble of hooves and clatter of horns knocking together.

The awkward looking longhorns were cunning and fast, and a hundred times that first day a still-wild steer would make a headlong break for freedom and a flanker on a nimble-footed cow pony would leap ahead to cut him off. Then began a game of hide and seek and thrust and parry through thickets and ravines until the cow was tired enough to trot back to the herd, to rest up until his next escape attempt. These relentless games continued all day, and for several days after.

The crew pushed the bawling longhorns over ten miles that first day and by the time we bedded down, everybody was thoroughly wearied. Overnight, the nighthawks slowly rode through the herd, singing or humming, calming the restless animals made jittery by the constant companionship of wolves.

After the first few days, under normal conditions, there was little vigorous driving to do. We were in open country, with few places for runaways or predators to hide. The herd was strung out over a mile or more, and the animals were allowed to graze as they were nudged down the trail. Bose usually rode point, and Charlie could be anywhere amongst the herd: checking on sick cows or cowboys, marking in his tally book, seeing what's for dinner or the general temperament of his men.

I roamed ahead, looking for safe places to water the herd or cross the creeks. The streams were running strong and clear, but in most places the steep banks had a drop-off that would cripple the cattle. The crossings where the banks were low and clear were also favored drinking places of the Comanche.

That sundown I had my bedroll laid out next to Charlie, Bose and Pierpont. Andy was getting on well with the other cowboys and had taken to spending his evening hours with them. Espinar had made a dandy pork-and-beaner supper and I could still smell the brown sugar and red pepper in the kettle over the fire. The cowboys were on their blankets around the camp, talking quietly, a few already dozing after that fine meal.

"You and Mr. Greeley have more in common than you think," Pierpont was saying to Charlie. "He has always been quite proud of his position at the forefront of the national temperance. He abhors spirits and the carnality and degeneracy that liquor brings."

"I ain't a foe of vices, Mr. Pierpont," said Charlie. "I think every man's entitled to a few. In moderation, they add a great deal of character. I, myself, am quite fond of that carnality topic. I'm as leery of a man who claims no vice as I am of pulling on an unchecked boot in tarantula country. But not out here, trying to sneak 2,500 cows through the Comanche nation. This ain't the place for exhibitions of whiskey fervor or card sharpery."

"Sometimes men's baser natures need to be constrained," said Pierpont.

"If they ain't hurting nobody, I don't see it would be a concern. I always figgered most of you angolmaniac reformers still had plenty of unfinished work back east," said Charlie. "God put us Texans out here and you Methodists back there for a reason. I believe that to be part of his plan."

"I'm not so sure that's accurate," said Pierpont.

"Douse the lamps and hobble your pie holes," Charlie barked, his head on his saddle. "We got cows to push in the morning."

The fifth morning on the trail, Ulice Jefferson got his horse gored and himself nearly killed. We were crossing a patch of brush country when a massive bull, one of those 1,500-pound beasts going on to Colorado as breeding stock, charged out of the mesquite like he was shot from a cannon. Ulice wasn't a great horseman anyway, but neither him nor his horse had time to react.

The big block head of the bull smashed the horse in the rump and the seven-foot of horn caught the horse behind the foreleg and sliced him open to his tail. The horse flipped ten feet in the air with Ulice and a bloody rope of intestine tangled in its legs. Then they all landed in a heap. The snorting bull spun around, looking for more action, but two cowboys charged up and chased him off.

The chuckwagon came up shortly after Ulice got dusted and Espinar was out tending to the boy. Another cowboy had ridden up and put the horse out of its misery. Ulice was a sixteen-year-old cotton-hand and struggled with agile horse work. He was maybe a little slow, but he was a determined worker. Espinar had already taken a shine to the boy.

"Brisk up, fellows. Look at that mesa over there," I whispered the next morning. Charlie was holding the herd to water and graze for a day, so I had taken some of the crew to look around. Pierpont had come along too. Nearly every day Pierpont asked if he could ride along. Sometimes I let him, if I wasn't going out too far ahead and the land was flat and easy. So far, he'd only got dusted three or four times, and had tolerated it without complaint. I made it clear that if he lost his seat while we were fleeing hostile Indians I wouldn't be stopping to pick him up. He accepted those conditions.

We had just topped a low ridge, a hundred feet higher than most of the rolling prairie. Two lonely cottonwoods stood along the crest. On a low mesa a thousand yards away, a line of a dozen bare-chested Comanche braves sat on their ponies. I got the binoculars out and watched them. One of them had a spyglass out and was watching us, too.

"Wonder what it is they want?" said Andy.

"Probably nothing more than to get under our skin. It's hard to figure why they do things," I said. "They have their reasons, and they will make those reasons known when they're ready. We'll just sit right here and let them know we're not looking for trouble."

"Quahadi," said Bose, looking through the binoculars.

"Yep, that's what I thought," I said.

"Are those hostiles?" said Pierpont.

"As long as they're not wearing paint, we don't have much to worry about. I doubt they've come for our hair," I said. "But hair's hair, and they'll take it if they don't think it's being guarded stringently enough."

"Think they're upset with us for crossing their yard?" Andy said.

"Just about guarantee it," I said.

"Maybe they're scared," Andy said. "I ain't ashamed to admit I am."

"Me and you both," I said. "But Comanche don't see things that way. They may be holding back for any number of reasons, but fear ain't one of them. They've let us see them, wanted us to know they're out there. Watching. They know we're well armed and well mounted. For a group that small, we'd be a handful, and they know it."

"Comanches is tricklish," said Bose. "Auguring their intentions is folly."

"Aren't they being rather bold, this close to the Army forts?" said Pierpont.

"I don't think they're troubled too much by the Army," said Bose. "As you seen back at Judge Jeffers place, the Army has its hands full worrying about insurrectionists. Texas ain't back in the Union yet, so the government really don't feel obligated to do too much. Folks out here is asking for help, but the Army is slow in providing any. The way they see it, a few primitive savages shouldn't pose nothing more than a slight annoyance. A threat to rebellious Texans doesn't constitute a need for federal resources or money."

"Yes, I can attest to that. The people in the east are just now understanding the full devastation of the great struggle," Pierpont said. "To say the government is war weary would be an understatement."

"Well, war weariness is a condition unknown to a Comanche. To a Quahadi, making war is the only reason to exist. A life without raiding or war would be unthinkable, dreary and meaningless. Basically dishonorable," I said. "They are either warlike or preparing to get in that condition. If they ain't acting warlike, they're plotting on how best to get warlike. Or sleeping and dreaming of being warlike. There is no second option. War is what they do. They're good at it. Other Comanche have gone to reservations, but not the Quahadi, the Wild Ones. The unconquered. They have never signed a treaty or attended a peace meeting and they refuse any parley with the whites."

"If you ain't their friend, you're their blood enemy, and they have dang few friends," said Bose. "And allegiances can be fleeting, at best. But I am curious about them over there. You reckon they might want to parley?"

"Maybe. They seem to want something," I said. "Bose, you come with me. The rest of you, just stay right here."

Bose and I trotted our mustangs down the hill. When we reached flat ground and started across the valley floor the Comanche rode off the butte and out of sight. By the time Bose and I had joined the others, the Comanche were back again. We tried to approach them again, but with the same result. They didn't want to talk, but they wanted to make sure we got their message, whatever that was. It didn't seem to be more than telling us they were there, and watching.

I wanted to send the message that we weren't there for trouble, so we dismounted and sat cross-legged among a patch of Texas Bluebells in the shade of the cottonwoods. We remained that way for a couple hours, quietly smoking, listening to the sounds of the hawks overhead, the honeybees buzzing amongst the wildflowers, and the horses' loud crunching of the good bluestem grass. The Indians did the same, under a line of trees at the base of the butte.

Around noon, in the distance behind us, I heard the rattle of pots and pans and Espinar's gruff geeing and hawing as he worked the reins of the mule team. To avoid the dust and debris and millions of flies kicked up by the cows, he always drove the chuckwagon a few miles ahead of the herd, looking for that night's campsite.

"Hold up, Espinar," I said, after riding back to meet him. "Better wait here for Charlie and them to catch up. We saw about a dozen Comanche a mile ahead. They didn't seem nothing other than curious, but you never can tell."

"I'll set 'er up right over there by the creek," said Espinar. "It's a good spot, and it was about time anyway. They ain't coming this way, is they?"

"Not on our heels, anyway," I said. "But they're out there. I sent Andy on back to tell Charlie."

"You don't seem to think much of journalists. Seems like few around here do," said Pierpont as we rode across some open country a couple days later.

"If you come to Texas for favorable opinions of northern newspaper men, you'll have little success," I said. "There have been some unkindnesses printed about the people of this state that have not set well."

"I've found that to be true so far," he said. "I can understand some of the resentment, though much seems unreasonable and misplaced. What's your reason?"

"I've known a few with good intentions. More whose intentions were not so pure. I knew some newspapermen around Fort Augustine during the Florida War. Reporters were frequent visitors to the fort on our Seminole Reservation, during the treaty negotiations and legal disputes. I met plenty during the Mexican War. I met more when I traveled with my brother John to Washington, D.C. He went there to negotiate for better treatment for our Black Seminole tribe after we were moved to the Oklahoma reservations," I said. "We made several trips. Few were fruitful, but I learned a good bit. Our tribe is literate. I speak in plain language out here, because that's the language that needs spoken. But don't let my trail manners fool you. I went to school. I can read, write and do sums."

"I look forward to some interesting discussion and debate," Pierpont said. "Hopefully with no prejudgements."

"Perhaps," I said. "I've read law books and studied Indian policies and treaties. We are part of the Five Civilized Tribes. We had towns and businesses. We had schools in Florida, European style schools, like yours. We were educated. We were productive. We were determined. The Five Tribes cultivated vast pieces of land, but a hundred thousand people were forced from their homes and marched across the country. You know the story of the Trail of Tears. That's us, too. Andrew Jackson couldn't have done it without your newspapers. The power of the printed word is great. I learned that early. More dangerous than the gun. The Mexican War couldn't have been fought without journalists on both sides of the border whipping up the frenzy. The Civil War would never have been fought without all the bloody shirt waving. And it's rarely just one side fanning the flames."

"You believe the Civil War shouldn't have been fought?" he said. "The war freed your people."

"I never said that. Just that it wouldn't have been fought without those gentle nudges in the newspapers. But it killed a lot of folks, and free or not, I understand folk's kids is mighty hungry. And as you have seen, there ain't a whole lot being done to fix that. Wars can't remove misery. They usually compound it. I've fought in three of them," I said. "The real war didn't end when the shooting stopped is maybe what I'm saying. There's going to be a long road ahead. Hard, drudging, mighty unpleasant and thankless work. Much less exciting to read about, and write, I imagine, than thrilling stories of dashing charges and gallant generals. I figure you scribblers and wordslingers will be off chasing some other breathtaking story before then. I guarantee the politicians will be."

"I see," said Pierpont.

"I'm real happy your Mr. Greeley wrote all those words about freeing the slaves. But you all get mighty reckless whipping those pens around, like a drunk with a six gun in a saloon. At least with a gun the other feller gets to shoot back," I said. "What did Mr. Greeley think was going to happen to the Indians when he wrote them words about going west, young man? To the Sioux and Cheyenne and Comanche? Why is it you think this Colonel Carleton and Kit Carson killed so many Apache and Navajo? What do you think domesticating the savages really means? Now you want to write a story about feeding these poor victims so you can feel good about yourselves. Ain't that what you're doing?"

"No, it's not," he said.

"Are you sure?" I said.

"It is that horrible on the reservations?" he asked, after a few minutes of silence.

"Not all. Not ours once we had cultivated and built," I said. "But it's still a reservation. To say I harbored a little bitterness wouldn't be overstating it. I try not to dwell on it."

It was several hours past dark when I reached the herd. As always, the nighthawks rode slowly through the herd, singing low and soft. I recognized Marcellus and Marius, two laborers from the same cotton field, and the white boy John Milton Wesley, son of their overseer. I whistled over so I didn't spook them or the cows, then sat under the stars and listened as they harmonized "Wade in the Water."

Marcellus, onyx black, tall, and skinny as a hay rake, with an Adam's apple you could perch a coffee cup on, sang bass. Marius, lighter skinned and slight, had the tenor. John Milton, who'd been raised just about as poor as the other two and picked cotton right beside them, held the baritone. I stayed for a while longer as they sang "Swing Low, Sweet Chariot" and "Amazing Grace." The cows seemed to enjoy the fine singing and I know I did. But I knew Charlie was waiting.

I rubbed my mustang down while savoring the aroma of the coffee bubbling over the campfire. I finished and turned him over to the remuda wrangler, then headed toward the fire. Most of the crew had finished supper and were lounging on their saddles and bedrolls.

Andy was sitting on a crate beside the wagon with a peppermint stick between his teeth, grinding the coffee beans for tomorrow. The grand smell coming off the fresh ground beans was as intoxicating as the liquor Charlie wouldn't allow. On the shelf beside him was a small stack of the red and yellow Arbuckles' sacks with the Flying Angel pictured on the front. For twenty of us, working hard all day, we went through a good five sacks a day.

Each one-pound sack of Arbuckles contained a stick of peppermint candy, and that was the enticement Espinar used to create an endless supply of eager volunteers to man the grinder. The clamor was so great Espinar had to keep a list to properly rotate the volunteers. With the constant annoyance of cowboys asking whose turn was next, Espinar had turned the upkeep of the list over to Ulice. He'd taken on the boy as his assistant after the hooking incident had busted Ulice's shoulder and wrist and left him useless as a cowboy. Charlie didn't mind, saying for all Ulice's efforts, he really wasn't catching on and had a tendency to get himself separated from the herd. Ulice was more than capable, though, for fetching water, feeding the fire, or stirring stew pots.

Sundown had brought a welcome coolness to the air and I could smell Espinar's pepper-heavy beef and bean supper bubbling in a kettle over one sweet smelling buffalo dung fire, and a fire-blackened five-gallon coffee pot over the other.

"I was starting to worry about you," Charlie said, sitting down next to me after I'd filled my plate and cup. "Thought maybe the Comanche got you. They out there still?'

"They're out there still, same ones I've seen for the past five days," I said.

"What's that going on yonder?" I said. "You fixin' to bury someone?'

A hundred feet or so away was a big pile of dirt. An unrecogniz-
able, grime-covered man was neck deep in a hole, feverishly throwing
shovelfuls of dirt over his shoulder.

"Oh, that's Clay," said Charlie. "He was getting too squirrelly. I had
to find something to work his fidgets out."

"You don't say," I said.

"He ain't cut out for the tedium of a cattle drive," said Charlie.

"Few is," I said. "Looks like a fine hole as holes go. Hope nobody
steps in it."

"He'll fill it back in," Charlie said. "That's his fifth hole today. He
was up all-night pacing, so I put him to work digging holes as soon as
the sun came up. He's been at it since."

"Well, I'll be," I said.

"I wonder what the hell those Comanche are up to," said Charlie.

"Just watching us. They never come closer, and ride off if I try to
holler at them," I said. "The band isn't getting any larger, so I don't expect
no imminent trouble, but tell your night boys to stay alert."

"I've got good ones out," he said. "How's the water ahead?"

"The creek's five miles ahead and running strong," I said. "Those
late rains are a blessing. Nice, easy slope that would allow the herd to
spread out and drink their fill. If it ain't fouled by the time we get there."

"Fouled?" Charlie said. "Buffalo?"

"Yes, sir," I said. "Regular buffalo crossing, and there's a good-sized
herd coming from the northeast. They're between the creek and us, and
the lead buffalo will hit the creek midmorning.

"No other place we can get to the water?"

"Not for miles. The banks are too steep. You'd cripple your cows," I
said.

"How big a buff herd?"

"Not that big, but several times larger than this herd. Ten thousand
or so, maybe, plenty big enough to foul that creek up good for three
days. Not to mention eating up all the grass."

"Gol-dang it. Well, I can't let the herd go three full days without
water. It'll be hard enough on them between the Concho and the Pecos,"
Charlie said. "You think you can nudge the buffaloes the other way?"

"Probably so. It usually don't take much to stampede a buffalo herd," I said. "Hard telling which way they'll run though."

"Take Bose and some of the steadiest boys with you and see if you can run them off," said Charlie. "Andy if you want, let him have some fun. He's been busting his tail. And Clay. Take five or six."

"Clay ain't exactly one of the steadiest," I said.

"I know, but he's letting himself get worked up over something," Charlie said. "He can get difficult if it's let go. Maybe shooting a few buffalo will take the edge off whatever his difficulty is."

"Shoot a few? You want meat?"

"Of course," Charlie said. "Espinar and us old hands have been looking forward to this day for a while. Dang it, but I love me a good hump steak drizzled in honey.'"

"Fine eating. We can bring plenty of fresh meat," I said. "He brought some honey?'

"He mentioned a bee tree nearby when we camped," Charlie said. "He says he brought a whole honey gathering suit the bees can't sting you through."

"Is that right?" I said.

"Looks like we caught up with the buffs," I said. We topped the gentle rise, and half a mile away the buffalo were spread out across the wide valley, feeding in belly-deep bluestem grass. They were drifting slowly toward the creek. Ray, Andy, Bose Ikard and Clay Allison and two other young cowboys had come with me to try to move the buffalo out of the way. The reporter came along, too. Charlie had allowed it but told him to stay the hell out the way.

The whole basin seemed to rumble with the grunts and bellows of 10,000 of the great shaggy beasts. The big, taut-muscled mature males, six feet tall at the shoulder and weighing a ton, stood guard at the edge of the herd. In the center, cows grazed and reddish-orange calves frolicked. On the rise across the valley, a pack of wolves lazed in the sun, waiting for a sick calf to fall behind or an adventurous one to wander off.

The valley was dotted with buffalo wallows, round, barren craters ten to twenty feet across, maybe three feet deep. In the wallows, bulls rolled violently. They thrashed and kicked, throwing up great clouds of dust and molted fur in their displays of virility.

"You ever have to drink from one of those, Bose?' I said, pointing at the closest wallow.

"No, but I've heard men say that by the time they found one, it was sweet as heaven's nectar," Bose said.

"Drink from it?" Pierpont said.

"Those holes are centuries old and will fill up with water after a rain and hold it for a good long while," I said. "Buffalo been migrating up along through here since before Jesus days. Millions of them every year. Every time one of them rolls, they pack the ground a little harder, add another layer of that thick, oily buffalo hair. Makes a sink just as waterproof as any made of porcelain."

"I'd have to be mighty desperate," Andy said.

"That's why you always get fresh water out here at every chance," I said. "It can be far between 'em."

"Of course, sometimes there's a good bit of buffalo piss in there, too, as that's how they mark their territory. Only a few thousand young hot bloods a year, is all," Bose said. "But you get thirsty enough, you'll drink it. Trust me. I know a couple fellers."

"That sure don't make it any more appealing," Andy said.

"You just never been thirsty enough," I said.

"Watch this," I said, pointing down range. It was earliest days of the rut, but there were already several big, long-bearded bulls strutting around, nose in the air, shaggy heads swaying. They sniffed each female and pissed a lot.

Two big bulls had squared off, snorting, grunting at each other. Their shoulders and broad back bunched with muscle and the thick, matted hair was caked with dust and dead bugs. Working themselves into a frenzy they pawed the earth and bellowed.

The younger bull charged, sprinting with racehorse speed toward his rival. He launched himself and their skulls crashed together like a cannon shot. Both bulls were knocked to their knees. They stood up, shaking their giant black woolly heads, bloody froth dripping down their beards, discombobulated. They backed up, gathered their senses, and charged again. And again. They crashed their skulls together, driving and pushing, their short, powerful legs digging. The dust erupted up around them as they locked up, bloodshot eyes wild, straining and thrusting, going for the hook. They bellowed and battled until the older one stumbled. The young challenger got his horn into the flank of the old-timer and ripped his belly open. The wolves on the ridge perked up at the smell of blood as the victor stomped all over his gashed foe.

"Might as well have a little fun," I said. "Ready, Bose?"

"Ready," he said.

"Boys," I said. "We need to ride around them, stay downwind, to the south. When we run them keep 'em headed north, away from that creek. Me and Bose will go down and get them started, and on our signal come whooping and hollering and shooting. But shoot them pistols in the air and don't get too close. Me and Bose will do the hunting. You just do the noise making."

"Well, then, I'm hunting too," said Clay. "I'd like to ride down on one of them big bulls and take those horns."

"You ever shot buffalo on the run before?" I said.

"No."

"The ones to avoid are the big bulls," I said. "These rifles we got ain't powerful enough for long distance buffalo kills. That's why we have to ride up close, and don't shoot until they're all running one direction. Killing a running buff means galloping up close and shooting them right in the heart or lungs. A moving target the size of a frying pan on a ton of muscle running full out. You make one wrong move down there, you'll get yourself killed. Or us."

"You ain't no better horseman than me, nor hand with a rifle," Clay said. "I never heard Charlie nor Mr. Loving say you was in charge of me. Ain't no colored man, freedman or no, ever gonna be in charge of me."

"Then your ears need cleaned. You go down there wounding a bunch of buffalo with wild shooting and get somebody hurt, you won't have to worry about who's in a charge of who," I said. "Just know where you're shooting. The heart and lungs. Anything else ain't much more than fly swatting. Shoot the young cows."

"I know how to kill game," he said.

"Maybe, maybe not. You're likely to just make them mad," I said. "Follow me but stay well back. The buffs can't see worth a nickel, but those big ugly noses of theirs work just fine."

"You don't need to concern yourself with me," said Clay.

"Andy, you boys, I hope you're listening to me, if you're wanting to shoot, too. Getting gored and stomped ain't no way to end your trail, you hear me?" I said. "Shoot the young cows, not the bulls, especially not the big ones. Their hide is tough as an ironclad, and the meat ain't much better. Stay shy of the bulls, and away from the front of the herd in general."

We rode slowly into the downwind side of the valley, single file. At a hundred yards away a few of the buffalo paused to sniff the breeze. A cow snorted noisily, followed by some anxious bawling. A bull at the edge of the herd bellowed, and suddenly every animal in the herd was on high alert.

"Woooo hooooo," Clay shouted at the top of his lungs and spurred his horse into a gallop.

"Dang it, Clay," I shouted, but it was too late, and we had no choice but to get running ourselves. We took off at a sprint and I yelled, "Come on boys. Turn 'em."

Bose was right behind Clay, then surged past him, toward the front of the herd, firing his pistol in the air as we whooped and shouted and waved our hats. The outer wall of buffs started jogging away, bumping each other, bawling, and then breaking into an awkward lope. In a few seconds they found their stride and were thundering across the prairie.

I felt the old excitement and so did my little palomino, mustang-blooded horse. We flew across the prairie and the horse's mane whipped my face as I leaned into his neck, rifle at the ready.

I chose a target and the little mustang seemed to know exactly what I needed. I rode in close, ten yards from the thundering herd. I pulled the reins and then my pony took over, surging in close enough to the buffalo to touch. I fired and my pony danced away as the buffalo crashed, flopped, and rolled. My palomino took me in close again and I landed another good shot. The buffalo coughed and stumbled. A squirt of bright red blood shot from its nose as it crashed to its knees and rolled over dead.

Ahead of me Clay rode up close to a buffalo, a bull, one of the biggest. He raised his rifle and fired, worked the lever on his Henry, fired again, and then again. He shot the buffalo four times, twice harmlessly in its huge hump, one that skimmed off its thick skull, and one that blew off the tip of its jaw. The buffalo didn't fall, or even flinch, and Clay forced his horse even closer. The wounded bull lurched to the left, the big head swinging out and up, trying to hook Clay's horse. The pony skipped easily out of the way, then flipped over in a cartwheel, snapping his leg in half in a prairie dog hole. Clay flew another 15 feet and landed hard on his back.

I spun my horse in that direction as Clay's crippled horse struggled to rise, its hindquarters in the air. The wounded buffalo swiveled his two thousand pounds of muscle around in an explosion of dust. He snorted and shook his big boulder of a head, flinging big red slobbers ten feet from his shattered jaw. The bull charged, caught the struggling horse and flipped it again. The horse crashed to earth almost on top of Clay and knocked him rolling. Clay struggled to a knee as the bloody-faced bull spun around for another charge.

"Heeeyaaaah," I screamed and spurred my hardworking little mustang at that charging bull. I raised my rifle to my shoulder with one arm as my pony raced over that ground. I squeezed the trigger and my first shot was a clear miss. The next shot also landed harmlessly, high in the hump, as the bull rumbled toward Clay. I swung the rifle down and up and fired again. The bullet missed the lungs by a mile, but did hit the bull square in the ankle bone just as that foot hit the ground. The leg exploded in a thick mist of red as the bull crashed to the ground, roaring in outrage and pain as it tried to rise. I took a steady shot and killed him clean.

"Thanks for saving my life I guess," said Clay, bloodied and torn, sitting on the ground in a slouch.

"You should have listened," I said. I started to mention the dark wet stain on the crotch of Clay's trousers but didn't. "Now do something useful. Shoot that poor suffering horse and then take that big knife of yours and get to butchering."

For once Clay said nothing and seemed fairly well cowed. He walked over to the quivering horse on the ground and put a .44 slug in its head, then went to the closest buffalo and began cutting. Andy collected the pack mules while Bose and I started our butchering. We found a young cow and removed the warm liver, sliced off chunks and dipped them in green bile. It was an Indian delicacy which had taken a little getting used to, years ago. Bose and I ate with gusto as the others looked on a little squeamishly.

After a short rest we all went to work and within a couple hours we had the canvas full of hump roast, rib steaks, tongues, and several huge livers. With hand axes we had chopped up the thick leg bones so Espinar could use the rich marrow in his cooking.

"Seems like a waste, killing all those buffalo," said Andy.

"Everybody's gotta eat. Nothing goes to waste out here," I said, pointing at the wolves and coyotes gathered eagerly around the far edges of the scene. A lazy swirl of buzzards was already taking form in the sky above us.

"The wolves fill up on these here dead ones, they're less likely to snatch one of those purty little orange calves. Or one of ourn," said Bose. "That's one way to see it."

"Don't care so much for buzzards and scavengers," Andy said.

"Why not?" Bose said. "They's all God's creatures. They're only doing what comes natural. The wolves and coyotes and buzzards will grow fat and thankful. Just cause they's ugly and have bad table manners, don't mean they shouldn't have a spot at the table. I mean, it's a good thing the gals in my life never thought that way."

"I suppose."

"Who wants to double me back?" said Clay after we'd about finished the dirty, bloody butchering job.

"Ain't no doubling unless we're being chased by hostiles, Clay," I said. "You kilt your horse your own self. A man that decisive should be able to figure his way back to the herd."

"How about you, John Milton, will you double me back?" Clay said.

"Nobody's putting extra strain on another horse because of your poor stewardship of your own," I said. "Best get walking."

"That's five miles back," he said.

"Closer to three," I said. "It'll give you time to mourn your horse."

"We can move some of that meat to the other mules, and I can ride one of them dumb critters," said Clay.

"I won't stop you, but them mules ain't never had a man on them," I said. "Your feet might hurt worse for walking, but in the long run, your bottom end would probably end up in better shape. I expect you'll land on it a time or two."

"I've broke plenty of broncs in my day," said Clay. "It's a mighty hard-headed horse that I can't get to see things my way in a fairly short time."

"Horses are horses, mules are mules," I said. "You ain't seen hard-headed until you've tried to mount a balky mule. But, by all means, be my guest. We can carry some of the meat behind us."

Bose held the mule steady while Clay bridled and saddled him. The mule fought the unfamiliar bit some, but didn't seem to mind the saddle, at least not until Clay sat down on it. The mule stiffened up, refusing to budge as Clay slapped at its haunches. Then the ugly creature laid his ears back and whipped its head around, sinking his enormous yellow teeth into Clay's shin and trying to yank him out of the saddle. The mule crow-hopped about five lengths then sprang high off the ground and jack-knifed open. He came back down to earth, bucking and kicking and twisting.

"Grab the apple, Clay!" Bose hollered through laughter, and Clay clawed for the saddle horn. The mule snap-kicked at the clouds and Clay went flying. He landed hard on his side on a pile of fresh buffalo dung.

"Gad-blast," Clay croaked, one hand holding the busted ribs he'd landed on. With the other he was unsteadily aiming his Colt at the mule which had loped off, showing a mouth full of yellow teeth and braying that sounded a lot like laughing.

"Why you cussing the mule? He seen what happened to your horse," said Bose. "I wouldn't trust you neither."

"I'll shoot that mule," Clay said and cussed.

"You ain't shooting nothing, Clay. Can't you get it through your thick head God didn't plan for you having your way today?" I said. "Take the loss and be still before you shoot your toe off."

"Aw, hell," Clay said, looking down at the wide swath of fresh buffalo mess on his shirt. Then he started laughing, and kept laughing until tears came down his face. He laughed harder than any downtrodden man I'd seen, and we all laughed right along with him. Finally he got up, holding his ribs, his hip, and favoring one leg. Bose had collected the mule and brought him back.

"Here's that mule you tamed, Clay," said Bose.

"You're all funny," said Clay, now rubbing the back of his head. "I get it. Lesson learned."

He took off hobbling in the direction of the cattle herd, limping. We watched him walk for fifty yards and then rode up next to him.

"Hold up, Clay," I said. "We'll get you horsed."

"No, I'll not take your charity now," he said.

"Have it your way," I said.

We rode on but after a mile I looked back and Clay was really struggling on his lame leg. It looked like a couple of the wolves weren't satisfied with the buffalo buffet and were trailing him.

"I'm not going to try to explain to Charlie how I got one of his cowboys killed with blood poisoning from blistered feet when I had five perfectly good horses," I said, after riding back to him. "Get up behind Andy."

"Behind him? I ain't riding behind him. Why, he's..." said Clay.

"On a horse and you ain't," I said. "Make up your mind Clay. Letting you blister your feet all up and die from blood poisoning probably won't make Charlie too happy. You dying because of notions in your head likely won't bother him at all. Other than the horse."

Andy stuck his arm out and Clay swung up. We continued on with no further words on the subject.

We had a feast that night. With the help of Ulice and some hungry volunteers, Espinar quick fried the tongue with onions and peppers. He seared the hump roast over a hot fire, then sliced it up and threw it in a pan with honey and tallow and hot red pepper. He added biscuits and roast sweet potatoes and boggy top peach pie. I couldn't imagine there was any better eating in the world.

"Sure you don't want some of this tongue, Andy?" asked Bose. "It is fine dining."

"No, sir. I seen what them horny old buffaloes was doing with them tongues, all wiggle waggle up in them cow's heifer parts," Andy said, shaking his head. "No, sir, it don't sound appealing. No thankee."

"It only tickles about halfway down," said Bose. "It can be quite pleasing if it's been peeled all the way."

"That boy's going to be plumb sour mouthed when he finds out what was in that prairie giblet sop I made," said Espinar.

Maybe Clay was humbled some, but whatever the reason, his mood improved. He was funny around the campfire, even at his own expense. Clay got excited and told us some tear squeezers about the hardships of serving in Forrest's cavalry in the last year of the war, and some side-busters of his times sneaking into the bawdy houses of Union-occupied Nashville's Smokey Row.

Several days of easy traveling over rolling grassland brought us near the Middle Concho River. Bose and I went on ahead, searching for a place to cross where the cattle wouldn't get bogged down in the soft sand of the riverbed.

We split up, going up and down river to find a flat spot. I rode my well-rested Arabian-thoroughbred runner that day, down in the riverbed, staying beside the water in the uneven shadows of willows and cottonwoods. I came around a long curve and the Arabian stopped short with a snort and toss of his head. Twenty yards away were a dozen bare chested Comanche braves, sitting cross legged on a sandbar while their horses drank.

For a second, the only motion was the slight flutter of feathers and the strips of ribbon and calico in their ponies' bridles. Even before I could pull a rein, the Arabian had whirled around and charged away. Whoops and shrieks came from behind me and I could hear the Indian pony hooves splashing through the water. I gigged the Arabian's flanks and he dug for the gap in the trees on the ten-foot bank ahead. We hit the 45-degree bank and the Arabian lunged upward so hard my head snapped back. I grabbed the saddle horn with both hands as the Arabian's hooves found traction and we vaulted over the rim. We'd sprinted a quarter-mile before I chanced a look back.

Behind me, the Comanche came boiling over the creek bed, faces etched in fury, whooping and howling. They were a blur of whipping feathers and flowing manes and slapping legs and repeating rifles in outstretched arms. The whoops were near. Shots popped and bullets whizzed by. I corkscrewed around and fired a couple shots as they thundered after me, leaning low on their ponies.

The Arabian was fast, but the Indians stayed close for a time. I tapped my spurs to the Arabian's flank and he showed his racing champion bloodlines. He peeled his ears back, and we were off. The wind whipped past as he stretched out like a greyhound racing dog, burning grass ten yards at a bound.

The ground flew away under the Arabian's pounding hooves as the war cries and gun shots faded. Before we'd reached the mile mark the Arabian had two hundred yards on them, and by two miles it was over five-hundred yards and gaining.

I had just taken a breath of relief when I saw a cloud of dust and riders coming over a knoll a half mile in front of me. They disappeared into a dip and when they sprang back up, I saw they were cowboys from the herd. They blew past me popping pistol shots at the Comanches. The whooping stopped suddenly, and when it started up again it was fading away, going the other direction, with much less enthusiasm.

I pulled to a stop and watched the cowboys chase the Indians across the prairie. Bose and Andy rode back to me.

"Stirred up a hornet's nest, did you?" laughed Andy.

"Lucky for me, it still wasn't no war party." I said. "Same ones that's been dogging us."

"Just a little deviltry, I suppose," said Bose. "More than likely just having a little fun. They can be the most aggravatinist rascals when they're a mind to. Their idea of fun ain't necessarily mine."

"They do have a peculiar sense of humor," I said.

"They sure do," said Bose. "And as soon as you think you're in on the joke, they'll lift your hair and the joke's on you. They'll find it dang funny no matter which way it turns out."

# COMANCHERIA
## JUNE 1866

"So, you coming out with me this morning?" I said to Charlie as I saddled one of the cow ponies.

"I thought I would. I'd like to see what that wagon train has to say before we bring the herd closer," he said. "Must be a reason they're coming this way and it likely ain't good."

I'd seen the wagon train coming our way for days, off in the distance, coming from the west along the Butterfield Trail. They were coming slowly, ten wagons, families walking alongside. A few head of livestock. We stopped a few hundred yards away and three men from the train loped their horses toward us. They had guns sticking out of every pocket, but other than the big man in front, they didn't look like the type of men accustomed to gun play. I recognized the large fellow in plainsmen clothes.

"Howdy, Bigfoot," I said to my old friend, Bigfoot Wallace. Bigfoot was about fifty, well over six-foot tall and 250 pounds. He'd packed on a good bit of table-muscle over the years, but he was still no man to trifle with. It was just a few summers past that I'd seen him hoist a snake-shy yearling foal on his shoulders and truck it over a flooded creek. He was famous in Texas, and plenty of his adventures had made it into the big eastern newspapers. Plenty more into the dime novels of the day. A Virginian, he had come out to Texas intent on killing Mexicans after his brother was executed by Santa Anna's Mexican Army at Goliad.

"Huzzah for Texas," Bigfoot said. Bigfoot had been there at the Battle of Salado Creek in the fall of '42, with Jack Hays, my first big fight. We were both youngsters then, but Bigfoot had already been stalking Mexican soldiers for six years, killing scores. It was his long-range marksmanship, and ferocity when it got hand to hand, that kept that much larger army at bay at Salado Creek.

That had been the campaign that had interrupted my pursuit of Eagle Claw and the Comanche. The Mexican Army, some 1,500 strong, had crossed the Rio Grande River with the intention of retaking Texas. Our company was part of 200 men under Colonel Matt Caldwell when we encountered the Mexicans seven miles from San Antonio.

Bigfoot and I were two of thirty under Jack Hays that acted as decoys to lure out the advance party of the Mexican Army. We expected about fifty cavalrymen or so to challenge us. Instead, the entire 500-man cavalry corps was already in saddle, lying in wait. They charged out after us and engaged us in a galloping gunfight for five miles.

We made it back to the main body of Texians, but the entirety of the Mexican force soon arrived. Outnumbered seven-to-one, we held our position throughout the day. That night, we counted sixty dead they'd left on the field, with evidence plenty more had been picked up and carried away. Only one Texan was killed. That still wasn't good enough for Captain Caldwell, Jack Hays nor most of the panther-blood Texans. We tried a sneak attack that night, but the Mexicans were gone, having left a hundred burning campfires to disguise their retreat.

"Your account with the Mexicans squared yet?" I ask Bigfoot after I'd made introductions. I'd heard he'd slowed down his killing of Mexicans to concentrate on killing Comanches, but that his heart wasn't really in it. During the War years, Big Foot had stayed with the Rangers in Texas, selflessly protecting the womenfolk with their men gone off to war. He'd had a lot of them to protect, and rumor was he protected a lot of their bed covers, too.

"Santa Anner still breathing?"

"Was last I heard," I said.

"Then I ain't done yet," he said. "I'd heard you'd got yourself kilt somewhere's in Tennessee during the war."

"Next thing to it," I said. "I guess I got a hard head."

"That's a blessing sometimes," he said. "What are you doing away out here?"

"Scouting for a trail herd," I said.

"Is that you? They said a herd was coming this way, headed to New Mexico, that you all had a bold plan to drive cattle to them starving Navajo," Bigfoot said. "I hope you succeed. Good lord, they're miserable."

"That's the plan," Charlie said. "We got some good hands. The stock has held up fine so far."

"Well, that shines," he said. "Them reservation Injuns is in a dreadful state."

"And you, where you headed with these wagons?" I said.

"I'm leading the folks back east. They can't take the Comanche raids no more," Bigfoot said. "It's a real shame, so many places been abandoned because of the redskin scourge. I can't say I blame them. Comanche have been running wild the last few years. We ain't got the men to protect the homesteads in West Texas."

"How far you going?"

"I'm taking them as far as Ft. Belknap," said Bigfoot. "I figure they can make their way back to civilization from there without wasting the talents of a skilled frontiersman such as myself."

"Had any trouble?'

"None to speak of, but there's a passel of Comanche back a way," Bigfoot said. "They looked us over real good, but never came after us."

"How many is a passel?"

"A good fifty, maybe more. They was painted, so it's a mystery to me why they let us pass," he said.

"Where'd you see them?"

"They was not two whoops and a holler from Castle Gap when I seen 'em, which is where I figure you're headed with them beeves," said Bigfoot. "I seen some tipis up, back behind the Trinity Buttes. It looked like they'd been there for a while and planned to stay longer."

"But they never bothered you?"

"No, sir, they never. It's a puzzle. We would have given them a fight, but probably not for long," Bigfoot said. "I'm telling you, though, you got some dangerous territory to cover before you get to Fair Carletonia."

"Carletonia?" I said.

"Col. James Henry Carleton, that's who you're going to see ain't it?"

"It is," Charlie said.

"That's what folks have been calling the Bosque Redondo. I guess it's what you call ironic that he's the one charged with feeding the Navajo. Since it was him and Kit Carson that run the Navajo off their land in Arizona and put them on the Long Walk," said Bigfoot. "Burned their crops, poisoned their water, and shot their horses and marched them there to starve. That ain't the thing gonna engender a lot of trust and goodwill."

"There's folks say he is a changed man and this ushers in a new era with the Navajo. Or something similar," said Charlie. "We even have a scribe with us to document the event. Says Carleton has found Jesus or something."

"Is that right? I heard a rumor he was getting ready to retire and run for Governor of Maine," said Bigfoot. "I hope the scribe paints a true pitcher. I was there in early spring. It is a sorrowful place. I've seen many a reservation, and none more wretched than that one. That location for the reservation couldn't be worse. The brackish Pecos water has the Injuns walking around gripping their guts with dysentery. Its poor ground, and cutworm has ruined their crops three years running. They had a rat epidemic so they brought in cats to eat the rats and the Indians ate the cats. They eat the rats, too. Probably about the only thing keeping them from starving. Carletonia, like I said."

"I heard they was in sad shape," said Charlie.

"Some of 'em went on the warpath. Cadete and about 300 Apache jumped the reservation. But instead of going back to Arizona, they are somewhere on the Plains committing mayhem. Not that I blame them," said Bigfoot. "The Army asked me to scout for them, to track Cadete down. I declined. I got nothing against no Apache. Now, if they would have been shooting Mexicans I would have gleefully marched along."

"Who is this Cadete?" I said. "I haven't dealt much with Apache."

"He's the chief of the Sierra Blanca Mescalero band," said Bigfoot. "What's worse, Luther Walsh is said to be wooing Cadete with promise of rifles he stole from the Army. They think that's maybe why Cadete didn't go back home. Waiting to get his hands on some guns."

"Rifles?"

"That's the rumor. That somehow Luther Walsh has got his hands on about 3,000 repeating Spencers out of the Ft. Smith armory and is arming unreconstructed Rebs and renegade Apache. They have hit wagon trains as far north as the Santa Fe and south to the Camino Real. The Indian rumor mill says he's also trying to entice Manuelito and his thousand or so braves that ain't been reservated. It's a hot time to be going Ft. Sumner way."

"Well, I'll be durned," said Charlie. "I sure hope they don't go after our beeves."

"That herd is a mighty attractive target," said Bigfoot.

"I reckon it would be," Charlie said. "But we got plenty of repeaters on our side as well."

"I don't believe they're close to us at the moment," said Bigfoot. "But Luther has an army in the making. He's already chased off several fair-sized army patrols sent to bring him in. If he keeps having success against the Americanos, he won't have no hard time convincing more renegade Apache to join him for some shoot-all-day rifles. If he really gets rolling, savages from the ends of the earth will be rushing to join them. If that happens, there will be hell to pay."

"They can't talk the Apache down?"

"Maybe, but I doubt it. Like I said, Carleton has made a career out of killing Apache and Navajo. And lying to them. That they are dubious of his intentions now seems understandable," said Bigfoot. "Folks at Ft. Sumner is also worried that if Cadete gets strong enough, he might entice Victorio or Cochise to come east and attack Carleton. They sure hate him bad enough."

"Cochise and Victorio answer to Cadete?"

"No, Cochise and Victorio are from different bands. Cadete is Sierra Blanca Mescalero. Cochise is Chiricahua, and Victorio is chief of the

Warm Springs Mimbreños. Them latter two share a torrid hatred for Carleton," said Bigfoot. "After what Carleton done to their father-in-law."

"Who?"

"The father-in-law to both of them rascals was Mangas Coloradas, who Carleton had murdered in '62. The old chief entered the fort under white flag, but Carleton had him arrested anyway," said Bigfoot. "Then Mangas was mysteriously shot trying to escape. The soldiers cut his head off, boiled it, and sent it to some big museum back east in Washington. They ain't forgot that."

"I reckon not," I said.

"Up until then, Victorio nor Cochise rarely bothered white folks," said Bigfoot. "They ran wild against the Mexicans which, you know, kind'er endeared me to them. I knew Cochise when I ran the mail for the Butterfield stage in the late 50s. He was a wood cutter for the stage line and rode along with me a few times on that long trip between San Antonio and El Paso. I wouldn't never had made it if the Apache hadn't looked kindly on me."

"Goodness gracious," said Charlie. "Like we ain't got enough to be concerned about with the Comanche."

"There's a small party I seen trailing us, you seen 'em?" I said.

"I have," said Bigfoot.

"What were they up to when you saw them?"

"Trailing you, like you said."

After waiting two days I took a few cautious pokes around the buttes Bigfoot had mentioned. There were plenty of cold campfires but I saw no sign of any recent habitation so we pushed on toward the Concho. It was easy traveling to the gradual, cleared slope of the shallow river and the cattle had plenty of room to spread out and drink their fill. At dusk we bedded them down on the east side of the river and posted extra nighthawks. There was good grass and the cows seemed content.

"We're going straight across the Llano, no stopping," Charlie said. "I've been pondering it, and I think its best that way."

"No stopping?" I said.

"We've been averaging about 15 miles a day. Bedding down each night would be six days without water in 100-degree heat, straight across dry scrubland," said Charlie. "Cutting that time in half would have advantages."

"It would," I said. "I'm in favor of it. Rough either way."

"Six days without water, or three nights without sleep," said Charlie. "I think it's a safer bet for everybody to cut our time in half, pushing day and night. We'll not stop until we reach Horsehead Crossing."

"You're the boss," Bose said.

"We'll lose cows either way," said Charlie. "Three fewer nights that the Comanche can stampede the herd seems appealing."

The next day the herd grazed and watered in the lush Concho valley while Bose and I roamed, looking for sign of hostile Indians. Espinar and the cowboys filled every possible vessel with water.

The sun had dropped and the evening started to cool when we set off across the Llano. We headed due west, across ninety barren, waterless miles to Horsehead Crossing on the Pecos. As much as the longhorns needed water, I wasn't over-eager to reach the river. Horsehead was one of the few easy crossings on the crooked, steep-banked river, which meant it was also heavily traversed by Comanche warriors coming up the war trail from Mexico.

"Move 'em out," Charlie yelled, and they did.

At daybreak we were five miles past the Concho, in the vast emptiness of the Llano Estacado plains. The treeless, windswept land was flat but for a few low buttes and mesas. Red dust covered the rib bones and buffalo skulls that were scattered between the bunches of grama grass and patches of sage and squat mesquite. The flatness was slashed with arroyos, steep red-dirt stream beds that ran with a few inches of water only every other spring or so. This was Comanche country, treacherous for man or beast.

The Comanche hunting party was back, seeming to harbor no ill will over losing their chase. They continued to watch, expressionless, just out of rifle range. Sometimes they rode along parallel with the herd, appearing and disappearing in the shallow dips and low buttes of the prairie.

On our western horizon we could see the Castle Mountains, which were twelve miles this side of Horse Head Crossing. The mountains were a range of 3,000-foot-tall mesas that rose suddenly out of the flatness of the prairie and stretched for several miles. Castle Gap cut the mountains right down the middle, between two flat-topped, steep-sided limestone cliffs that resembled the parapets of a castle.

The mile-long gap through the cliffs was the road used by the old Butterfield Overland Mail stages, wagon trains and Comanche raiding parties. In some places the cut was flat and grassy, one-hundred yards across. In others it was rocky and just wide enough for a wagon to squeeze through. The turret-like bluffs provided a perfect site for ambush. It was a risky passing, but we had to go through it. The horses and cattle would not survive the two more waterless days it would take to bypass the Gap.

"That don't look good," said Bose, as we rode forward. A column of vultures circled silently above the Gap. We approached cautiously, hiding for an hour in some mesquite bushes three hundred yards away to study the remnants of a wagon train. There were five wagons, mostly burned. A dozen dead men and the same number of mules were scattered around the ground, most with an arrow or two sticking out. Wrinkled, waddling bare-headed turkey buzzards, coated in dried blood and bits of flesh, swarmed over the scene, gorging on the dead men and mules.

Seeing no sign of human activity, we galloped to the scene, shouting. Crows wheeled and darted, cawing angrily over their interrupted feast. The vultures hissed and grunted, refusing to leave their feeding until we put a couple shots into them.

The attack had come where the rocky slopes rose sharply on both sides and narrowed the pass to just fifty feet wide. The ground was rugged and broken, splotched with low-growing scrub mesquite and stiff, thorny greasewood shrub. Spanish Dagger spikes rose above prickly pear in the caliche covered slopes. Two wagons would have had a difficult time passing in this spot, especially in a flurry of arrows, but at least one teamster had tried it. He had tipped over for the trouble and was still trapped underneath, his bloody white skull showing where his scalp had been.

On every charred wagon-tongue was at least one blackened thing that had once been human. Shimmering green horse flies swarmed the dead, all of whom were stripped, scalped, and mutilated. Some of the men had been tied spread-eagle, staked out and slow roasted to death over open fires, a favorite Comanche method. Their eyes had been cut away, black, empty sockets crawling with flies. The work of Comanche, but there were too many bodies here for it to have been the work of the band following us.

"I'd say it's a good two days old, but hard to tell out here in this heat," I said to Charlie, after he had ridden up.

"I reckon this would be the work of the large band Bigfoot warned of," said Charlie.

"I expect so," I said.

"Kind of a strange looking train. These ain't settler wagons," Bose said. "Whatever was in them wagons is gone. Don't appear to be no women's things in here. No food nor clothes nor goods of a homesteader sort."

"Cleaned out slick as a whistle," I said. "Comanche don't generally take off with parlor furniture and bedding. What was in those wagons that they would be cleaned out so thoroughly?"

"Hard telling," said Charlie. "But this one here, all bloody and bloated, I do believe is Sacramento Simms. I can tell by that big scar under his chin. He was a freight-line mule skinner. Killed a man some years back and fell in with some unscrupulous sorts. Was wanted for selling guns to some Kiowa last I heard."

"Gun runners?" I said.

"That's what I heard," said Charlie.

"Can't imagine what else would be cleared out so thorough," said Bose.

"That would fit, both Sacramento and this here," said Charlie.

"Working with Luther Walsh?"

"Easy to see it," Charlie said. "But I've got a couple thousand thirsty cows to worry about."

"I better see what lays between us and the river," I said. "I'd guess the bunch that did this is long gone by now but can't take nothing for granted with these jaybirds."

"I'll come along with you," said Bose.

I knew of a few springs in the Castle hills, so Bose and I filled our canteens with fresh water, strapped on all our extra pistols, checked our spare cylinders and loped off toward the Pecos. We found the crossing, a narrow clearing pinched between moat-like banks that dropped twenty feet straight down. The riverbank was littered with the skulls and bones of mustangs and other wildlife poisoned by the gyppy water or crippled by falls over the years. Otherwise, we saw no sign of trouble and headed back.

"We clear ahead?" Charlie shouted, when we met the herd about four miles from the river. The poor, alkali covered, bawling longhorns were in misery after three days without water. Their lolling tongues nearly dragged the ground.

"Yes, sir," said Bose.

"I think we should probably part the herd, and send the strong half on to water first," said Charlie. "I held up the slower ones back at the gap for half a day. Maybe that way they won't get trampled in the rush to the river."

"Probably a good idea," Bose said. "Let's just hope too much of that water don't kill them."

"Some will perish, but it can't be helped. They're wild range critters used to living rough and drinking gyppy water if that's all that there is," said Charlie. "It's a gamble, but we got to chance it."

"Just get the flankers up here, and I'll show them where to point the cows. We have a nice level approach, but it's not wide. Get some men down river so they don't drift."

"We'll have to keep those cowboys awake for the next twenty-four hours," Bose said. "If they're gonna hit us, right here would be the spot."

"I know it," Charlie said. "Espinar will have both coffee pots going around the clock."

"Get out of their way and let 'em travel," Charlie shouted back at his cowboys. The cattle could smell the river and were coming our way in a sharp boned jog, the big red brindle Judas steer leading them like they were cavalry.

I stayed alongside as the first gangly longhorns lurched into the river and the dust-heavy cowboys hooted and croaked hoarsely. At dusk, for nearly a mile the river was filled with cattle soaking to their shoulders.

Espinar had the big five-gallon coffee pots going and had unfurled a long tarp from the wagon to provide some shade. Ulice stayed busy, handing out brown gargle and biscuits to the exhausted cowboys staggering in.

"Saddle up a fresh hoss afore you set," Charlie yelled at the incoming cowboys. "And check your weapons. We can expect devilry from the Comanche tonight."

"They've been watching close enough all day," I said. The twelve Comanche had shown themselves several times throughout the day. "Good time for them to jump us, they think we're worn out from getting these cows across the river."

"Exactly what I was thinking," said Charlie.

"By gum, you do make a fine pot of coffee," Charlie said to Espinar after a few quiet sips. "Dark as night, strong as love and hot as Hell. Keep it bubbling. We need to keep the boys perpendiclar one more night."

"I'm on it, boss, whatever these cowboys need," Espinar said. "We'll not run short of steaming Arbuckles. Biscuits are warm. Stauncher stuff will be ready soon."

Some cattle had drowned falling into the water, or broke a leg or neck, but considerably fewer than Charlie said he had expected. His spirits were high as the cowboys wandered in. There were piles of thick, juicy steaks from the few unfortunate beeves that had darted past the cowboys to their doom. We toasted their sacrifice as we savored the fresh beef, thick sop and boiled potatoes, fried onions, hot biscuits, and boggy top berry pies. And coffee. Gallons of coffee. As we devoured that sumptuous spread Charlie made an announcement.

"Gents, we're at the halfway point. We're on schedule, maybe a little ahead. Fine job, fine job," said Charlie. "We're over the worst part of it in far better shape than I'd hoped for. I just gotta ask you to stay awake for one more night. The Comanche have been watching us, as you know. They know we're tired, and probably expect us to be careless. And it sure looks like a heller of a storm brewing. I expect they'll try us tonight. You agree Pete?"

"I do," I said. "I don't think they want our hair, but it's a good time for them to try some mischief. Especially steal some cows now that we've gone to the trouble of crossing the Llano, the Pecos, and watered 'em good."

"That's what I'm thinking, too," said Charlie. "I propose we let them have fifty or a hundred head. We're tired, and the Comanches love to spook a herd. But these cows is still tired from that long dry spell and the mad rush to the river. I doubt they'll run far, even if stampeded."

"A hundred cattle?" said some cowboys.

"We have at least that many I thought we'd lose by now," said Charlie. "Ones that'll drop over dead before we cross another two hundred more miles over New Mexico scrubland."

"Yes, but why make it easy for them?" said someone.

"Why make it hard for us?" Charlie said. "Kinder sticks in my craw, too. I hate to do it, but I hate to bury cowboys worse. Especially when it could be avoided. Like I said, we've got cows I expected to lose."

"Why not just run them some over, as an offering, if they want tribute?" grumbled Clay.

"Nah, with Comanche, even if we dicker for a few, they'll want to steal a few more. That's just the Comanche way," Charlie said. "We've been fortunate so far, more fortunate than I would have guessed, and with no loss of life. That's just the way I want to keep it."

"Pretty fair reasoning," I said.

"Take a hundred of the weakest, move them to the outside and let 'em wander off a little way. We'll keep a strong line of cowboys between the cutouts and the main herd," said Charlie. "When the Comanche hit, we start our own stampede of the main herd up this horseshoe bend in the river. The Comanches can't get at them from the other side, and the trees are thick enough at the riverbank it should keep too many from falling in. A natural corral."

"I'll form the line," I said. "I want Bose out there with me between the cutouts and the herd. And Ray and Braswell. Andy and Marcellus. And John Milton. Espinar, if you want to come."

"The cook?" hollered Clay Allison. "Ain't that a sham. Taking a damn bean-tender in front of a known fighter."

"Sonny, I was fighting Comanche when you were wet nursing," said Espinar. "Well before that."

"He knows how to shoot better than you, and when not to shoot even better," I said. "And that's the point right now. We're not trying to ignite an Indian war. There's a small band that's been following us. They get a few head and nobody gets hurt, maybe they'll go away. We get into a shooting fight with them, they might bring back the bunch that raided those wagons we passed. The whole Comanche nation if they want. We'll have trouble every step of the way to the fort."

"But make no mistake, boys. Strap on your second pistols, and make sure you got plenty of loaded cylinders. Just hold your water and don't start blazing away. It won't be easy with screaming Injuns galloping down on you," Charlie said. "I agree with Pete. If they were after blood, they'd have already attacked."

"We're not going to shoot back if they're attacking us?" said a cowboy.

"You're not going to shoot if all they're doing is hooting and waving blankets at the cattle," Charlie said.

"Sounds like we're cowering to them redskins," said Clay.

"Shut up, Clay, this ain't the time for nonsense," Charlie said. "In the middle of a dang storm you're unlikely to hit anything anyway. And if you do, it's just as likely to be one of us."

"Gives the warrior a little more honor that way, him stealing the cows," I said. "Letting him think he struck a blow against the Americanos."

"That's what I was thinking," said Charlie. "As long as it don't embolden future raids."

"Hard to say what emboldens a Comanche," I said. "They're a mercurial lot as I've ever met, though I've seen Sam Colt disembolden more than a few. They know we're well armed and prepared to fight. Maybe that will be enough, and they'll settle for a few head. They can't move fast while trying to drive cows and there's no place to hide more than a couple head."

"They probably had better summer plans than herding cattle," Charlie said. "Comanche don't care much for drudgery."

"Prairie etiquette. Good manners can go a long ways if their intent isn't warlike to begin with," I said.

"I reckon if we get much of a storm, the herd's likely to stampede anyway," said Charlie, as thunder rumbled and a streak of lightning crackled across the sky. "I'd rather have the Comanche run them into the canyon than out of it. Worst case scenario, we'll have to round up a bunch of cows tomorrow. This just might prevent that."

"Just might," I said.

I selected a calm horse and sat waiting in the inky night beside Bose. We'd pushed about fifty weakened cattle out onto a sage flat. The six of us formed a line and posted up between them and the main herd. At dusk, the coming rain had cooled the air quickly. Thunder and lightning roared and flashed and the black clouds rolled overhead. I pulled my hat off and turned my face to the heavens to feel those big blissful raindrops. Behind me, the cowboys kept the jittery cattle of the main herd milling in a tight circle.

"Can't make it too obvious," said Bose of our line of defense. "It's not like they just started stealing livestock yesterday."

"Like Charlie said, I figure the biggest deterrent to them stealing more than a handful of cows is that no Comanche wants to be slowed down by cattle long," I said. "Let's hope they play along and everybody goes home happy."

A spectacular lightning bolt arched across the sky and crashed to earth. The flare of light flashed just long enough to spot the line of mounted Comanche on a small mesa.

"See them?" Bose said.

"I did," I said. "They're not close enough yet, but better let the others know which way they're coming."

"You don't really expect those boys to hold their fire, do you?" Bose asked.

"No, I expect them to run away as fast as their horses can carry them. That's what any sane person would do if a horde of screaming Comanches suddenly descended upon them from the blackness of a thunderstorm," I said. "One thing, this way they can save a little face themselves if called into question as to why they didn't think to fire their weapons."

"Ain't you the ever-thoughtful gentleman," said Bose.

"I try," I said. "Mostly I just don't want any wild shooting causing a stampede before we're ready."

We sat in the dark and waited through several more minutes of pouring rain, lightning flashes, and cannon booms of thunder. A lightning bolt crashed to the ground and the Comanches came charging at full gallop, flapping blankets over their heads and clanging cowbells.

I fired my pistol twice in the air while Bose and the others sprang into action, whooping and hollering and blocking the cutouts from turning back to the main herd. Torches had been prepared near the campfire and I saw them burst into light. They whipped through the darkness as the main bunch of cowboys went charging hell for high leather, running the herd toward Charlie's makeshift holding pen in the bend of this crooked river. The confused cattle in the cutaway herd dashed and darted in every direction. I thought I might have to give the raiders a hand, but they finally got the cutouts surrounded and driven off.

I was tucked away in a sparse thicket of mesquite, surprised at how well it had gone when I heard the pounding of hoof beats behind me. There was a howl like a wolf and then a Comanche war lance blasted me across the head. The mighty blow nearly unsaddled me. I was stunned and seeing triple and grabbed my saddle horn to hold on. I was expecting a death blow, but the Comanche vanished into the blackness. I was slumped forward, thinking to wretch, when Bose rode up alongside me.

"That Comanche, he just ran by and counted coup on me and run off," I groaned, hearing myself slur. "He could have killed me easy."

"He did?" Bose said. "What the hell for?"

"I don't know," I said, and fell unconscious off my horse.

"We've tarried here about as long as we need to. Don't want to give the Comanche the idea they can waltz up in here and take free cows anytime they take a notion," said Charlie. "I reckon we'd best head on in the morning, if you ain't seeing double no more."

We'd grazed and watered the herd for two days, and the gyppy water hadn't killed too many of them. Now we were turning north, up the New Mexico alkali flats.

"My vision's fine, but this headache is lingering," I said. "Espinar gave me a dose of laudanum. I expect I'll take another and doze for the night and be refreshed by morning."

"Refreshed enough to ride drag for a while?" Charlie said. "I'm a little concerned about the boys I have back there. They're doing a dandy job keeping the cows from hightailing it, but they're young. I'm concerned the Comanche might try to hit us again, from behind. Those boys ain't experienced in reading the signs of danger around them."

"I'm not much a cowboy," I said.

"You don't need to be. Like I said, those boys are doing a fine job at that," he said. "Just watch our back trail. Just keep looping around there, watching for signs of anyone trailing us."

"Sure," I said. "I can do that."

"Good," he said. "Bose will ride scout until you make sure we ain't being followed by cattle thieves."

It was probably a good idea to send me back there. The two cowboys who had been assigned to ride drag were Dewey and Denny Jameson, 16 and 17-year old brothers of destitute situation, orphaned by the war. Their father and older brother had been in Hood's division and both had been struck down by Yankee bullets at Chickamauga. Their mother went down to a broken heart soon after. Their pa had been a close friend of Charlie's. They were good boys, but still green.

We followed the twisting course of the river through this desolate shrub desert. Days were dry and brutally hot. The heat not only came from the sky, but rebounded up from the hard-baked ground like a blast furnace. Animal heat rolled off the herd in a nostril clogging cloud of flies and manure-flecked dust. All the men were ashy white with alkali trail dust, hats pulled low with their bandannas up to their eyes. They looked more like highwaymen than honest cowpokes, but that still wasn't enough to keep the sand and alkali dust out. Cattle were falling out every mile or so, and lanky, leering wolves followed along behind the drag men.

Returning from a loop around our back trail I was surprised to see the shape of a third drag rider trudging his horse through the heavy drag dust. I held back awhile to make sure it wasn't a bandit sneaking up with his face covered. After a few minutes I determined it was Clay Allison. I would have almost preferred a bandit. I was curious as to why he was there but didn't savor a conversation with him, so I did another loop along our back trail. Two hours later I came back around and found him still there so I rode up beside him.

"Balmy weather we're having, ain't it?" I said, pulling up beside him as the herd plodded along. He grunted something and made a great show of pulling his bandanna even higher. I ignored him for a while but decided to keep a close eye on the youngsters back here with him. Clay wasn't doing much except complaining about everything, so I butted in every time he would get to haranguing too much. It wouldn't take much complaining to sour impressionable youngsters in this over-baked, foul-smelling drudgery of staring at the behinds of 2,500 alkali sick cows day after day.

"Why are you so dumpish?" I said, when he started in again.

"It's mighty dull music, if you ask me," Clay said. "I'm back here for punishment."

"Narrowly avoiding that wagon train massacre, and having Indians shadowing us trying to stampede our herd ain't enough for you?" I said. "Not to mention a buffalo hunt? Well, if I'd signed up for a safari I couldn't imagine a better time."

"We should be hunting down and shooting holes in them Comanche that's been doggin' us. It's a cowardly display in my opinion."

"Have you shared that opinion with Charlie, or Bose?" I said.

"To hell with Charlie. And double hell for that haughty Bose, and you, trying to boss me like I'm some field hand or something. This is just a waste of my skills." said Clay. "Riding drag... Eatin' drag dust... Ain't a job for a white man."

"You can ride off any time you want," I said.

"Freedmen's Bureau protecting all you jigs, ain't right," he said.

"Why do you say things like that? Are you trying to provoke me?" I said. "Because eventually I'll get provoked. I've held back for Charlie's sake, but the job's tough enough without such nonsense from you."

"Is that right?" he said.

"I ride for the brand, same as you. Like Charlie said, ain't no black, white, Yankee or Johnny Reb out here," I said. "You need to come to terms with that."

"Or what?"

"The terms might come to you."

We stopped for the night and I headed for the campfire and some much-needed coffee.

"Who wants the candy?" Espinar shouted, holding up the night's first package of Arbuckle's.

"My turn," said Clay.

"No, I'm up," said Marius, the slight tenor singer. Ulice consulted his list and said it was, indeed, Marius's turn. When Espinar handed Marius the sacks, Clay glowered and started pacing and huffing in excited indignation. Marius pretended not to notice and carefully laid the red-and-white striped peppermint stick on the drop table, saving it for later. He sat down on a crate beside the wagon and poured the dry beans into the grinder, cranking the coffee mill between his legs. He hummed contentedly as Clay stomped around, glaring at him.

With a curse, Clay took three long steps and grabbed the candy. Marius leapt up and the two of them got in a tussle, knocking into the wagon, falling over some boxes, and kicking over a pot of beans Espinar had soaking.

"What in tarnation are you doing Clay?" I yelled.

"I didn't do anything. This clumsy jigaboo just knocked over our supper," Clay snarled.

"That's just like you, Clay," I said. "Bullying people and throwing a tantrum when you don't get your way."

"You best be ready to pull them pistols if you want to down talk me," said Clay.

"That's enough Clay!" shouted Charlie.

"No colored's gonna boss me around," said Clay. "I've had my fill of all these blasted unnatural changes!"

"Changes don't have nothing to do with it, Clay. I rode these Plains for nearly thirty years as a free-living man," I said. "I'd of killed you then. I'm less inclined to do so now, but don't push it. You don't call no man unnatural."

"You're right, he ain't bossing you no more," said Charlie. "Because you're fired."

Clay twisted around to face Charlie with a murderous look.

"Don't look at me all horns and rattles, son, or I'll cut a switch," said Charlie.

"Don't talk to me like I'm a boy," said Clay.

"You are a boy. I thought I hired a man. All you done since you got here was complain and shirk," said Charlie. "Grab you a horse and set out. Don't come back around our fire."

"There's Comanche out there," said Clay.

"You're an all fired gunman. Shoot 'em," said Charlie. "Or complain 'em to death, but you ain't my holler no more."

"That ain't right, said Clay, to the sound of half a dozen pistols being cocked and pointed at his heart.

"That's the only choice you got," said Charlie. "Unless you want to ride to Ft. Sumner tied to the spokes of that wagon wheel. You need to cut dirt. We got sleeping to do, and you're preventing it."

# HORSE THIEVES AND STOLEN RIFLES
## JULY 1866

I'd ridden through this area before, and knew where a shaded little pool in a freshwater creek was hidden a mile or so away. The trees and shrub bushes along the river's edge weren't big and didn't offer a lot of cover or shade, but it was the best I'd get out here in this barren country. The vigilant Comanche stayed away for a couple days after the stampede but had returned. I'd come within shouting distance of them and they'd still shown no outward display of hostility. Since they'd had plenty of chances to take my hair and hadn't, I'd decided to take a bath. I watered my horses good, laid my things out right, and jumped in.

Two hours later I was stretched out on my horse blanket, sunning my nethers, dozing and daydreaming the day away. I was pondering my future when I heard the men walking toward me.

"Sorry mister, but we're gonna have to take that fine horse of yours," a voice said a second after I heard the bushes break. I jumped up, armed only with the muslin towel in my hands.

Two men had emerged from the dense brush and rocks fifty feet away. They were walking along the stream towards me with guns drawn. Behind them I could see four or five more coming down the high gravelly bank. Further back on the rim I saw a man holding some horses.

I recognized Ezra Smoot, and his big, lumbering swagger out here where stepping lightly prolonged life. Gid Smoot was beside him. The other five were young, nervous, wide eyed. I recognized Reuben Higbee, one of Porter's youngest sons. I halfway recognized the others.

"We'd pay you for the hoss, but we don't have time to negotiate,"

Ezra said. "Your herd will probably catch up to you by nightfall. All you gotta do is sit here in the shade and wait for them."

"You all really need my horse that bad? Stealing horses is a hanging offense out here," I said.

"Yes, sir, we mightily do, but that dasn't need concern you," Ezra Smoot said.

If it had been one of the cow ponies, I might have just gone along. But it was the Arabian, and no amount of money nor amateurish bad men was going to take him while I was still kicking.

I made a quick survey of my situation and was glad I'd taken the time to lay my weapons out within easy reach. My saddle was on the ground about five feet away, behind some chest-high brush and rocks. Looped over the pommel was my holster holding two loaded Colts and a 14-inch Bowie knife.

I eyed my assailants as they walked toward me. There's a difference between bullies with a gun and gun men, and it's a difficult thing to hit a running man with a pistol even from ten feet away. From thirty paces, only the most dead-eyed gun slick could hit a moving target with any consistency. Except for Ezra and Gid, these boys didn't impress me as gun slicks of any sort, except perhaps the sort to die young. Ezra and Gid, I took as the type gun slicks who made their reputation gunning drunk farm boys and pushing around shopkeepers. They'd have to be quick on the trigger, and steadier than I took them for. Still, it was possible. Even the worst shot gets lucky. But so was it also possible they were setting to shoot me where I stood, without me even giving them a fight. That's what I would expect from Ezra. I wasn't about to do that either.

"That's about far enough," I said. I pointed my towel covered hand at them, with my finger under it pointed out like a gun.

"What are you going to do, shoot us with that old rag?" Ezra laughed. But they had stopped. It was a good enough bluff to show me they were susceptible to feints.

"I won't shoot you, but them up there will," I said, nodding my head at some imaginary person behind them. They hesitated for just a beat as their eyes flashed toward the rim. I dove to my left, doing a little flip and roll over my saddle as some wild shots passed overhead. I snatched my gun belt and bullet pouch as I came to rest behind the rocks. I rolled some more, up the grade through the sharp caliche and wide patch of low growing prickly pear cactus. The horse thieves were slow, and their bullets pinged off the rocks and stitched up the ground behind me.

I was scraped raw and full of cactus spines as I scrambled through the rocks and brush. I looped my pistol belt over my shoulder and kept a Colt in my right hand as I crawled up the sloping, hundred-foot long embankment. Below me someone shouted and a flurry of bullets ripped through the brush. The shots were nowhere close, and I could tell by their cursing they had already lost track of me. The Higbees had picked a bad spot to try to ambush me, and I had a lot better idea where they were than they did of me. After a half hour of belly crawling through the sage and rock I'd flanked them and squeezed up under an overhanging ledge to wait.

I had a lot of experience lying still and quiet but it didn't sound like the horse rustlers did. I couldn't see them, but I could hear them clearly in the jumbled boulders and thick foliage thirty feet down. They were loud and dumb, tripping, cursing, huffing, and grumbling. I had counted on them not expecting one naked man to try to maneuver around and take the fight to them, and I was correct. Huddled close together, they were bickering over who would stick their neck out to look for me.

I had plenty of bullets, but I was no great pistol shot either. I was buck naked, and they had my horse. I couldn't retreat, but I wasn't really in position to charge. I could hide out and wait for the herd to pass by, though they could be miles away. There might or might not be a slew of Comanche raiding parties and bandits between me and them dumb cows.

"Go around there and get him," I heard one say.

"You go around there and get him. This was all your brilliant idea," said another.

The squabbling continued as they walked further downstream, beating the brush looking for me. I made my way upstream, staying near the rim of the bank until the horse thieves' own mounts were between me and them. The man guarding the horses was seated on a rock, out in the open with his eyes fixed on his companions. He would be easy to overpower. The only bad thing was that they did have possession of my Arabian. I Indian-slithered across the ground until I was right behind the horse tender.

"Say a word and I'll slit you," I said, after I came up behind the man quiet as a cat and brought my big knife around his throat. I poked the point of my blade under his chin. "Comprende?"

He nodded so vigorously he jabbed himself and let out a little scream. I gave him a smart cuff with the pistol and told him to shut up and not move. He didn't, and the slothful Higbees hadn't even noticed his kidnapping. I stuffed a hankie in his mouth and tied his hands behind his back with a pigging string from my bullet bag.

I slipped among their horses and pulled two Henry rifles from their scabbards as the horse thieves continued beating the brush for me, cussing, and almost shooting each other more than once.

Time passed, at least an hour, and then I heard the Higbees coming back my way. Their guns were holstered and they were walking carelessly about a hundred yards away, paying no heed to anything around them. Some were cursing me, saying they'd fill me full of holes for tricking them with my towel. Others were laughing that they got my horse anyway. When I was ready, I sat the horse tender on top of the boulder and tickled my knife under his jaw again. Then I yanked the gag out and kicked him in the back.

"Now, holler!" I shouted.

He hollered plenty as he flew off the rock with his hands still tied behind his back. His legs flailed as he cussed and plummeted ten feet, crashing down in a mixed bed of horse crippler and cat claw cactus. He screamed and thrashed and raised to a knee. He stood up, then tripped down the slope and knocked himself out on a rock.

102

His screams had alerted the others and they shot wildly, the bullets cracking off rocks and zipping through the tree branches above me. I slid between two rocks and emptied the rifle into the rattling brush hiding the Higbees. While they ducked and dodged and tumbled down the slope I scrambled further up the bank until I was hidden by shrubs and the shade of the ledge. I laid there for a while, listening to the moaning and cussing. I'd hit at least one of them.

I was planning my next move when I heard the pounding of hooves coming fast. Two, maybe three, horses were galloping my way. I squeezed tighter under the bank as two big shadows soared over me.

I watched, gape-jawed, as about twenty feet down the bank, two horses landed in a violent explosion of dust and gravel, skidding almost sideways down the loose caliche embankment. In the roiling cloud Bass Reeves held the reins to his big white horse in his mouth and rapid fired two pistols into the bushes. Right behind Bass Reeves, Britt Johnson's big bay swerved and careened down the slope as Britt fired his pistol into the brush.

Bass sprang off his horse as it slid, landing light on his feet and still blasting into the bushes. Britt kept firing and I jumped up and emptied the second Henry into the tangle of brush where I'd last seen the Higbees. They may have shot back, but in the furious barrage we had unleashed, it was hard to tell. The shooting stopped, and it was silent except for the loud moaning and cussing of the wounded Higbees.

"You boys throw out your pistols and come out with your hands up. Otherwise I'm going to head shoot these blubbering sons-a-bitches," shouted Bass, looming over two Higbees sprawled at his feet. There was blood on their shirts and their hands were empty and raised. "Be quick about it, or you'll find what you just got was only one small piece of the hell we'll unleash on you."

"I can't," choked out one voice. "You got me in the leg."

"Well, get to crawling then, all the way out where I can see you," Bass shouted. "Throw your pistol out here."

"Here's mine, you son of a bitch," shouted another voice, deeper. A Colt came arching out of the bushes and landed in the dust.

"Give it up fellers. I'm bleeding to death," said a quivering voice in the brush. After a good deal more cussing than I'd expect of a Mormon another pistol landed in the dust. A man stood, supporting himself by leaning against a stone.

The others, looking halfway dazed, came out with their hands held high. Gid Smoot's left sleeve was wet with blood from the top of the shoulder down. A bullet had taken a chunk out of the tip of his shoulder. He pressed a hankie to the wound.

"Howdy, Bass. Britt. I sure am pleased to see you fellows," I said. The Higbees continued their chorus of cussing, generally emphasizing each other's stupidity. Most of them had suffered some sort of wound. The horse watcher was awake now, and cussing too.

"I'm shot in the head," sobbed Titus Cluff, staggering out of the brush with his hands pressed to his brow. Blood from his wound had gushed down his hands to his elbows.

"No, you ain't, you big baby, you're barely hit, if at all," I said as I took Titus's shirt off him and tied it tight around his bloody head. There was a deep slice across his forehead, but most of the bleeding had stopped. "And you definitely ain't shot in the head. You cracked it open on a rock, most likely."

"He ain't dying, I am," said the dust caked, leg-wounded Furman Haight who had dragged himself through the bushes. He was bleeding bad, from a wound just above the knee. I made a quick tourniquet out of his shirt and twisted it tight with a stick. The blond-haired boy beside him didn't look shot, but was covered in blood and had a badly busted nose. Bass had booted him a good one in his dismount. He hadn't been cussing like the others and looked pretty shook up.

"What's your name kid?" I said, as more moans came from around me. Britt and Bass kept pistols on the gang while I finished inspecting their wounds.

"Zach Petty," he said.

"All right, Zach," I said. "Hold this tourniquet stick tight for a few minutes while I try to make a bandage. Loosen it every little bit to see if it's still gushing."

"Help me, somebody help me," said one Higbee crumpled against a rock.

"It's Eldon," said Gid Smoot, sitting down in the dirt. "I reckon he's done for. He took a slug right in the belly."

"It hurts," groaned Eldon Jukes as I bent to check on him.

"Gut shot is a rough way to go, but you brung it upon yourself," I said. "Here, let me see."

Eldon took his hands away from the wound. The shot had barely nicked his side, just deep enough to skip off a rib bone before going out his back skin. Painful, but not fatal. Not unless infection set in. Riding a horse was going to be mighty unpleasant. I lifted the horse watcher to his feet and led him down with the others.

They cursed us blue for a solid three minutes after we made them hobble themselves by pulling their trousers down over their boots and lying face down on the bristly creek bank. I suppose it made them especially leery since I was still running around naked in a two-gun holster.

"Who's the boss of this inept outfit?" said Bass.

"Ezra, that's him down there," Zach said. "Dead as a wagon wheel."

Ezra Smoot was lying on his side, indeed dead as a wagon wheel. He'd taken one right through the chin. A few feet away was another dead man, face down with another bullet hole just beneath his left shoulder blade.

"You shot him in the back," said Gid, as I rolled the dead man over. It was Reuben Higbee.

"Well, this ain't good," said Britt.

"Why are you boys doing this? What are you doing out here stealing horses?" I asked, looking at the dead men on the ground.

"We needed one in a hurry. Ezra's horse stepped in a gopher hole," Furman Haight said. "We're after Wildcat Bob Ketchum. There's a $1,000 reward on his head for killing three people in a stage robbery. We aimed to collect it."

"Based on what I saw here, you all really ain't cut out for that kind of work," Bass said. "School girl dilettantes like you all shouldn't be waving pistols at no one, especially not bands of killers like Wildcat Bob has. If you ain't no better at ambushing people than what you just now exhibited, your bones are gonna be bleaching out there on the prairie. Stealing horses is even above your abilities, apparently."

"It was more like borrowing," Gid said. "We really didn't mean no harm. You're with that trail herd a couple miles back, ain't you? That herd will be along soon. You coulda just took you a siesta and waited for them. We know'd that herd would catch up to you afore sundown. It's Charlie Goodnight's outfit, ain't it?"

"No, it was flat out robbin'. That's a blooded horse you were trying to steal, worth all the horses you got there and twenty more," I said. "They'll be no argument on that point, or I might start contemplating some real gut shooting."

"I expect ya'll be best served taking that advice," drawled Bass after another round of insults from the horse thieves.

"You going to behave yourself?" I said to Zach. He wasn't running his mouth like the others. In fact, he'd barely uttered a word since the shooting stopped.

"Yes, sir," he said, looking down, thoroughly beaten.

"Alrighty then. It looks like your compadres there are sufficiently subdued enough we can let them up. Long enough to tie them up anyway," I said. "Get the ropes off them saddles."

After we had the bandits roped securely to the trees I threw their saddles and guns into the deepest part of the pool. After that, I pulled my drawers over my thorn-riddled legs and dug some bacon and biscuits out of my saddlebags.

"You sons a bitches just going to sit there and eat while we're bleeding to death over here?" shouted Gid Smoot.

"I don't see the point in us standing," I said as Britt piled kindling for a fire. "Shootouts is hungry work."

"Exhausting," Bass said. "Just ask Ezra there. He ain't moved since we got here."

"Well, you rotten..." screamed Furman, with the tourniquet.

"You'll bleed out at the same rate, us standing or setting, eating or having hunger pains," said Britt. "More you talk, though, faster you bleed. Something to consider."

"Hunger makes a man cranky, too," I said. "Probably something you'd best avoid."

"I'd offer to share mine with you boys, but why waste it on someone we're likely gonna hang," said Bass.

"Hang?" said Eldon.

"On an empty stomach, that would be my vote," said Britt. "Leave us be, if you know what's best."

"It hurts," said Eldon.

"I reckon it does. That's generally the point of shooting someone," Britt said. They were a bickering bunch, and I couldn't tell if they were more upset about their dead kin, being forced to surrender, or facing the wrath of Porter Higbee.

"I'm bleeding to death," said Furman.

"And ain't nobody bleeding to death with that nice tourniquet on. Now we just need to remember to loosen it so he don't lose that leg," said Britt. "Going hungry don't help a man's memory about such trivial matters. Just let us eat in peace, before we faint away from hunger and forget all about you."

"These ropes are digging into us. This is might uncomfortable," said Tobias Hoagland, one of the younger bandits.

"You keep running your yap I'll make you as comfortable as old Ezra there," said Bass. "He ain't complained a bit and that's how I like it."

"When my pa finds out about this, he's gonna hang you on a meat hook," said Areli Higbee, another of Porter's sons. He was the other Bass had kicked in the jaw when he'd vaulted off his horse.

"You and all them pistols," snarled Gid. "You all gonna need a bunch more guns than what you got now. You may have got the drop on us this time, but you can't whip all of us."

"Got the drop on you?" I said.

"Son, you're a real idgit, you know that?" said Bass. "I reckon I won't be taking advice from no shot up Higbee, especially no gunfighting advice. I can't move without tripping over some dang leaking Higbee or another."

"I'm tired of this ear-beatin'," Britt said. "Them trees ain't stout enough to hang all these fools. You wanna shoot 'em?"

"I could go either way," Bass said. "I don't really want to waste bullets on 'em. If we'd thought to replenish our ammunition before throwing their guns in the water I'd go along with it. But punishment is due. It's too hot to get wore out giving them a thrashing. Want to drag them from horses?"

"Could do that, as long as we use their own horses," I said. "Powerful hot for thrashing."

"Drownin' would be cool on a hot day," said Bass. "We could drown 'em."

"We could do that. How's that sound, fellers?" I said to our grumbling captives. "You want drug or shot? Relish a dip? Thrashing is an option, but as mouthy as you all are, I'd probably get irritated and shoot you anyway."

"You know, taking a dip does sound inviting," said Bass.

"You're all going swimming while we're tied up and suffering this way?" said Eldon.

"Why not? Can you think of a better way to pass time?" said Bass. "It's a hot one out, but you boys got it cool there in the shade."

"We could just leave them tied up there, leave them to the fates of the prairie, like they was set to do to you," said Britt. 'Someone will show up, two legged, four legged, or feathered. But someone will."

"You gonna leave us out here bleeding and all?" Gid said. "Comanches might show up."

"You're fretting over nothing, thinking way too far ahead," said Bass. "It'll be dark soon and the wolves will come. Could be a panther around. Thought I saw a track. The Comanche's a good two day's ride off. I suggest you stay real quiet."

"Panthers?" gulped a young bandit. "You got no right to tie us up and leave us out here."

"Banditry was always a gamble. That's a chance you took when you decided to rob me. This is a mess of your own making," I said, which only prompted a round of cussing.

"Where you figure those church boys learned all that bad talk?" Britt said.

"A mess like this, I probably should check with Charlie before we make any drastic decisions on the fate of these boys. I am in his employ, and his crew will be facing the ramifications here. I best not be making any ex parte rulings," I said. "He plans to make this a regular trail and he'll not want to be worried about a horde of vengeful Higbees each trip."

"I'm agreeable," said Britt. "You figure the herd's seven days or so from the fort?"

"About that, I calculate," I said.

"If you don't mind, maybe we'll ride along with you for a few days," said Britt. "We need some time to ponder these new developments. Mutual defense is probably a good idea."

"Sound reasoning," I said.

"Our horses is played out, too," said Bass. "You reckon Charlie can find us a couple cow ponies to ride for a few days, give ours a little respite?"

"He'd be happy to," I said. "We lost a cowboy aways back. We got spare horses."

"Hey, mister," said Zach a few minutes later. "Can I talk to you, please? Away from these here fools. I'm done with these crazy people."

"What's on your mind?" I said.

"I don't know what he is, but Porter Higbee ain't no holy prophet. I want away from that lunatic. He's raving distracted, is what he is. He's a bully and a loudmouth. My pa lost his fool mind a few years back and dragged us all off to join him," said the boy. "I been looking for a way out for years. I sure would like to join up with you all driving them cows."

"You shut your mouth," yelled Gid Smoot.

"If I'd knowed how stupid these here was, I never would have joined up with them," the boy said.

109

"That kind of misjudgment of character almost cost you a neck stretchin," said Bass.

"I know it. I don't plan on repeating that mistake, if you'll just give me a chance," he said. "I ain't taking up with their outlaw ways."

"Horse thieving kind of disputes that."

"I can't disagree, but that wasn't my idea."

"Porter's going to kill you," screamed Eldon, who then went to whimpering quietly after Bass clouted him a good one in the ear.

"You need to shut your damn mouth," snarled Gid, apparently in charge now with Ezra and Reuben dead. I'll kill you my own self."

"Oh, shut up, Gid. I was gonna get shed of you first town we came to," said the youngster. "There ain't much you can say to push me around now, since we're likely going to hang anyway."

"You'll find out how Porter deals with apostates," said Gid. Once he said that, I figured the protests of the young boy were genuine.

"They're loco, all of them," said Zach.

"You'll burn in Hell for that remark," said Gid, right before Bass's heavy boot caught him right upside his head and sent him to slumber.

"Anyone else needing a love tap?" said Bass.

"All right, Zach," I said. "You convinced me. Or more like Gid convinced me. You try anything and I'll shoot you dead without a thought. Understand me?"

"I do," he said.

"Didn't expect to see you out here," I said to Bass and Britt after the bacon started sizzling in the pan.

"We were told the girl we're looking for is with a band of Penateka that was camped near here," said Britt. "We've been following this group of about fifty or sixty braves. I reckon you seen the burned wagons at Castle Gap."

"Hard to miss," I said.

"That was the work of that Comanche raiding party," said Britt. "They carried off 800 or 1,000 brand new U.S. Army Spencer Carbines.

That's our best estimate anyway. Could of been considerable more they'd already made off with before we reached them."

"800 rifles?" I said. "How'd you discover that?"

"We snuck up on them a week ago, after we saw smoke coming from the Gap. We watched them high-tailing out of there with a string of twenty or so mules and pack ponies strapped with crates," said Bass. "Every brave had a shiny new Spencer carbine across his saddle. I guess they was in a hurry and hadn't tied one of the crates tight enough. It hit the ground and broke open. A bunch of rifles come spilling out. They were the new Spencer repeating carbines. 24 to a crate. We counted about forty crates."

My rescuers had seen the herd a few miles back and Britt rode off to fetch them. When Charlie and a group arrived I was stretched out on my belly on my saddle blanket, naked as a jaybird. Bass was intently working the tweezers, pulling the cactus thorns out of my rear end.

"Well, of all the odd and wonderful sights there is to see on the prairie, I can honestly say that this is one that's never even slightly crossed my mind," said Charlie.

"Take a pitcher," I said.

"I'll just commit it to memory instead," he said.

"Throw a dollar in the tip jar if you're gonna sit there and oogle my bare behind," I said. I had a lot of thorns.

"What about them over there? Did they pay?"

"Well, there's two that sure paid dear," Britt said.

"I reckon. Boy, I'm sure glad all the Texas hoopty girls ain't as touchy as you," said Charlie. "Wouldn't hardly be a cowboy without a hole or two in him."

"I know one about to get a leak," I said.

"Now, darling, you just lay there and look purty while I figure out this mess you stirred up," Charlie said, and even his horse seemed to be smirking at my predicament. "I reckon there's an interesting story behind all this."

"They tried to rob me of my horse."

"I see you still got him," said Charlie.

"Yep."

"That's some long odds. How'd you manage that?"

"They weren't real bright," I said. "And slow to boot. And then these two paladins came charging out of nowhere and saved my bacon."

"Well don't that just beat all," said Charlie. "You say they gonna live?"

"Appears that way. Except for the dead ones, who appear beyond resuscitation," I said.

"They explain themselves?"

"They had plenty to say, hardly none of it nice either," Britt said.

"You don't say," said Charlie.

"I figured you might want to have a word with 'em," I said.

"They got names?"

"Higbees, Haights and Smoots. Maybe a Hoagland down there. I guess Ezra there was running the show until he got clipped," I said. "You might want to hear about these rifles before you weigh in on the fate of these reprobates."

"Britt told me," Charlie said. "That is a frightening number of armed Comanche."

"Yes, sir," I said. "We might have a real problem on our hands."

"All of Texas might have a real problem on its hands," said Charlie. "Britt said they were across the river, headed north to the Caprock."

"Yes, that's what I'd figure. Cache the guns in the canyons there," I said. "There could be a few still prowling about though. I'm more concerned about what I got stirred up with the Higbees."

"They come to steal your horse," Charlie said. "You dealt with them justly, seems to me. Me and the crew stand with you. I'd be mighty disappointed in any man that allowed his horse to get stoled."

"Just wanted to make sure," I said. "I reckon they'll be some severe afterclaps to this."

"I reckon," shrugged Charlie. "Looking that bunch over, I ain't exactly trembling in my boots."

"Porter's a different story," I said. "He's mighty formidable, and you know it. Up to you what we do with these here."

"We're fairly formidable ourselves," said Charlie. "Let's sleep on it. Too late tonight for a hanging, and where we gonna find a sturdy enough tree anyhow?"

"The boy's probably not far wrong when he says Porter is a lunatic. He crossed that line several years back," said Pierpont.

"How many years back did your pa join them?" I said to Zach.

"In 61, right after the war started. We moved out here from New York, where we had a farm. Sure wish we'd never left."

"So you were with him during the Bear River massacre?" Charlie asked Zach.

"I was fourteen," Zach said. "I wasn't there. My Pa and brothers were though."

"Zach, do you know what Porter's up to?" I said.

"I know some," Zach said. "Porter says we are wandering in the wilderness like Moses fleeing Egypt, searching the plains for the promised land to establish his New Zion. He preaches that from our current trials and tribulations a new scripture and new nation will emerge. That we are to build this city and bring salvation to the miserable savage redskins, the Comanches to be exact. He preaches that we have found the land of milk and honey in the Palo Duro Canyon. That is where he'll build the New Zion."

He reeled that off sounding like he'd taken a double dose of laudanum and someone was whispering in his ear. His face was slack and his eyes were faraway.

"That's quite an undertaking," Charlie said.

"Yes, sir," said Zach after a second, brightening a little. Like he was snapping out of that little trance he'd been reciting. "All them rifles you're talking about? Those was intended for us."

"What?" I said. "Porter Higbee is trying to buy near a thousand rifles?'

113

"More than that. He got one shipment of rifles, from Luther Walsh, but wanted some more," said Zach. "That burned out wagon train was supposed to be delivered to Porter."

"How many men does Porter have, and where are they?" I said to the kid.

"Several hundred. More than two hundred armed men, but only about fifty or seventy-five in Texas right this minute," Zach said. "We got little settlements scattered all over, but they ain't meant to be permanent. There's one in the Sangre de Cristo Mountains. Others in Colorado and Mexico. One in the Nebraska Territory. The folks there are farming, cutting lumber, things like that, amassing the food and supplies we'll need, waiting for Porter to summon them. He's got men set out along the Santa Fe Trail, and others, that rob wagon trains that look worth robbing. Once everything is ready, they will go to the Palo Duro and convert the Comanche, who he says is the Lamanites."

"Goodness gracious," said Charlie. "Like Texas ain't got enough problems right now. Convert them to what exactly?"

"Convert them to Shizzites," said Zach.

"The who?" I said.

"Shizzites. Porter claims we are the last tribe of Jared."

"Who?"

"From the writings of the prophet Ether in the book of Mormon," said Zach. "Jared fled with his people from the Fall of Babel and sailed to America. A few thousand years before it was America."

"No kidding?"

"No. Not according to the Book of Mormon. Though it's Porter, and not the book, that claims we are Shizzites. I've read the book of Mormon many times. Seems like that's all we did. A whole lot of scripture reading. It's true what he says about King Shiz," said Zach. "After Jared's tribe was in America for a few hundred years, divisions and feuds opened up. King Shiz was the last anointed king of the Jaredites, and he was killed by his rival, the evil king Coriantumr. Porter claims him and his blood kin are the only descendants of King Shiz."

"Ain't that something?" said Charlie. "I've never heard such."

"I told you he was off his rocker," said Zach.

"And the Comanches are who?"

"The Lamanites. They came to America in Bible times, too. They were a powerful prosperous nation, but they fell into sin. Because of that, God cursed them with dark skin and that's where all the Indian tribes come from. It's our purpose, says Porter, to convert them all to Shizzites to join us in the war against the Gentiles and the apostates."

"Is that right?" I said. "And just how does he expect to do that?"

"Through the power of the Sword of Laban, Aaron's sacred Breast-plate of Judgement, and the Golden Plates. Porter says, with the sword and armor and holy book of prophecy, he'll bring the savage heathen to salvation. Or else."

"The what all?" asked Charlie. "That's a fanciful tale."

"No, I seen all that. It's true he's got them things. He says they are what gives him his prophecies and such. He'd had himself another vision before all that, the one that sent him into the Palo Duro where he found them things," said the boy. "The armor and sword give him power. For guidance, he has seer stones he calls the Urim and Thummim, and that big thick book he calls the Golden Plates, covered with gemstones and gold. The book is full of strange writing and colored pictures. Only Porter is able to interpret it. I don't know if they actually give him visions, but the armor and all that is real enough. A big steel sword three feet long with all kinds of jewels in the hilt. A sure enough steel breastplate with more jewels in it, too."

"A story book, then?" said Charlie.

"No, it ain't no story book," Zach said. "I never seen anything like it."

"Sounds like a story book, pictures and all."

"I don't rightly know what it is. Peculiar pictures and gibberish," he said. "Words in letters I've never seen."

"And you say he's got two hundred armed men believing this?"

"At least that many. He's got them set up in twelve companies, or legions, as he calls them. Mostly all led by his brothers or sons," Zach said. "He calls his legion commanders the Quorum of the Twelve Apostles, just like the old church. Eventually he wants fifty men in each of them legions."

"Well, I'll be dogged," said Charlie.

"What do you think of all that?" Bass asked. I'd been quiet.

"Interesting," I said.

"Sure, but you sure seem to be mulling it hard."

"He must have found the armor and sword of a Spanish Conquistador left here 300 years ago, when Coronado came through," I said. "I don't know about any visions or prophecy, but I wouldn't be surprised about the breastplate and sword. Francisco Vázquez de Coronado crossed right through the Llano Estacado and the Palo Duro Canyon looking for the Seven Golden Cities."

"How do you know this?"

"My father was Spanish. He told us stories of the great Spanish explorers and conquistadors," I said.

"No kidding?" said Charlie.

"The book he's talking about is most likely an Aztec or Mixtec codex, that Coronado brought up from Mexico. Probably written in Latin, or Aztec. Maybe some Spanish. Aztec priests wrote them before the Spanish conquest of Mexico. Somewhere between a scroll and a book, many in gold leaf. It's a pictorial history of the life. Their history and religion and culture. Pictures of their gods and ceremonies. Plenty of Aztec warriors. Astrology. Anything you could imagine."

"Ain't that interesting," said Britt. "You know, they'll never do it, but nobody loves that religious hocus pocus more than a Comanche. Too bad they usually tire of it soon and scalp the missionary and eat his liver."

Toward dusk, six men rode toward us across the plain, looking unfriendly. We let them come, but we had our guns on them as they approached. They were led by a man, tall and fit, with a sun weathered face. He had the look of a formidable fighter.

"I'm Purnell Higbee," the leader said. "Those are my men you got there. My kin. What has happened here?"

I allowed Gid Smoot to give Purnell his version of events, and then I gave him mine. The two differed wildly, in that in Gid's version, I had somehow crippled his horse, lain in wait for the seven of them all on my lonesome, and then molested them after throwing their saddles in the creek.

"You can talk to them, Charlie. I'm about talked out with Higbees," I said when I'd finished my recitation. Bass and Britt nodded along, rifles up, keeping a close watch on the Higbees. Four of Charlie's cowboys stood ready alongside them.

"They tried to steal this man's horse and leave him stranded out here in this desolate land. They are poor excuses of horse thieves and gunmen," said Charlie. "We're fixing to decorate a cottonwood with them, first sturdy one we come to. Or first town we come to. Makes no neither mind."

There wasn't a plan to hang them, but Charlie wasn't a man to cower in a confrontation. The prospect of warmongering zealots adding to the hazards on his cattle drive had put him in a bristly mood.

"Now, see, I can't allow you to do that," said Purnell.

"Mister, how you planning to stop us? I don't reckon you got the guns, gumption nor guts to do so," said Charlie. "Sounds like you boys need to be more particular about whose horse you set out to steal, and stop cornerin' them that's meaner than you. This ain't Utah, and we ain't no settler families."

"You need to watch how you speak," said Purnell.

"You boys think you're tough. Well, I don't think you're so tough," said Charlie. "Back shooters and molesters of old ladies, more likely."

"That's mighty jaundiced tone you're taking," said Purnell. "I'm trying to be reasonable here. I'm not near so rigid as my brother Porter, but you killed two of ours and he does take the blood atonement literally. It's best we come to an understanding here. He'll likely not be wanting to discuss the matter much."

"Yes, so we've heard."

"I won't dispute that these boys you got under arms are a bunch of idgits, with the dead ones dumber than any, but that still leaves me with a dilemma. The men you killed are Reuben, my nephew, and Ezra, my brother-in-law. Ain't so sure but what Reuben is both nephew and brother-in-law, his mother being a Smoot," said Purnell. "Personally, I don't mind the loss, but you know, who wants a cold matrimonial bed.?"

"That's rich, coming from a polygamist," said Charlie.

"Well, four cold beds is colder than one," said Purnell. "I'm married to two Smoots, a Schmidt, and a Ludlow. All them boys you roughed up is related to 'em. Likewise, my brother Porter is married to two Smoots, a Cloward, and a Hoagland."

"Sounds mighty cozy," said Charlie.

"My brothers, Preston and Prosper, both married a few Smoots, too. There's a bunch of Smoot girls. Sixteen of them I believe. So, you see this could get touchy," said Purnell. "Them Smoot girls is a good looking bunch, or was when they was younger anyhow. Now they all kind of tend toward stoutness and favor their father. My first wife has grown a mustache."

"On purpose?'

"No, dammit, not on purpose, and not to my liking, neither."

"I was only asking to be polite. No reason to get snippish," said Charlie. "Though I can see why you'd have a raw nerve over it."

"I'm bound to see my wives receive satisfaction in this matter," Purnell said. "And uphold Porter's dictates."

"In that case mister, you deserve whatever quick death comes your way," said Charlie. "It would probably be a blessing."

"Some days I feel that way, but we're getting off the subject here. The point is, them you shot up is close kin to my wives. They got a lot of brothers. If you keep shootin' them up, it'll be rough on me, and that'll come back on you," said Purnell. "Letting you hang those boys would be looked at harshly by their sisters and such."

"He shot Reuben in the back," said a wounded Higbee.

"Is that true?" said Purnell.

"I shot him where he was at when we started shooting," I said.

"Are you saying he was running away?"

"I said he was stupid, not cowardly, if that's better," I said. "I don't think he was running. If he was, I probably wouldn't have shot him."

"Porter ain't going to take this well."

"Seven of them came at me. I'm upright and they ain't," I said. "Your ire should be directed at their breaking of the Commandments and their unskilled sinning and lack of preparedness for a life of crime. Tell 'em not to cripple their horses and think they can buzzard somebody else's."

"You can tell Porter Higbee I'm not in the habit of catering to the whims of some hell-bound deviant," said Charlie. "Stealing horses is a capital offense."

"No need for ugly words, Mr. Goodnight. Unless you want to pursue hanging them fellas, or engage in gun play, we'll take our men and light out," said Purnell. "The dead one and his brother ain't the brightest boys, and then again, I don't think they really intended no harm."

"What do you think should happen to these boys?" Charlie said to me. "It's your horse."

"In light of all that, the rope might be merciful," I said. "But I really don't care what you do with these trifling outlaws. It won't be long before they get gut shot in another robbery, or die of thirst after ruining another horse. They need to find a new line of work. They ain't cut out for this."

"Based on the situation as it stands, I harbor no hostility toward you. It would be fine with me if our paths never crossed again," said Purnell. "I ain't so sure how this will all set with Porter, but it is my sincere hope we can remain at peace."

"Best way to assure peace is to stay the hell out of our way," said Charlie. "I see any of you irksome Shizzites near my crew or these cattle, and my men will be under orders to shoot. Do you understand?"

# REACHING FORT SUMNER
## AUGUST 4, 1866

The sun was blazing down as we crossed into the reservation a day south of Ft. Sumner. I rode with Charlie and a small group a few hundred yards ahead of the herd. Pierpont came along to record, as he called it, the historic event. Five miles from the fort a small column of cavalry rode toward us. I was surprised to see Bigfoot Wallace with them.

"Greetings, gentleman," said the Captain. He was a man of about forty with steel gray temples and the weathered, stern face of a man who'd spent a life on the frontier. "Captain Tim Hardy at your service."

"Pleased to meet you," said Charlie. "I'm Charlie Goodnight, and this here's Bose Ikard and Pete Horse. These other fellas is Marcellus, Braswell, and Ray. And Mr. Pierpont, the journalist. I appreciate the escort."

"Harrington Pierpont, with the New York Tribune," said Pierpont. "A pleasure to meet you, Captain."

"Ah, yes, Mr. Greeley's man. I heard you was coming," Hardy said. "Admirer of the Colonel, I understand."

"I am, yes," said Pierpont. "I believe he is a good man. He's accomplished some great things."

"He's accomplished some big things, no denying," said Hardy. "I reckon it's your journalist's job to make them great or not."

"Didn't expect to see you again so quick," I said to Bigfoot.

"I got that wagon train to Belknap and headed directly back here," said Bigfoot. "Sounds like there's an epic ruckus brewing. I ain't about to miss it."

"Is that right?"

"I'm sure the Captain and the Colonel can fill you in," said Bigfoot.

"Are you expecting trouble?" said Charlie.

"Hard to tell what to expect," said the Captain. "These Indians have been waiting for this beef for a long time. They're getting restless. Cadete and three hundred Mescalero Apache warriors have already jumped the reservation and are somewhere on the Llano. Manuelito has a hostile bunch holed up a little ways to the west of us."

"So, that situation ain't calmed down none?" said Charlie.

"No, not by much. And we heard you had a run in with some of Porter Higbee's clan. That's no good sign, either. They've become a problem, big and looming larger," said Hardy. "Colonel Carleton would like to speak to you about that."

"Speak to who about that?"

"Any of the three of you that might be interested in helping track Higbee down."

"I don't think that's anything we was considering," said Charlie.

"I suppose not," said the Captain. "But we're in need of experienced scouts. We need men that know the Palo Duro and the other Panhandle Canyons. The compensation would be more than generous. It's a desperate need."

"Have you no scouts of your own?" I said.

"We do, some Tonks," said Hardy. "One is a son of Placido, who I understand was an old friend of yours."

"Are they not eager for this mission?"

"No, it's not that," Hardy said. "Maybe a little too eager. Brave as badgers."

"Which son?" I said. "Charlie or Little Spots?'

"Neither," said Hardy. "Red Bear. Really Placido's brother's son, but you know how the Tonks are. After the brother was killed, his wife and sons became Placido's. He's a youngster."

"Whose son did he become after Placido was killed?' I said.

"No one's. There are barely any male Tonkawas left after the Wichita Agency massacre," said Hardy.

"Well, I suppose we could talk it over," said Charlie. "But I don't expect to be volunteering. I'm already committed to driving another herd up from Texas just as soon as I can ride back there."

"I reckon I'll follow Charlie," Bose said.

"If you would just consider it," the Captain said. "I'll ride up ahead a bit, so just follow me to the cattle pens and we can start getting them weighed."

"No need for that," I said. "I'll listen to what the Colonel has to say. Sounds like me and Porter might be headed for trouble down the line anyway."

We crossed the reservation a few hundred yards ahead of the cattle. A few excited Navajo children, dirty, disheveled and hungry looking, came out to watch the procession of cowboys and longhorns. Bigfoot had not exaggerated the state of misery. The adults, in frayed calico and pieces of castoff Army uniforms, sat in front of sun-baked hogans, just thatch-roof mud huts, watching with the look of defeat. It was a look I knew well. I'd seen it on my people and the others who had been forced onto reservations. These downtrodden, hungry-looking Navajo had the life beaten out of them. They bore no resemblance to free and fearless Plains Indians dodging in and out of thundering buffalo.

"So, is this it?" said Pierpont as we rode past a row of shabby hogans. "I thought there might be more of a reception. That the natives would be a little happier at the arrival of the herd."

"These people have a sadness in them that cows won't cure," I said.

"They've seen herds meant for them before that just kept on going," said Hardy. "They get some of what's left behind. Maybe. Old and sick, or bloated to busting with Pecos River water. The last Indian agent we had here cheated the Indians out of their beef, flour, blankets. Anything and everything. Sold them to settlers and mining companies. He double billed the ignorant Indian Bureau back in Washington as a topper. Quite an operation, but he's finally on his way to Federal Prison now, thanks to Col. Carleton."

"My lord, that's a dismal looking group," Pierpont said.

"I suppose you can see why the Comanche are fighting so hard," I said. "I hate what they done to me personally, and to others, but I can't disagree with them on principle. I sure don't blame any that jumped this reservation. It's not a fight they're ever going to win, though."

"It's not just the Indians," said Pierpont. "I thought there might be some celebration."

"What was you expecting, a brass band? Or hugs and big pats on the back?" said Charlie. "We done our part like we said we would. Drove some cows from one place to another. Not sure what's so spectacular about that."

"Well, Mr. Greeley seems to think it's a grand accomplishment. Now that you've established the trail, many more herds will follow. Enough to feed everybody, including new settlements throughout Colorado and beyond," said Pierpont. "It will bring a new prosperity. To everyone, including these poor souls."

"Mr. Pierpont is under the impression that Col. Carleton is trying to atone for some of his earlier sins by running off the corrupt agents," said Charlie to Hardy, ignoring Pierpont. "Maybe cleaning up his record to run for office."

"A good many back east believe he could be a force in politics if he chooses to," said Pierpont."

"Hard to say what motivates Colonel Carleton. He's a complicated man, but he is working hard to jail the crooks, and at the other agencies. It's a slow process," said Hardy. "He may be trying to atone for his sins, but the Federal Government isn't in no rush."

"I suspect that's true," I said.

"Just so we're clear," said the Captain. "I'm career Army, since 1850. I led a regiment in the war. I don't care much for Carleton's tactics against the Indians. However, he was the one with enough courage to honestly investigate Porter Higbee and the Mountain Meadow Massacre."

"Yes, so Mr. Pierpont has been telling us," I said.

"I was there with him, with the 1st California Dragoons. He was a major at the time. We arrived at the scene of the massacre in '59, two years after the event. Those damned Mormons hadn't even buried them, and animals had got to the bones. We found about seventy skulls and buried them and put up a cross. Out of about 150 people. It ain't right, and they need a reckoning. Now Porter's planning something big, and it's going to be our job to bring him to account."

"How do you plan to do that?" I said. "I understand he's gotten pretty powerful."

"I'll let Colonel Carleton tell you all about it," said the Captain. "I can't really tell you much about it just now."

Charlie and the cowboys drove the herd to the holding pens while Bigfoot and I rode on to the fort to meet Col. Carleton. He greeted us in his office with cigars, brandy, and iced water. Instead of sitting behind his large desk he joined us at a round table near the opposite wall.

"Can I get you anything else?" Carleton said as Bigfoot vigorously puffed his cigar alight.

"Do you have any wine in the house?" said Bigfoot. "I have a powerful thirst."

"I'm sure we can find something," said Carleton. He nodded at his fresh-faced orderly and the young soldier hurried out the door.

"This cool water is all I need," I said, quickly drinking the first glass and filling another from the pitcher.

"I'm proud to finally meet you, Mr. Horse. Mr. Wallace has been regaling us with some of your adventures," said Carleton. "From your days riding with "Devil Yack" Hays and the Rangers, when you gentlemen whipped the Comanches all across Texas."

He was a hard-eyed man of fifty with bushy mutton chop sideburns covering his cheeks. It was hot outside and not much cooler inside but Carleton wore his double-breasted frock coat buttoned tight and all the way up. He was still lean and looked campaign ready.

"Just call me Bigfoot. I don't always come to the call of the other," Bigfoot said. On the table beside the pitcher and stone jar holding the ice was a bowl filled with lemons and limes. Bigfoot had already quartered several with his Bowie knife and sucked the juice from them.

"Thank you, Colonel. I rode with Jack Hays, and we had our successes," I said. "Jack is the greatest fighting man I've ever known, and I've been proud to know a good many. All across Texas might be stretching it. Mr. Wallace has been known to gild a detail."

Devil Yack was what the Mexicans called Jack Hays. Bravo-Too-Much was the Comanche, Tonk and Apache name for him. Mild as a church deacon until the foe was engaged. Ferocious as a tiger until the foe was vanquished.

"You were with Hays, Sam Walker and Ben McCulloch at Walker's Creek in 1844?" he asked. "Hays and 15 Texas Rangers charging 200 Comanche braves?"

"Close enough. We were a crazy, fearless bunch back then. Rogues and wanderers. It is hard to exaggerate Walker's Creek, but don't always go by those tall tales of the Rangers," I said, as the orderly entered the room with his arms full of corked green bottles. "Some of them were probably spun by a Ranger who was embarrassed of pocket, seeking strong whiskey or a warm bed for the night. A good many of us stayed that way. The government sure never paid us."

"Outstanding, youngster," Bigfoot grinned as the boy set the bottles on the table. "I'm putting you in for promotion forthwith. All the way to Major General if you can procure me some white sugar."

The boy looked nervously at Carleton. When Carleton nodded the private hustled down the narrow hallway and returned with a palm sized block of white sugar. Bigfoot took out his knife and started shaving it off into his glass of iced brandy and fruit juice.

"Well, now, that's a fiction right there if I ever heard one," said Bigfoot. "Implying a Ranger would string a whizzer. Why, I never..."

"Huzzah for Texas," I said to Bigfoot and tipped my glass to his.

"You men are legends in these parts, all of Texas. I imagine you always will be. It's a discredit to the state of Texas that the Rangers weren't better compensated. It's a discredit to the Army that they have not tried to study Hays' methods. I think you'll agree that the Army has never understood how to fight Comanches," the Colonel said. "No imagination. And most of the officers that have come west since the war ended have no interest in finding out how. They're more concerned with suppressing Johnny Reb and any insurrectionist grumbling until they can get transferred back east. Captain Hardy is an exception, but few officers relish assignment out here."

"Captain Hardy said you were looking for some scouts to chase down Porter Higbee," I said, watching Bigfoot squeeze another lemon half into his mix of brandy and wine.

"Yes, indeed we are going after Porter," said Carleton as Bigfoot stirred his drink with his knife blade. "I'd like you to ride along. Scout for us. Interpret with the Comanche, if need be."

"I'm not signing on to fight Indians," I said. "I had my fill of that years ago. I'll defend myself but I'm not looking for no fight with Comanche."

"Understood. We're not going after the Comanche. Porter Higbee is the immediate problem," he said. "It wasn't Walsh that killed Judge Jeffers. Nor the Comanche. It was Porter Higbee. He just keeps getting stronger and stronger selling his Armageddon prophecies."

"Why did Higbee kill the judge?" I asked.

"I'd say it served several purposes. Judge Jeffers was a federal prosecutor before he was a judge. He was with me in Utah, leading the investigation into the Mountain Meadow Massacre," said Carleton. "Jeffers was relentless. The church hindered our investigation at every turn. Witnesses were intimidated. Some were murdered. Many fled the territory. There were assassination attempts on Judge Jeffers, but he persisted. We had prepared a solid case. Then, of course, the War broke out and there were other priorities."

"We heard he harbors a grudge against you as well," I said. "For the same reasons."

"I'm sure he does," said Carleton. "But I doubt he'll come against me here with a regiment of cavalry and a howitzer."

"But if he gets his hands on all those guns that just seem to float out of Army depots on their own, he might," I said.

"You heard about the guns, then. He still won't have enough men," Carleton said. "Now, if he recruits a few hundred Comanche, who knows?"

"Or Cadete's Apache," Bigfoot said. "Them little bands of Comanche I've crossed don't have no interest in aligning with no white man, and don't believe any of their people do neither. Not even the most eager for blood. Cadete's boys is an entirely different matter."

"Yes," Carleton said. "Or the Apache. Those rifles are a powerful attraction to any renegade band that wants to fight the Army. That would apply to Cadete's band, or Manuelito and his Navajo band that remain defiant and unvanquished."

"The government is planning to bring Porter back for trial on all those charges?" I asked.

"I'll be blunt. For the sake of this mission, let's just consider him adjudged guilty. Or an invading foreign adversary," said the Colonel. "I have no keen interest in bringing him in. Nobody in the government does. Few think it could be done anyway. Frankly, the last thing we need is some huge trial where he becomes a martyr."

"You don't think there will be more trouble if we just kill him?"

"Maybe. The thought in Washington is the group will disintegrate if he's gone," Carleton said. "Personally, I'm not so sure. Zealots love their martyrs. There have been a few that left Porter and they don't describe it as real pleasant. Without Porter's vengeance to worry them, we figure others will leave. We may offer amnesty to some that are still with him."

"Yes, we met a boy on the trail who was trying to leave them. He rides for us now," I said.

"Is that right?" said Carleton.

"Zach Petty. His pa took the family into Porter's clan a few years back. Zach was with some of Higbee's men that tried to steal my horse," I said. "He told me he'd been trying to get away from them and I believe him. He's worked out good so far."

"I heard there'd been an incident," he said. "Tried to steal your horse? I guess it didn't go as planned for them."

"I still got my horse. Killed two of them, including Porter's son and one of his lieutenants. A few more took some lead, but I imagine they survived."

"Porter's son. That ain't going to set well," said Carleton.

"I imagine not. All of them that got shot was close kin to Porter or his wives, apparently. Purnell said he'd overlook it, given that it occurred during the commission of a felony," I said. "But he didn't think Porter would be so forgiving."

"No, he's not the forgiving sort," Carleton said. "The man should read the Good Book more."

"Sounds like he's trying to write his own, is the problem," Bigfoot said. "Now, what exactly is it you are proposing?"

"Porter's planning to build a city in the Palo Duro, or one of the other canyons east of the Escarpment," Carleton said. "The defector told you that, I assume. We plan to pursue him there."

"He did, but the whole thing sounded a little far-fetched. You're sure the Palo Duro is where Porter Higbee is?" I said.

"He's got temporary camps here, there, and scattered in half a dozen states and territories. All very remote from civilization. Higbee himself was sighted riding along the Canadian River, headed east with a wagon train and a bunch of armed men," Carleton said. "That was ten days ago. It looks like he's getting set to establish something with some permanence."

"You're still after Higbee even knowing the Comanche have got their hands on 800 rifles?" I said.

"So far I've only heard rumors of that. Do you know that for a fact?'

"If you believe Britt Johnson, which I'm inclined to do," I said. "He said he saw a Comanche raiding party leaving the scene of burned out wagons. He saw a line of ponies carrying rifle crates. One fell and busted open and some guns slid out."

"Yes, I know Britt. If he says that's what he saw, then I expect he's right. The problem is, that's only a portion of the stolen Army rifles that have made it to Texas," said Carleton. "I'm sure you've already been told that was at least the third large shipment stolen from the arsenal at Ft. Smith. And those are only the ones we know of. Ft. Smith isn't the only arsenal in the country, just one of the biggest."

"I seen that bunch that took the rifles," said Bigfoot. "They didn't just happen upon them wagons. It was clear bad intentions were foremost on their minds."

"That's a whole lot of problems," I said. "How does that happen, from an Army arsenal at Ft. Smith or anywhere else?"

"They did it pretty much the same way they divert the food meant for Indian reservations. Some of that comes from Ft. Smith, too. The same thing happens other places. With the war finally over, there's a whole lot of war material getting destroyed, sold or moved. Crooks and cheats ooze out of every corner wherever the Army is buying, selling, or transporting," said Carleton. "The Army has made arrests in Fort Smith. Luther Walsh was apparently the mastermind. Of one of the rings anyway. We know there's more. He had people working on the inside, in the Quartermaster and the Armory. People could divert shipments and cook the inventory. Layers of bogus purchase orders. Who all has those guns now, we don't know. Not with certainty. Walsh had been keeping some, selling some to Indians, and had this big deal cooked up with Porter Higbee."

"That's a sizable mess, all right," Bigfoot said.

"Luther Walsh wants to start as many fires as he can. His strategy is to keep the Army fighting Apaches, Navajo, or Porter Higbee so we won't have much left over to fight him," said Carleton. "So now he's in the gun running business and stirring unrest. We had a plan in place, waiting for those guns to be delivered to Higbee. Then we were going to swoop down on both of them. The meeting place was supposed to be south of here along the Pecos, but that meeting never happened. Apparently, because the Comanche swooped in instead."

"Walsh is trying to re-fight the Civil War?" I asked.

"He is said to have the financial backing of the Knights of the Golden Circle," said Carleton. "The Knights are said to have castles in the Sangre de Cristo Mountains and beyond. Defeated Confederacy or not, they still have wealth and power. They can buy a whole lot of weapons. If not stolen from our own arsenals, they can get more from Europe. New Mexico is a powder keg just waiting to blow. Texas is a hotbed for Rebel sympathies and some of the malcontents have made it here. You're familiar with the Knights, I assume?"

"I've had more than my share of run-ins with them," I said. "The folks that killed Lincoln. Still have some grandiose ideas of setting up slave states in South America. Cuba. I know they have deep pockets and friends in high places."

"Yes, that's them," he said. "Very grandiose. We haven't seen them, but it's a rumor. If Luther doesn't already have their backing, he's trying like hell to get it."

"Bigfoot told me some of those reservation Apache have taken up with Luther and have been raiding and terrorizing folks," I said.

"That's what we heard as well," said the Captain. "Honestly surprised you didn't have more trouble. There's plenty that don't want to see the beeves make it to the reservation. It's a whole lot easier to recruit hungry young bucks to the war path than fat, lazy ones. Manuelito is about whipped. Tired and about starved out. We're in some fairly hopeful negotiations with him but if he was to suddenly have a few hundred rifles, and unlimited ammunition, he'd likely not be so acquiescent."

"I don't relish a scrape with Manuelito. Old Bullet Hole. Gad, he would be a rank one to tangle with," said Bigfoot, sleeve-wiping his mouth after draining another lemon. He'd collected a pile of fruit peels on the table in front of him. Carleton motioned at the orderly and pointed at the nearly empty fruit bowl. The private hurried toward the door.

"I can see why Porter's become a priority," I said. "That explains a few things. Sure don't paint a prettier picture though."

"Then, of course, there are the Comancheros," said Carleton. "Something's going on there and we don't know what it is, exactly. After being especially busy these past six years, they've gone suddenly, and oddly, quiet.

The Comanchero were rough-living, uncouth traders from New Mexico, shiftless vagabonds of all races and nationalities who engaged in every manner of criminal behavior and brutality. Anything where a profit could be turned. They made their living trading with the Plains Indian tribes, primarily the Comanches, which is how they got their name. But they traded with anybody, for just about anything. Almost all of it illegal. For decades the Comanche had stolen Texas cattle and horses and traded them to the Comanchero for such things as tobacco, beads, knives, paint, and pots and pans. In recent years that trade had expanded to include a large amount of guns, ammunition, and whiskey going to the Indians. Hostages were also traded to the Comanchero, to be sold into slavery, or, if their families had any material wealth, to be sold back for a ransom, as Britt Johnson had arranged.

Comanchero business had thrived during the War, when most all the soldiers went back east. The Indians stole hundreds of thousands of horses and beeves. The Comanchero bought them, then sold them to government beef contractors, who then sold them to the Army to feed soldiers or reservation Indians. Often times, these same cattle were stolen and sold two, three, or more times. The Army would buy them, the Comanches would steal them, sell them to the Comanchero, and the Army would buy the same cows all over again. Sometimes the impatient Comanches wouldn't even wait until the Army took possession of the cattle. The Comanche would brazenly steal the cattle from the Comanchero and force them to buy them back. The cattle business was not for the meek.

"So, that's been happening here," I said. "Your own cattle have been stolen and sold back to you?'

"Yes, it happens," bristled Carleton. "We're basically forced to buy, otherwise these people really would starve. The soldiers would get pretty hungry, too. That's another fire to put out."

"They haven't chose sides with Walsh or Higbee?" I said.

"Other than maybe selling them stolen cattle or horses, no," he said. "You know the Comanchero aren't really much for face-up fighting. I'm not going to allow them, or anyone, to steal this herd, though. These Navajo are near death without food."

"Them Injuns ain't the only hungry ones," said Bigfoot. "I'm a tad peckish myself. Is there anything in the larder?"

Without waiting for an order from Carleton the orderly whipped out the door. He returned quickly with a platter full of enormous smoked turkey wings and fried potatoes. Bigfoot slathered it all with Tabasco and dove in elbows wide.

"You know the canyon land as well as they say?" asked Carleton.

"Yes, I know the canyons. I've been through them many times," I said. And I did. I'd been through them at least twenty times in twenty years. The Palo Duro. The Tule, Blanco and Yellow House, and all the smaller ones between and below them. The places of many languages and tears. Of families torn asunder. The valleys of wailing and ransoms.

"Looking for your sisters and mother, I understand," Carleton said. "A tragic thing."

"Yes."

"And never any luck?" said Carleton.

"Lucky as far as not getting killed and having my hair pinned on a battle shield, I reckon," I said. "I found one sister. She was lucky. She was unmolested, for the most part. Kept chaste so she could be sold for a lot of gold to be a concubine to one of Santa Anna's generals. My mother and other sister are gone. It's been almost thirty years."

"I'm sorry to hear that," said Carleton.

"The Canyons would be just about a perfect place to start up some secluded religious colony," I said. "Plenty of food, water and tillable ground. It's a good place to winter since it blocks the wind. Sure wouldn't be much contact with the Federal government. Just that one little problem. The Comanche."

"Yes, we need to get to the Higbee clan fast. We need men of superior skills and experience," Carleton said. "Kit Carson's a general himself now, in the Colorado Territory, or I'd call on him."

"From the looks of the reservation, appears he's already done plenty," Bigfoot said. He'd never cared much for Carson, the esteemed Indian-killer and dime novel hero. Neither had I.

"It's a failure, I'll admit," Carleton said. "Believe it or not, I am trying to improve things until we can find a better location."

"Why not let them find their own location, like back to their homeland?" I said.

"That's not my decision," he said. "But I've earned any invective you might hurl. I'll accept it."

"I'm too tired from pushing cattle to hurl anything at anybody," I said. "I've had good men tell me you're trying to do better. I'll accept that. For now."

"I've been out here since '62, most of it out actively campaigning. I'm no chair bound memo-writing general. I was out fighting, which was my job. I'll not apologize for that. However, I was not watchful of those entrusted to feed the conquered people. I will apologize for that. It was not always this way. In the beginning, we had men in charge who had fought the Navajo and respected him. Those men would not see a worthy opponent cheated," said Carleton. "Then those men were transferred to fighting units in the east, and the sneaking, thieving scoundrels and carpet baggers came west to plunder the ignorant red man. We can discuss it further at a later time, if you're inclined. But right now my priority is stopping Higbee."

"Captain Hardy implied you had a bold plan to put him down," I said.

"It's been my contention we've needed Jack Hays-style units to fight the Indian. Now, I think we need that type unit to track Higbee down. I need men that know how to trail like the Rangers, live like them, move like them, and fight like them. There ain't a man in New Mexico other than you two at the moment."

"We can't teach your men that," Bigfoot said. "Not in time to go hunting."

"No. I know that. I don't believe one ordinary army unit can ever move fast enough to catch them. We need elite units and Captain Hardy has a company of forty men, ready to go," said Carleton. "A small, fast, well-trained, heavily-armed long-range force to track Higbee down and flush him out."

"Yes, Captain Hardy told me a little about the unit. You said well trained," I said. "You never mentioned experienced."

"No, there are a couple veterans, and a few galvanized Yankees serving out their enlistments," said Carleton. "But it's true, for the most part they are youngsters that saw little action, or were simply too young to serve."

"This will be one hell of a spot to find out who's got it and who don't," Bigfoot said to Carleton. The turkey wings had been reduced to bone and Bigfoot was leaned back in his chair, rubbing his ample belly.

"Is it ever a good time for a man to face battle for the first time?" Carleton said. "You either learn or you don't."

"I'm just saying, the way Hardy explained it, we're going to be way out there on our own," I said.

"Agreed. But the boys signed up for some adventure, some fighting. This is miserable duty here at the fort. Chopping wood. Digging latrines. Dealing with the woes of the Navajo and the occasional half-drunk renegade. Dirty, thankless, and dangerous. We fight smallpox, measles and other disease more than hostiles," said Carleton. "We lose men to boredom and desertion. These boys relish the thought of getting out and doing some real soldiering. They are itching for a fight."

"Not too eager, I hope," I said. "And just forty men? Whether it's Higbees or Comanche, or even Walsh, forty men wouldn't stand a chance against them."

"That's only part of the equation. I propose to emulate the old Ranger tactics to engage and harass them," said Carleton. "Just hold him in place long enough for the converging columns."

"Converging columns?" I said.

"Yes. It was something we had been planning for the Comanche, but we're going to use it now. That should show you how urgent Washington thinks the Higbee problem is," Carleton said. "Four columns. A total of over 1,500 troopers. A column of four hundred from here, another coming north from Texas, one west from Kansas, and one from Colorado. I will lead the column from Ft. Sumner personally. If it would happen that one of the other columns makes first contact with the Higbees, then they will follow the same plan. Hold them in place until all columns concentrate."

Carleton took us over to one of the wall maps beside the two crossed cavalry swords on the smoothed log wall behind his desk. It was a map of the Texas Panhandle. Carleton traced his finger along red lines that led from bordering states, across the wide, white space that made up the prairie, to the flurry of squiggly lines that represented the canyons and badlands of the Caprock Escarpment.

"How do you plan on communicating out there?"

"We'll communicate with a series of gallopers," said Carleton. "We will meet a large supply train in 45 days, and they will reprovision us for another 30 days."

"Sounds like a bold plan," I said. "And a foolish one, being in Comanche territory this time of year."

"Forty-five days is only the contingency plan. We want to finish this up before September, before Comanche moon. Put the Higbee issue to close finally, precisely so the Army can defend the frontier," said Carleton. "We need to be able to meet the Comanche with force when they come on their fall raids. They are brazen and murderous enough as it is."

"Yes, I've seen the deserted homesteads," I said. "And if nobody makes contact?"

"We'll have to head back eventually. If we see any Comanche out there, we'll try to talk peace with them if both parties can be civil that long," Carleton said. "But my assumption is they won't be too welcoming, and we'll have to shoot a bunch of them. That would advance the wishes of some."

"Like I said, I won't hunt Comanche for you," I said. "Once Porter ain't the target, I'll be riding on. And this Higbee fight sounds like something a whole lot bigger than what I need to be getting into, anyway."

"Yes, but two things to consider. One, Porter will come after you eventually. If he murdered a judge with a squad of armed bodyguards, he'll come after you. I know that. You know that," Carleton said. "Two, whatever the reward is, you'll get the lion's share."

"How much is that?"

"At least $5,000. Split between the two of you. I wouldn't ask you to risk your life for less," said Carleton. "I promised shares to the men that volunteered for this mission, which really isn't legal. I can't give them much, and wouldn't anyway. They're good boys, but they'd desert tomorrow if they suddenly had $200 in their pockets. I don't blame them. It gets awful stale out here."

"Understand," I said. "I will not obey orders I consider suicidal. Or idiotic."

"I ain't keen on taking orders from no man, in uniform or no," said Bigfoot, looking down at the platter of bones. "But I'll fight this Higbee for you. A tussle with a danged-old Shizzite might be just what the doctor ordered. I've been off my feed of late."

"Captain Hardy is as solid as they come," said Carleton. "He got a lot of medals in the war, and he didn't get them by getting his men murdered in reckless charges. Like so many."

"Tell me about this reporter," Carleton said after Bigfoot had excused himself to go take a nap.

"What about him?"

"What's he like?"

"I thought you'd met him," I said.

"I have. Under different circumstances," Carleton said. "Early on, back when I prided myself as a great Indian fighter. My way of thinking, over the years, has changed. These Navajo have been wronged, and I intend to make things right with them."

"The same ones you and Carson ordered shot on sight?" I said.

"I was given an assignment," said Carleton. "But I'll also take responsibility. I'm not sure rehashing it right now solves much. I've killed plenty of Indians in the past, I'll kill more if that's the order I receive. If it's a legal and humane order. But watching them starve is not what an honorable officer does. I'll kill 'em, sir, but I don't intend to cheat them. Or sit by and allow them to be cheated."

"Interesting," I said. "As far as the reporter, he's tolerable."

"Can he ride with the column without being a hindrance?"

"Yes, surprisingly, he can," I said.

"Good. He'll be riding with you."

"Me?" I said. "I thought you meant the main column."

"He wants to be at the forefront. He says he is an accomplished horseman," said Carleton. "He tells me he never slowed the herd down any."

"Well, to be truthful, he did a whole lot better than I expected," I said. "But a herd moves fifteen miles a day at best. We'll be riding fifty miles a day some days. Aside from all the shooting that's likely to happen."

"He said he was game," said Carleton

"I'll leave him in the dust if he ain't," I said.

"I expect Captain Hardy would make that decision," Carleton said.

"I'll leave him in the dust, too," I said. "If we're going to do it the Jack Hays way, well, let's do it. But if you ain't gonna do it right, don't do it."

"I agree," said the Colonel.

"And when is your column going out?" I said.

"We'll leave in a week, ten days," said Carleton.

"I'm not hunting Comanche for you," I said. "We wait any longer than that, we'll run right into them."

The next day we said our goodbyes to Charlie, Bose, and the rest of the crew. Charlie and Mr. Loving conducted their business and happily reported back that the Army was buying all the steers, 1,600 of them, at eight cents a pound paid in gold. Mr. Loving and some of the cowboys would drive the remaining 800 breeding stock up to the Colorado mining country. Charlie and Bose would take the $12,000 and return to central Texas to put together another herd before the coming of winter. Britt and Bass had already ridden out, still dogged in their search for Coralee Tucker.

"I guess we'll have to part ways here," said Charlie. "I got obligations I wish I didn't have. If you haven't caught that sidewinder by spring, maybe I can join you in looking."

"If we haven't caught him by spring, I'll be looking to buy some of your cows and setting up my own operation," I said. "I hope to be far away from the Palo Duro before the Comanche moon rises."

"You ain't got a lot of time," he said.

"I know it," I said. "But it sounds like this is something needs done."

"It does, sure enough," Charlie said.

"I reckon you best get on back, catch on with the next herd Charlie's gonna be bringing up," I said to Andy later.

"No, sir, I'm coming with you after Higbee," Andy said.

"This ain't the place for you to be sharpening your teeth on. That's as rough a group as I ever crossed, and I don't reckon they're gonna be surrendering. They may want to go out in some holy blaze of glory. There's likely to be a whole lot of dead men," I said. "A lot of us won't be coming back. That's the kind of job this is."

"You're going," he said.

"I've done this kind of thing before," I said.

"And there was a time you hadn't," said Andy.

"I guess I can't argue that," I said.

# THE GREEN GABLES
## AUGUST 1866

"What are we going to do until we ride out?" asked Andy on our second morning in town. "That bed sure feels better than the ground."

"That it does," I said. Carleton was paying for our room at the Westward Hotel while we awaited orders from Washington. Andy, Zach and I shared a room with three broke-down beds, a thunder pot and a blue-flowered enamel sink bowl. There was a sun-faded Arabian rug that looked like it had taken a load of bird shot and a bureau that looked like it had lost a fight with a puma.

The room was above the Green Gables saloon, in a long, narrow adobe two story. The rooms on one side of the upper floor housed the Westward Hotel, the other side held an eight-room brothel. The brothel didn't really have a name. Just the Westward.

The room had a view of the main street of Tornado Town, which looked about like any other fort town. Maybe a little more perilous than most. There were the usual general store and apothecary and restaurants. There was a Chinese laundry, livery and blacksmith shop and newspaper office. The majority of the businesses were brothels and saloons, which attracted a rough crowd of teamsters, traders, explorers and soldiers. Just about everybody carried a gun, and most looked like they carried battle scars. There was apparently enough fractiousness and villainy in town to keep two undertakers in the black.

"I ain't never spent any time in a real town before. Me and Zach would like to have an explore," said Andy.

"We can enjoy a little leisure, I reckon. Just be about your wits whilst out trampoosing around," I said. "Fort towns attract some coarse louts. Don't do wandering off too far. I expect Col. Carleton to summon us at any time."

Five days passed with no express rider from the east for Carleton. We took to lounging in the Green Gables, playing checkers or poker for matchsticks. We took our meals there and it was satisfying fare after a long trail drive. Espinar was a fine cook, but a little variety was pleasant.

Truman, the convivial owner and bar dog of the Westward and Green Gables, was a long-time friend of Bigfoot's. He didn't allow for gambling except for matchsticks, which just about eliminated card cheats and gunfights. He said he wouldn't sell liquor, except it's hard to run a liquor establishment without it.

Truman was so happy to have an eastern journalist of Mr. Pierpont's stature lodging in his hotel that he'd given him the finest suite for the duration of our stay. Included among Pierpont's perks was the companionship of Kansas City Stella, a stout prostitute with a bicep that would have been the envy of any Army muleskinner. Bigfoot preferred to camp outside town at night but would come in during the day and drink prodigious amounts of brandy smashers made with crushed ice from a two-ton block brought down from the Sangre de Cristo mountains.

The inside of the saloon was dark and cool under the three-foot-thick adobe walls. The tables seated about fifty freighters, soldiers, and frontiersmen. Trail dusty young men in range clothes and bits of Rebel uniforms stood hip-cocked at the bar, thumbs hooked over low-slung cartridge belts as they practiced their desperado sneer on folks they thought they could bluff.

Along the walls, mounted trophy deer and elk and buffalo heads protruded between posters for Durham tobacco and Tennessee whiskey. An eight-foot-tall stuffed grizzly bear stared from the corner. Polished brass spittoons were strategically placed on the sawdust covered floor. Above the bar was a life-size painting of a nude buxom beauty. Her dignity was intact only because of two strategically held six guns and the shaggy black beard of a monstrous buff. Her eyes said come hither, but her hardware made me leery.

Two brown skinned women in gauzy Mexican blouses and bright, flared jarabe skirts sashayed between the tables, swinging their hips as they balanced trays of beer bottles and shot glasses. A few other women in tight satin dresses were selling something else.

Bigfoot was in the Green Gables, wolfing down his second big plate of mystery meats, German cheese and scrambled eggs when I joined him at the table. That man ate more eggs than anyone I knew. Eggs prepared any manner of way, it didn't matter. If it was an egg from anything this side of rattlesnakes, he'd eat it with a grin. He claimed buzzard eggs were mighty fine eating, which I doubted was true, and doubted he knew for sure, since buzzard eggs were normally laid in high cliff-side caves or the tips of tall trees. They'd have to be mighty fine eating to go to all that trouble.

"Sure glad you ain't sleeping in my room tonight, Bigfoot," I said. Bigfoot's love of eggs and sausages often made for odious companionship on the trail. More often than not, he rode at the end of the line. Especially if there was no breeze. "You're gonna end up with a case of the fecular bloviations that'll drift a buffalo herd."

"It'll only be my business if I do," he said. "That's why I prefer sleeping under the stars."

"That there, Mr. Pierpont, is the West," I said. "Being neighborly."

"Yes, very considerate," said Pierpont. "I suppose."

"Mr. Pierpont has been wondering if you'll share some of your experiences with him," I said to Bigfoot. "He's purchased new journals from the mercantile to record all the drama transpiring around him."

"Is that right? Well, I always enjoy chatting with scribes and wordsmiths, Mr. Pierpont. I'm quite a lover of the verse myself," said Bigfoot. "Why I heard of this one tale about this feller from Nantucket. I suppose that one blurs the lines between fact and phantasm to where it takes scribblers like yourself to puzzle out."

I looked up as Clay Allison strutted through the batwing doors. He was followed by half a dozen old plainsmen and hunters in well-worn buckskins.

Clay had traded his faded cowpuncher garb for an all-black with silver trimmings Mexican pistolero get-up. He wore a black shirt and tight black charro jacket with pearl buttons and silver embroidery on the collars and cuffs. A wide-brimmed, silver-banded black sombrero was on his head, and black vaquero trousers with silver conchos flared over his pointy new, stitch-designed black boots. Around his waist was a red sash and a pair of pearl handled Colts on a gun belt with more silver sparkling.

"Howdy boys," said Clay with a big smile and a black cigarillo dangling from his lip. "Mind if we set?"

"Hello Clay, fellers," I said, judging Clay to be in a conversational mood. "Pull up some chairs."

"Looks like you got the herd through all right," said Clay, as the waitress fetched our drinks.

"Sure," I said. "We never had no problems."

"Ya didn't?" said Clay. "Ya mean, other than shooting some Higbees."

"Other than that," I said. "And some knot-head cowboy wanting to re-fight the Civil War around the supper wagon."

"Well, I do feel bad about that, mostly letting Charlie down," said Clay. "I know my mouth just goes a running sometimes when it shouldn't, so I really ain't mad at ya for saying that. I was just so dang tired of cows, cow stink, cow noise and cowboys. That ain't my callin'."

"It's honest work, Clay," I said. "You're a good hand when your temper ain't running you."

"Nah, not for me," said Clay. "Listen, rightfully, I owe you for saving my life from that buff."

"If you say so," I said.

"I do, so let me give you a head's up," Clay said. "There's a whole bunch of Higbees and Smoots and that clan camped outside town. They are mighty upset you kilt that Ezra. They say you shot Reuben Higbee in the back. And the ones you didn't kill is mighty embarrassed and angry that you got the drop on them the way you did. They are talking Blood Atonement."

"I appreciate the warning, Clay," I said.

"They're strapped up and wearing 'em low," said Clay. "They are determined to put in the time and go through some hardships to find you."

"They're here in Tornado Town now?"

"Hard to say. They're around close by. Most stay shacked up a few miles away, at an abandoned farm," said Clay. "But they keep people in town around the clock. There's always at least a dozen of them in shouting distance anymore. Jubal and Jude Haight was in town when the herd got here, but lit out soon after. I imagine old Porter is plotting your demise as we speak."

"As for the dead Higbees, I never shot first, and they were stealing my horse," I said. "And none of it was by ambush or calculation."

"I never believed for a moment that it was," said Clay. "I know you ain't no back-shooter. But that ain't the way Porter sees it."

"Where's Purnell stand if gun play breaks out?" I asked.

"He surely hoping it don't, and that's sincere," said Clay. "But, you know, if you kill some more of his wives' brothers or whatnot, he won't have no choice but to come after you."

"Those boys were just woeful armed robbers," I said. "And even worse as gunmen."

"No argument there," Clay said. "But there's enough of them, they're likely to hit something by accident."

"Thanks again for the warning, Clay," I said. "Let me buy you a beer. We got time for that?"

"I'd be pleased with a beer," said Clay. "I felt like I owed you. That's a rough bunch."

I knew a couple of the other men who joined us at the table. I knew of the others. Experienced, tough as bullhide men who'd spent years adventuring and exploring across the plains and mountains of the west. The youngest of them was over forty. Besides Clay, they were One-Eyed Bill Hoover, Barney Olmsby. Nat Simmons and Matt Simmons, and old Bones McGraw.

"Barney, how'd you old gristle heels end up with a hot head like Clay?" I said.

"He said he could shoot," said Barney.

"As long as it ain't a buffalo," I said.

"Ain't funny, Pete," said Clay.

"As long as there's action, Clay's a fine hand," I said. "If the drudgery wears on, you best have a shovel handy and a hole for him to dig. He can be a handful."

"You talk like I ain't in the room," said Clay.

"I speak plain whether the subject is in the room or not, Clay," I said. "You'd prefer I spoke behind your back?"

"A fella could get irritated listen to people black mouth him like that," he said.

"I ain't black mouthing nobody," I said. "But get as irritated as you want. I don't have obligations to a friend keeping me holstered."

"Clay, I know this man, and when I ask him a question, I know he'll speak the truth," Barney said, taking out his 14-inch Bowie knife to clean the dirt from his nails. "He's treated me respectful with the truth, and you too, if you'd realize. If you want him to speak different, then act different. Might be best you find another spot to drink."

"I reckon," said Clay. "Maybe I need to dig me a hole."

"No need for that," I said. "Let's all just calm down some. You come into riches to get them britches? And them fancy Colts?"

"Ran into Miguel Ángel Venegas. Notice the extra buttonhole right here?" said Clay, lifting the vivid silver silk kerchief billowing around his throat. He pointed to a small hole in the shirt fabric right where his collar bone connected below his chin. "I punched his ticket on the Iron Horse to eternal fire. Had a $500 reward on him. Fifty a head for his two amigos."

"Well, it's a mighty purty suit. Particularly the hanky," said Bigfoot.

"I'll get shed of this hanky onct I get the hole sewed up," Clay said of his shimmering bandanna. "It's a bit more fooferaw than my tastes run to."

"I think it's right purty," said Bigfoot. "More generally so on a gal, I reckon."

Clay shot him a glare but let it pass.

"You took out the Black Angel?" I said, and gave a whistle in admiration. Venegas had spent some years in a Mexican prison. When he came out, he was not a better man for it. He'd become an even more brutal sodomite and had been taking out his hatred on the young sons and daughters of Mexican farmers across the southwest. He'd made the mistake of kidnapping a visiting dignitary somewhere along the line. That got the rewards and writs out on him.

"He was a bad man," I said.

"Yes, and I reckon he's suffering for it now," Clay said.

"That must have been a hot time, you bedding him down," I said.

"He interrupted a meal I was enjoying at the table of a Mexican family outside town," Clay said. "I was doing some work for them, and they'd been letting me sleep in their barn and board my horse until I figured out my future. Pedro is a right nice feller, and his family treated me like I was one of them."

"You're doing farm work now?"

"Well, I was having me one of my moods when I rode over the hill and seen old Pedro trying to dig a well. I told him, hey, you need holes dug, I'm your man."

"No kidding?"

"Nope, got him a nice well dug," said Clay. "And a whole slew of post holes. I hung around a few days. His wife is a mighty fine cook. Better than Espinar by considerable bounds."

"Where does Venegas come into this?"

"He come up, him and his gang, on the run from some law or another. Busted through the door right as we was setting down to a dinner of goat stew and tamales," said Clay. "They said they was taking horses, the tamales, and Pedro's fifteen-year-old daughter. They mistook me for some sheepherder. That's a danged insult a man can't take. I shot Venegas right through the table, then got one more and Pedro blowed one in half with his scattergun."

"Is that right?"

"It is," he said. "And I made out right smart. I took the $500 reward from Colonel Carleton himself. Me and Pedro split the other hundred, and what we made selling their saddles, boots, and guns to the mercantile. The horses they left was decent ones, too. I kept one as a spare and Pedro kept the others. Settled his hash, settled my squirrels down. And I got me this slick pistoleer outfit."

"See, Mr. Pierpont, nothing goes to waste out here," I said.

"Too nice of a suit to bury with some low-down buzzard like Venegas," said Clay.

"It's fittin'," I said. "Try not to get no more buttonholes in it."

"Ain't planning on it," Clay said. "But that reward got me thinking. Now, me and these boys are going after Porter Higbee."

"Going after Porter? He's got a hundred men. Maybe more. Maybe many more," I said.

"I know," said Clay. "But those boys, they're crack shots with those Whitworth rifles they got, and they got a forty-pound bench-rest gun, too. We figure to take him from far out, and then hide out somewhere for a while."

"How you going to collect your reward that way?"

"Well, I reckon they'll bury him, and we'll go back and dig him up. Bring his head in," said Clay. "I ain't shy about digging holes."

"Colonel, you know there's Higbees down in the bottoms," I said to Carleton the next morning over breakfast in his quarters.

"Yes, I'm aware. They come in pretty regularly," Carleton said. "It's mostly the younger ones, though. The ones he knows we can't tie to stolen Army rifles or any other crime. None that had any involvement in Mountain Meadows. There's little I can do about it. I can't arrest a man just for being related to an outlaw. Nor do I have any real authority to run them out of town."

"What is their business in town?"

"Mostly just drinking and acting swinish. But nothing meriting a showdown with the Army," said Carleton. "We know they always keep a few spies in town, but they are spies that don't commit crimes."

"Doesn't seem to be good policy, letting them mingle with the troopers," I said.

"It's a bit of a game. Not all the soldiers they get drunk are indiscreet, and I have my own agents down there too. We probably have information revealed we don't want, but that's impossible to control," said Carleton. "As a trade-off, my spies also get information from the Higbees once the whiskey hits and they start bragging about some plot or another. I feed them some bad information, and see what they do with it."

"I see," I said.

"We're not interested in the little fish, anyway," said Carleton. "Although I'm sure we'd prevail, we'd gain nothing, and possibly lose valuable men, if we try to scrap with every Higbee we see."

"I suppose," I said. "Porter appears to have no shortage of Shizzites. Enough to cause considerable carnage."

"The who?"

"The Shizzites," I said. "You didn't read up on his theology while you were investigating him?"

"I did. I don't recall any Shizzites, though."

"I suppose not. Porter hadn't been ex-communicated and started his own sect back when you knew him. My understanding, from what Zach says, this Jared fellow in the Mormon Bible led his tribe across the seas to the land that is now America. The last honest King of Jared's tribe was King Shiz, killed by an evil usurper, Coriantumr. Shiz's descendants fled and scattered, and these are who Porter's claiming are the chosen people," I said. "Now Brigham Young is Porter's Coriantumr. Porter is leading the Shizzites, the tribe of Jared, to unite all the Indian tribes, which are the Lamanites from the Mormon Bible. You knew about the Lamanites, I reckon?"

"I did."

"That's what the boy says the Mormon scripture says, and my understanding, them in Higbee's clan do a whole lot of scripture reading," I said. "That lost tribe of Jared. That's the whole idea behind this new Zion."

"No kidding," said Carleton.

"The Shizzites are Porter's new Danites, the men you investigated before. Some of the older ones were actually Danites," I said. "He's got them set up in twelve companies, or legions as he calls them. One led by each of his brothers, about twenty men each. But he plans to make them larger."

"We knew he had some military organization, and we'd heard tell of his Quorum of the Twelve Apostles," Carleton said. "I wasn't sure exactly how it fell together. That part is very secretive, even amongst the loose-lipped and whiskey addled."

"Most of the Quorum are Porter's closest kin," I said. "They've been practicing their trade by robbing wagon trains, joining in some Indian raids. Even going down into Mexico and picking fights with some of the bandit caudillos across the Rio Grande."

"I knew they'd been raiding and robbing. I know they're powerful. Still, I think it's unlikely they'd ever succeed setting up a theocratic state. But who knows?" Carleton said.

"It's all pretty hard to accept, but I've seen what zealots can do," I said.

"It remains unclear whether Higbee and Walsh are in cahoots or at odds. If Porter's Shizzites throw in with Walsh and the Knights of the Golden Circle, we could, in fact, have another war on our hands. The government, the people, are sick and tired of war and death, and maybe even more, paying for them. Certainly, people do not want another prolonged conflict," said Carleton. "If these forces out here are allowed to combine, grow stronger, and bring in all these hostile Indian tribes, the government might feel a lot of pressure to just let them take a piece of ground. That's why we must nip this in the bud. We need to strike hard, fast and with finality."

"I agree," I said.

We'd been in town over a week when I noticed Andy had started following Clay around, and had assumed a swagger of his own. Zach was following Andy around doing the same thing. Clay was enamored with a Mexican saloon girl named Rosalita and Andy was spending a lot of time with a petite blond prostitute named Eunice.

"I can't tell you what to do and what not to do, but some of them girls have a case of regrets you'll carry with you the rest of your life," I said to Andy that afternoon in the Gables. "It's a business transaction, don't go getting googly eyed."

"I understand them things," Andy said. "I ain't completely wet behind the ears."

"And don't get yourself in no shooting scrape over her," I said. "Plenty of whiskey bent pecker-brains habitate these saloons, believing the guile spun by them gals swooning all over 'em."

"Now, Pete, when did you get so callous?" said Half-Chin Annie, draped on my legs. She was Cleveland Annie when I'd first met her in Austin in '45. Texas had just been granted statehood and the town was celebrating. But after a few weeks I was broke and bored and went looking for my Ranger Company. Then she got broke and lonely and went back to getting paid for her favors. Some months later in a San Antone saloon two drunks slapped leather and a bullet clipped Annie's chin. It was just a graze, but the wound bled a lot and she wore a thick bandage for several days. People speculated a large chunk of chinbone had been shot off. It hadn't, there was just a little welt of a scar, but a sudden influx of whores from Cleveland led to the new name.

"Our good times was twenty years ago," I said. "We was just spreeing."

"Pete, I'm crushed," Annie said, eying Bass Reeves like a hungry wolf eying a tied goat. Sadly for Annie, Bass had made it clear that his marital vows to Nellie Jean would not be broken. It was the same with Britt and his Mary, who he'd faced the Comanche nation to retrieve. So, here she was on my lap, her one true love, with her vasty alabaster bosom overflowing her blouse. I'd noticed her eye-stripping a couple young cowboys, too.

"I leave broken hearts wherever I go," I said.

"Well, didn't that month we spent in Austin mean nothing to you, you as frisky as a young colt?" she said.

"Sure, but you kept breaking colts. That was a long time ago," I said.

"A girl's got to make a living," she said.

She was still a looker, just getting a little hard around the eyes. But that will happen in her profession. Few women on the Texas frontier didn't have hard eyes. Most got that way from digging and scraping every day trying to make a life, with one eye on a bunch of hungry kids and the other watching the horizon for Comanche raiding parties. Annie probably wouldn't make that trade, and I wasn't going to ask her. I figured she'd take it wrong.

"Eunice is a nice girl," Annie said. "But Mag Borge thinks she's his girl. And he always has some follow-a-longs with him. He's due back in town any day now."

"Who?"

"Magnar Borge, Big Mag," said Annie. "He's a pimp. He floats in and out of Luther Walsh's circle, but has avoided getting his name on a wanted poster. He's from Norway or somewhere. Big fellow, pale as a wedding dress, with white blond hair. His complexion and all, he can't be out in the sun long. He goes from town to town in a covered hearse, gambling and running whores. He's in the saloons all day, keeping his ear open for anything Walsh might be interested in. Gold shipments and payroll wagons and such. Sometimes he gets run out of places, but the law can't seem to hold him long for anything. He pays well for information on good robbery prospects. Sometimes he'll hire his gunmen out."

"What law is that?" I said.

"Other places. Ain't no law out here west of the Pecos," Annie said. "But he's usually not this far from civilization, though I've run into him from Santa Fe to St. Louis. The man has a fierce bad temper, and he usually has three or four thuggish dimwits and half a dozen poorly used girls with him. Lately some of Porter Higbee's men have been chumming around with him. He set his girls up in the rooms over The Mystic Saloon a few weeks ago."

"If he's got girls, why is he coming over here bothering Eunice?"

"He's trying to recruit her and Rosalita, and some of the other new girls," said Annie. "Though he pretends like he's got feelings for Eunice, that she wouldn't just be one of his whores. That kind of thing."

"Why don't you run him off?"

"I warned him, and Truman warned him, but Truman said he can't keep him out of the bar entirely," she said. "That could lead to gun play. Or Big Mag just offering Eunice a wad of cash outright to leave. At least here I can keep an eye on her, and maybe she'll realize what a scoundrel Big Mag really is."

"She's still here," I said.

"Yes. He hasn't made an outright offer to her. He knows that would be crossing a line," she said. "We've told her about him, us that's been around. In here, maybe she'll see. This life is plenty hard enough without a man like him."

"So I understand," I said.

"Yes, and he's due back. He went up to Taos for something, supposed to be back this day or next. I had expected you all would be long gone by now, and there would be no reason to trouble you with it" she said. "You might want to warn your young friends."

"I have warned them about the dangers of fort towns, but they're growed," I said. "They don't want to hang out with old folks. Same situation as Eunice. They got to make their choices."

"Sure," she said.

"Whatever happened to Jed, Jethro, whatever his name was, the silver miner?" I said.

"Jeth. We got married, moved to Dallas," Annie said. "We was happy for a few years, and then his money run out."

"I see."

"It wasn't like that," she said. "He run out of money because he was spending it all on whores. You know Dallas. Whores on every corner. I was a good wife to him. He had to have his whores and that life. I can't figure men."

"Hard to figure," I said.

153

"I would have gone back to whorin', to pay our way until he found something, to keep us and that little house together. But that idea didn't appeal to him," she said. "Said he didn't want no whore for a wife."

"Ain't that something," I said. "Sounds like you're better off."

"Maybe. It was nice for a while though. You still got some of that coltishness to you," said Annie sleepily, the afternoon sun coming in through her bedroom window. "Lots more scars than you used to have, though."

"Comes with the life I chose, I reckon," I said. Me and Annie had spent the last week in her suite above the Green Gables. All I'd had to do was pay for the room.

"What are you planning to do now?" she said. "After you plant this Higbee."

"Planting Higbee won't be no easy task, I figure, even with a thousand soldiers," I said. "Planning for after is probably a fool's folly."

"It's that bad?"

"It could be," I said. "But I figure Higbee's coming for me, regardless."

"Then post up some of them young bucks, let that rapscallion Clay Allison get him," she said.

"Clay's liable to get everybody with him shot. He's too wild," I said.

"Where'd you get this one?" she said, running her fingers along a bullet scar. "It's new."

"The War," I said.

"The war, hunh? Terrible thing," she frowned. "Turned out good for your folks though, I guess."

"Sure," I said. "I could barely ride through Texas, all them happy cotton pickers dancing in the road. Maybe if we can stop people from killing Freedmen's judges things will improve."

"Still, it's better, ain't it?"

"Sure. Lots better," I said. "Just not quite what people was expecting, I think. Maybe they'll figure it out."

"You know, I've got some money put away, for if I ever found a nice fella that wasn't trying to rob me or pimp me," she said.

"I hope you find him," I said.

"You and me, we're good together," she said. "Why, we have us a regular courtship almost."

"Crossing paths every three or four years ain't like no regular courtship I ever heard of," I said.

"More regular than any other man," she said. "It's always real pleasant."

"Stop it," I said. "Give me my drawers."

"It's getting too late," I said to Colonel Carleton. We'd been stuck in Tornado Town for over two weeks. "It will be September in a very few days. We need to get a move on."

"Yes, I'm aware," said Carleton. "I'm not happy about the situation either."

"Couldn't we take a few men and get started?"

"We have to wait for orders. I can't move without them," Carleton said. "It's not my choice at all, but orders are orders. You understand that. Your pay has already started if that's an issue."

"No, that's not an issue," I said. "The issue is getting out of there before the Comanche go on the warpath."

"I won't hold you to our agreement. The Army is creating needless hazards. For you, for my men, for civilians," said Carleton. "I think it's a vital mission to save many lives, maybe prevent a war. I tell you, as an Army commander and on a personal level, we need your help. But I'll harbor no ill will if you want no part of this bungling."

"Fair enough," I said. "I'll stick. For now. A couple more days."

"If we haven't heard in two days, then, yes, we'll just have to move. No options. I'll defend that position to my superiors if need be," Carleton said. "Or you can ride on back home. Your choice. No hard feelings."

"Fair enough," I said.

"Have you met any of the men yet?'

"A couple of the enlisted men. Captain Hardy and the Lieutenant that's coming with us. He seems an earnest sort."

"Payton means well, but he's a little excitable. He's a West Point lad who was too young for the Civil War. He has two older brothers that rose to general and colonel," he said. "The men are trained, they are skilled. I'll hand that to him. That was his doing. But I do need to handle him with a tight rein."

"This might not be the best job for him then," I said.

"Yes," he said, with a glum shrug. "But like I said, he's a West Point Man. His brothers have influence. They have political aspirations for him, for themselves. They think he needs some glory first. The Army really isn't the place for political aspirants."

"Isn't the reporter here to help your own political ambitions?"

"Don't confuse someone else's political ambition for me for what I may want for myself," Carleton said. "Same as you, I've had a long, hard career fighting Indians and Rebels. Once I get these Indians fed, and fixed so they can survive on their own, with a little stability, my military career closes. I'm done. Now all I want is a little peace. Go back to Maine. Unlikely I'll ever pick up a gun again, even to hunt. I'll have some time for real reading. I may write a book, chronicle some of my experiences. But not for a political career. Not to fight with fools and wallow with hogs all day."

"No, I suppose not," I said.

"Negroes hold elected office now. You've had a remarkable life, and are educated," said Carleton. "Would you want to be a politician? Or more to the point, even be around them?"

"I'd sooner get tortured by Comanche," I said. "Spit roasted and lathered in Tabasco sauce."

"Exactly," he said. "So the reporter can write as many blood-and-thunder stories as he wants. I'm not interested."

"That's good to hear," I said. "But Lieutenant Payton?"

"Captain Hardy is a good man," said Carleton. "Rock solid. He'll keep a leash on him."

"Let's hope so," I said. "This ain't the spot for recklessness."

"Indeed, it's not," said Carleton. "Well, a certain amount maybe. Otherwise it wouldn't be the Jack Hays way, would it?"

"Don't go mistaking boldness for recklessness," I said. "If Jack was reckless, I'd have been dead long ago. Jack was bold, but he was smart. He had a chess board in his head, staying always a step ahead of the Comanche, or Mexicans, or whoever we were fighting at the time. It's a rare combination."

"It certainly is," Carleton said. "Lt. Payton is not all bad. He has skills, just no experience, maybe a little too eager for my taste. But he's done an excellent job getting these men ready. He has drilled them, for hours every day, in the riding and shooting skills your old company commander required. I'd be honored to demonstrate."

"Sure," I said. "I'd like to see what you've got."

Carleton was right. Lt. Payton had done a good job with the men. When Jack Hays commanded his Ranger company, he didn't take just any volunteer. A man had to be tough enough to endure the punishing rigors of hard-riding patrols in extremes of weather. He had to possess exceptional horsemanship and gun skills. Jack had developed some tests so aspiring Rangers could prove they could shoot it out with a swarm of mounted Indians.

These men passed Jack's qualifications. For three hours I watched the forty men ride at a full gallop while shooting bean cans off fence posts fifty feet away. They hit ten out of ten times, just like Jack demanded. In the second round, they had to ride like thunder with their reins in their mouth, shooting the bean can with both hands. They did that, too, and then galloped past and shot the bean can from underneath their horse's neck. After that they showed how they could lean out of their saddle and swoop up a life-sized dummy at a dead run.

"Impressed, Mr. Horse?" Col. Carleton asked.

"Very," I said. "But them bean cans don't shoot back."

Later that afternoon I went to the Green Gables. Bigfoot Wallace had just finished a big plate of eggs and we were hunched over a table, drinking Sangria and playing chess. Other tables held some casual card players and some checker games. Clay, Andy, Zach, and a couple young cowboys had some tables together, laughing with Eunice and Rosalita and some other girls on their laps. Pierpont was at our table with Kansas City Stella, the stout prostitute, draped across his legs. They had gotten quite chummy.

"Have I earned the sobriquet cowboy now, you think, Mr. Horse?" beamed Pierpont. His mouth and sleeves were both smudged pink by his third - or fourth - pint jar of Bigfoot's sangria. Or perhaps it was Stella's lipstick and rouge.

"Why sure you have, as much as any man ever earned it. I reckon your bottom callouses is as thick as any man's," I said. "That is the tell sign of a real cowhand."

"Indeed, they are," laughed Pierpont.

"It's still a mighty cute bottom," giggled Stella.

"Looks like the drive has shaped you in several ways. Has your opinion on vice changed some? Will Mr. Greeley be seeing any of these libations on your expense account?"

"Well, now, I reckon what a man does out here is his own business," Pierpont drawled in a dead-on imitation of Charlie Goodnight. "A fair amount of vice gives character to a man, as long as he ain't no ear-beatin' braggart and general annoyance."

Bigfoot howled with laughter so hard he nearly rolled out of his chair, and I had a good guffaw myself. I don't think Stella actually knew who Charlie was, but she was giggling hard, bouncing up and down on Pierpont's lap with them, jiggling all over.

"And keeping your baser natures constrained?" I asked.

"Not for long, he don't," whooped Stella and Bigfoot nearly hit the floor. "Though I've never heard it called one of them before."

"I'll give you credit. You handled yourself pretty well out there. I wouldn't be planning no solitary excursions just yet, though," I said. "But you've earned yourself a spell of vice and relaxation. I won't tell nobody."

"If Mr. Greeley walked through that door right now, I'd be the first to tell him of the wondrous resuscitative and invigorating powers of vice," Pierpont slurred. "In moderation, of course."

"Of course," I said.

Instead of Horace Greeley, Magnar Borge walked in through the door, and he came in like he was looking for a dog to kick. He had a single pearl-handled six gun riding low on his bleached linen trousers and a murderous scowl across his face. Big Mag was white from top to bottom. His skin was almost albino pale and snowy hair fell over his collar. His white straw planter's hat and white linen suit were amazingly clean. Narrow-toed boots of white snakeskin or lizard were on his feet. He had a gang of men with him, including a few Haights and Hoaglands from the Higbee clan. Big Mag glared at Eunice and Andy as his group took one of the long tables and sat.

"Eunice, get over here," he shouted after a good five minutes of evil glances. He slapped the table hard and the room went quiet.

"I'm with Andy," she said, with a quiver of fright in her voice. "I'll talk to you later on."

"You will talk to me now. Grab that Mex girl and get on over here," he shouted, but Eunice and Rosalita made no move to get up.

"I reckon they'll stay put," said Clay.

"Ah, hell, here we go," I said to Bigfoot.

"Ain't our fight," said Bigfoot.

"No, not unless the Higbees try any back shooting," I said.

"The girl's with my friend," said Clay. "You tend to your business and we'll tend to ours."

"Who is this cabron?" laughed Mag to the crowd. "Butt out, greaser."

"Did you just call me a greaser?" said Clay. Clay was sunburned bronze and still had his neatly trimmed coal-black mustache and chin beard. His eyes were black as onyx. He had on a dead Mexican bandit's flashy clothes. The light was poor. Clay vaguely looked Mexican, but that didn't lessen the insult.

"I did," bellowed Big Mag. "You look like a Tijuana alley cat screwed an inbred sheepherder."

"Sure," said Clay. "'Cept we ain't in Mexico, and I ain't seen any sheep."

"Did you steal them pistols to use, or just to get your pitcher took with them?" said Big Mag.

"Darling, let me up," said Clay. With a half-sad smile he patted Rosalita on the rear end and lifted her off his lap. "Just stand over there against the wall for just a second."

Without looking at Big Mag, Clay licked the end of his just rolled cigarette, gave it a twist, and lit it. He lifted his eyes to stare into Mag's and blew out a slow cloud of blue smoke. Clay moved slow, taking a drink and then carefully setting his beer bottle on the table. He leaned forward to stand, then bolted up like greased lightning. His chair slammed over backwards and he fired from the hip. His first shot missed Mag Borge by five feet and hit Jeziah Haight square between the eyes.

Big Mag clawed for his cannon and Clay's second shot hit Mag's six gun as he yanked it from his holster. The third shot hit Mag in the left hip as he spun away from Clay's blazing pistol. Mag's gang returned fire, but Clay stood straight, firing with both Colts as the bullets whizzed past him. Myron Hoagland caught one right in the middle and he folded up like a camp chair. Earnest Haight took one in the calf as he dove behind an overturned table. The rest of Mag's gang stampeded out the batwing doors, tripping and falling.

The Big Mag clan had cut loose probably close to twenty shots, but the only thing they'd killed was some beer bottles and a lamp chimney. A couple spittoons had taken shots below the water line and were leaking out.

People cautiously rose from the floor and from behind knocked-over tables. They checked themselves and their companions for wounds and bruises. Other than the wounded gunmen, there was little damage but for some bruises or scrapes. Everybody but Pierpont. He was flat on his back with his arms outstretched like an angel's wings. His face was covered with blood, and a large red pool was growing underneath him. I thought he was dead until I heard him snoring. On closer inspection, there were no bullet wounds. In a few seconds his eyes opened. They were a little lopsided and bleary and his first few words made absolutely not a lick of sense. After a few tries, he finally got it right.

"What happened?" he said, slightly slurring. "Am I shot?"

"No," I said. "I believe you took some friendly fire."

In the scramble for cover, Stella had walloped Pierpont in the nose with the elbow end of one of those burly arms, hurling him backwards out of his chair. There was no way to know if it was the elbow, or the loud crack of his head hitting the floor, that had knocked him out cold. Stella brought a wet cloth and was cleaning Pierpont's face, offering tearful apologies.

"Did Clay get Big Mag?" asked Pierpont.

"Just winged him. Mag is hurt less than you are, but you couldn't tell it by the bawling," I said. "His sidekick, Myron Hoagland wasn't so lucky. Took one through the belly. That's him you hear loudly leaking out in the corner. A doc has been called for, but it's a pulpiteer that's needed. One of the Haight boys is growing cold, too. Stone dead."

"Killed?"

"Means the same out here," I said. "That's one dandy of a goose egg you got on the back of your head. You seeing all right?"

"As long as there's three of everybody," he groaned while Stella tenderly ran a wet cloth over his scalp. "It would probably be best not to mention this to Mr. Greeley at the Tribune."

"I wasn't expecting to talk to him," I said.

Within an hour, Pierpont had thick, dark maroon rings around both eyes. His broken nose was swollen and glowing red. He had a knot on the back of his head the size of a plum and was complaining of pain and dizziness. Annie found him a nice big dose of laudanum and he went to take a nap.

# THREE

# THE PALO DURO CANYON
## SEPTEMBER 4, 1866

After the shootout with Mag Borge, Carleton decided we should move out before a horde of trigger-happy Shizzites swarmed in, looking for revenge. We left the fort the next morning, headed northeast on an old patrol road toward the Canadian River. Captain Hardy led Lt. Payton, forty troopers, a surgeon and a farrier. We had twenty spare mounts and five mules toting water kegs and supplies. Bigfoot had come for the adventure, and I was happy to have him. Andy and Zach and the scribe Pierpont had come along too, and I wished they hadn't.

The first days we rode over miles of flat prairie covered by patchy buffalo grass toasted golden brown by the late-August sun. Prairie dogs chirped angrily at us as we passed by. Jackrabbits, antelope and prairie chickens scurried out of our way and into the thickets of sand sage and mesquite an acre or two across.

The only animals that were not of a nervous and furtive disposition were the ever-present vultures. They were never out of eye shot. Sometimes they were close enough I could hit them with a rock. Sometimes they circled miles away and maybe that high in the sky. But they were always there.

We reached the Canadian River and dropped down into its deep, red-clay walled valley. For two centuries the river valley, more than thirty miles wide in some places, had been the trade route for hundreds of Comancheros. Every year, thousands of stolen horses and cattle were herded through here. More than twenty parallel roads, trails, and paths wove through it, filled with deep ruts carved by the Comanchero's two-wheeled, oxen-drawn carretas, the rough wooden carts used in their pack trains.

The Comanchero had built crude trading points and rendezvous sites in the many narrow side canyons and caves in the walls of the Canadian. Most of those remained vacant now, after the Comanchero moved to more remote trading sites in the canyons east of the Caprock Escarpment. The Comanchero were not any kind of organized fighting force, and we had little to fear from them directly. And it wasn't quite time for the motley lot of thieves and degenerates anyway. They normally didn't appear until the Comanche returned from their wide-sweeping September raids across Texas and the bordering states.

If the Higbees had passed this way it wouldn't necessarily be easy to tell. The pathways in the river valley were also rutted by the wheels of countless iron-rimmed wagon wheels, from when it had been called the California Road. It had been heavily traveled by those headed out to the California Gold fields, coming from Ft. Smith and passing through Indian Territory. After the soldiers went east to fight the War, the Comanche ruled this land again, and many fewer wagon trains risked it.

"You've noticed those Comanche following us, I reckon?" said Captain Hardy. We were out in the open, having left the Canadian and riding south toward the Palo Duro. In a mesquite thicket off to the west, sitting perfectly still on their ponies, was the same small bunch of Comanche.

"I've noticed," I said. "Same ones I told you about at the fort. I've been seeing them for the last six weeks."

"Six weeks?" he said. "You don't seem too concerned about them."

"I'm not much concerned about them," I said. "Now those ones ahead of us have me a little uneasy."

"Ahead of us?" snapped Lt. Payton. "Why didn't you say anything if you've seen Comanche ahead?"

"I just did. But I haven't seen them yet, just saw some sign early this morning," I said. "I followed the trail for a while, hoping it would turn out to be that bunch behind us. It ain't. It's another ten or so, probably cooling off at Rattlesnake Springs for the afternoon."

"And they're watching us?"

"I imagine they are, now that they've noticed us," I said.

"What do you think of that?" said Hardy.

"I'm not sure what to make of it," I said. "Those behind us stole a few cows once. They still ain't painted, so that's a good sign. But you just never know with Comanche. They can be patient when they want to be. Maybe they're just gathering their forces."

Toward evening I came across the third small group of Indians since leaving the fort, single families or small bands traveling from one village to another. One was going to a wedding. They didn't tell me much I didn't already know, or strongly suspect. I paid them generously with sugar and flour and cloth for the women and some tobacco and new knives for the men. A couple packs of Arbuckles sealed the deal. Yes, Higbee had many men, wagons and guns.

The next morning we saw the circling column of vultures and rode toward it. Topping a small rise, we saw a buffalo wallow fifty feet or so away from a dead, bare-branched cottonwood tree. A flock of buzzards sat in the branches, engorged crops bulging, sedated by their gluttony. More hissed and grunted and waddled off their feast of the six dead men in and around the twenty-foot hole. The men had used dead horses as bulwarks, and a shimmering black blanket of scavenger birds ripped at the bodies. I took a detail and we rode cautiously toward the scene.

"You don't think that's Bass and them?" Andy said as we batted at the swarm of green horseflies. There was still a few inches of water in the wallow, and two scalped men were face down in the reeking, green gruel.

"Nah, ain't none of these fellows Negroes," Bigfoot said. "They may be burnt black, but they never started out their day that way."

"They put up a fight," I said, looking at a couple hundred empty rifle cartridges in and around the wallow.

"These is the fellows that was with Clay Allison back at the fort," said Bigfoot.

"Think so?'

"One-Eyed Bill Hoover. He finally got a matching set," said Bigfoot, holding a severed, scalped head out at arm's length. He gave it a vigorous shake to get the flies off. One-Eyed Bill's long, silver beard was so blackened and stiff with blood it looked like it had been dipped in a tar bucket and left to dry. "They took out his good eye, but never touched the one that was already sewed shut."

"Who is this one?"

"This one here is Barney Olmsby," I said. "And I think that's Nat Simmons. Maybe old Bones McGraw over there."

"That was Clay's outfit, but I don't see him," Andy said.

"Who done it?" asked Zach.

"This is Comanche work," said Bigfoot. The grass was matted with blood around the six dead men. Three had been burned to a char over large fires. They'd all been scalped and mutilated, gaping wounds full of maggots and heads dismembered. Dried ropes of intestines had been strung out by scavengers. "That's a rough group of men right there. Not the brightest, but more than capable. How long you figure they been like this?"

"In this heat, a body don't take long to go bad," I said. "Maybe only a day or two."

"Sergeant, get a detail to bury these men," said Lt. Payton.

"That's just a waste of time," I said. "We stop to bury all the men Higbee and Comanches kill, these soldiers of yours going to be broke down long before we find him."

"Harsh to say, but it's true," said Bigfoot.

"It's not right to leave these men out here like this," said Payton.

"Birds gotta eat," I said. "Out here, you're going to see a whole lot of things that don't seem right."

"Buzzards growing fat following Higbee's trail," said Bigfoot.

"I suspect they're going to get fatter before this is over," I said. Bigfoot asked the good lord to look over 'em as we rode past the dead men in the wallow.

After reaching the Palo Duro Canyon we rode along the rim for two days, looking down into the great crevice that separated the western High Plains from the rolling grasslands of the Great Plains to the east. From the canyon rim there were few gradual descents. Mostly, the 1,000-foot-tall red-rock walls dropped almost straight down. The Prairie Dog Fork of the Red River ran through the center of the Palo Duro, and many tree-lined creeks and streams cut through the canyons, feeding the Red, Brazos, and Colorado rivers that flowed all the way to the Gulf of Mexico. At a hundred and twenty miles long, the Palo Duro was the largest, but far from only, of the Caprock Escarpment's canyons cut by the rivers. More canyons ran for another eighty miles south, and the dozens of side canyons created a network thirty miles across.

One and a half million acres of narrow canyon and sharp ridges in the Palo, and at least triple that for the Caprock in its entirety. Throughout the canyon there were reddish-orange hoodoos, tall rock spires the wind had shaped to look like totem poles. In some places the canyon floor of the Palo Duro was twenty miles across, flat, and lush with waist-high grass. In others it narrowed to a farrago of bristly sandhills, flat-topped mesas, steep red-dirt ridges and straight-drop gorges and arroyos. Countless miles of narrow slots cut through the walls of the Palo Duro. Some that ran straight, some that circled around, and others that twisted off to nowhere. With openings not much more than a crack in the rock, they could be either a passage to safety or a trap. They looked the same from the outside.

Comanche legend said that long ago, the land was flat and surrounded by mountains. A giant eagle tried to claw his way to the top of the mountains, but the earth was slick and gave way, causing the bird to slide down to the base. He tried to claw to the top again, but again he slid down, leaving more deep gashes in the earth with each attempt. He clawed and clawed furiously, sharp talons slashing deep into the ground, only to slide down each time. The mountains wept in pain and the tears became a flood that gushed down the deep gouges, creating the many canyons. The red of the canyon walls, they said, was the color of the wounds that the giant bird left.

We searched end to end of the Palo Duro, then spent the next three weeks criss-crossing the rugged canyons east of the Caprock. We rode over numerous switchback trails, past the waterfalls and rocky outcroppings of the Cita canyons, through the deep gash of Tule Canyon to the 34-mile-long Blanco Canyon and the countless smaller canyons branching off in between; The North and South Prong Canyons, the Crawfish, Mulberry Canyon, Little Sunday, Double Mountain Fork canyon and others just a few hundred yards deep. We looked in them all and continued on further south through Yellow House Canyon and started back up again.

We followed the Comanchero cart trails, and the roads the bandits pushed stolen livestock over. For the number of wagons and horses the Higbees were said to have, they had done a good job of hiding their tracks among those left by the two-wheeled carretas. I found some faint sign of recent wagon wheels but they split up, joined and split up again several times. That was the old Comanche way of avoiding the few cavalry and Ranger patrols that had pursued them into the canyons. It was difficult to tell how many wagons there were, and impossible to know who was in them.

There were unshod pony tracks, Indian or mustang, and some shod tracks. None of the latter were fresh, though, and the trails soon faded. There were many game trails that small herds of buffalo and deer and smaller animals followed to the streams to drink. We found the ashes of old campfires, but they were small. Just big enough for six Comanche or two white men.

We slept in unlit camps, mostly living on corn dodgers and hard tack, buffalo jerky, and coffee. Every third day we'd make a stew or bacon and beans. In the heat and uncertainty, we stopped at every water hole and rested our horses often.

We were being watched, but by whom I didn't know. Probably several different parties. The same Comanche band made no secret of their interest in our affairs, although they came no closer. The Comancheros were staying hidden if they were there. Other than the rare occasions when they joined Comanche raiding parties, they were too few, and too poorly led or organized for a fight, even with only a small column of cavalry. But I knew if Higbee hadn't seen us with his own lookouts, certainly a flood of Comancheros had rushed to tell him of our presence, for a nice reward of a few guns or barrels of whiskey.

The sun was blistering and the air stagnant along the red-dirt trail and I had decided it was about time for me to ride on. If Higbee was somewhere in the Caprock, he'd forted up in one of these high-walled, narrow-entry canyons, and even 1,500 men couldn't peel him out of there. The Comanche continued to shadow us from a polite distance, but loped off if we sent a patrol that way. The constant sight of the Comanche had become a source of conflict between Captain Hardy and Lieutenant Payton. I'd seen them in several heated discussions.

"The Comanche are not our concern right now, Lieutenant. They've shown no inclination towards belligerence," said Hardy as Payton railed on about the Indians on a mesa more than a mile away. We had stopped for the day, in a nice patch of shade beside the Prairie Dog River.

"They're ghouls," said Payton. "Just stalking us like wolves or buzzards."

"That's the way it is out here, Lieutenant," said Bigfoot. "If they ain't actively displaying any agonistic behavior, why is you letting your feelings get all hurt?"

"Well, I don't like it," said Payton. "We need to ride out there and confront them, to let them know to respect our authority. That we won't play games with them."

"Sonny, it ain't a game, but it is. If you knew Comanche, you'd know that they're trying to bait you," Bigfoot said. "They'll take you one checker at a time. Rushing off after 'em is what they want. Pick us off a few at a time or wear down our horses."

"Don't call me sonny," snapped Payton. "I've been out here plenty long enough to see that all the Comanches are good for is raiding homesteads and lone wagons. When faced with real fighting men, they will scurry away like rats."

"You clearly ain't met a growed Comanche warrior then. Nor even half-growed, likely," said Bigfoot.

"I'm a little concerned about Lt. Payton," I said to Captain Hardy after Payton had stomped off red-faced. "How many times has he asked to take a squad and go after those Comanche?"

"Several," he said.

"He knows we're not out here hunting Comanche?" I said.

"He's been told," said Hardy. "Repeatedly."

"Having that reporter around to write about his glorious charges ain't helping any," I said.

"No, it sure isn't," said Hardy. "It was a fool's move to let him come along."

"Probably," I said. "At least he ain't fell off his horse yet."

"A wonder of wonders," said Bigfoot.

"I know we been putting it off, but don't you reckon it's time to go pay Jose a visit?"

"You're probably right," Bigfoot said.

"Who are we discussing?" asked Hardy.

"Jose Tafoya," I said. "You know him."

"I know him. His band of cattle rustlers and thieves is a big reason we had to get Texas cattle," Hardy said. "He's a friend of yours?"

"Not hardly, he ain't," I said.

"That rotten son of a rabid she-wolf," said Bigfoot. "I'd like to cut his gizzard out with a dull, rusty knife. There are accounts there that ain't settled."

"But for a price, or imminent threat of a noose, he might decide to help us," I said. "Jose's that kind of fellow."

"For a man who has chosen such a life of banditry, he does have an unnatural fear of getting hanged," said Bigfoot. "There's many other jobs where the likely outcome ain't a neck stretching."

The column waited while Bigfoot and I rode cautiously down Los Lingos Creek, to where it became the North Pease River, deep into the Valle de Las Lagrimas, the Valley of Tears, where the mothers and children were traded. Down to where steep walls suddenly enclosed the valley and the creek banks stayed green with sweet grass for the buffalo. Down to where we'd rescued Cynthia Ann Parker and ruined her life. Down to the darkest part of my mind.

I'd prowled this valley too many times, searching the trading sites during their fall trading season. I'd attended many of those rendezvous that sometimes lasted weeks, filled with horse racing, shooting matches, brawling and debauchery. I ignored the drunkenness and lechery while studying every face and listening at every conversation for word of my loved ones.

Jose ran just about the biggest gang of scoundrels and cutthroats. He could have lived comfortably on his sheep ranch in New Mexico, but instead he lorded over an outlaw kingdom and small army of desperadoes. Years ago, his men had tried to kill me more than once. On another occasion, Bigfoot had slain five of his men in a single battle. Things had calmed down, but nobody had forgotten it.

"State your business," a voice shouted as we came into a clearing. I could see the guard posts and sentries in the caves and ledges in the rocks above us.

"To see Jose Tafoya," I shouted.

"And who might you be?"

"I'm Pete Horse and this is Bigfoot Wallace," I said.

"If that's who you is, you ain't no friend of Jose's," the voice said. "He'd probably be mighty pleased if we shot you down right now."

"I'm sure he would be, briefly," I said. "But if we don't come out of here safe and sound, there's an army column coming in."

"Is that right?" the voice said. "Sounds like a whopper to me."

"Want to chance it?"

"What business do you have?"

"Just a chat, a friendly call," I said.

"Toss them guns down," the voice said.

"No, don't think so," I said. "You just go tell Jose we're here."

In a few minutes we were riding into Jose's stronghold of adobe brick and wood plank buildings. He had a small lumber mill, a blacksmith, and a gunsmith. Some solidly built cabins and a long bunkhouse. There was a store, saloon, chicken coop and a couple small sheds. Corrals held about fifty horses, and in the valley beyond were another hundred.

Jose Tafoya wasn't seven foot, but close to it. By far the tallest Mexican I'd ever seen. Not scarecrow skinny, but no spare flesh to him, except maybe over his eyes. His bushy brow seemed to have an extra layer of thick flesh in there. His chin was big and square. His hands were huge, bigger even than Bass Reeves' bear traps and his feet were the size of beaver tails.

"My man said you had a sack of gold for me if I could help you with a problem," said Tafoya.

"A small sack," I said and laid ten gold eagles on the table. "We're looking for Porter Higbee."

"Well, I can't tell you where he is, he'll kill me. Not for no measly hundred dollars," said Tafoya. "He has many men. They know you're here. They're watching you. I'm sure they watched you ride in here."

"That much we already had figured," I said.

"You are extremely foolish to come after him with forty men. That should be all the information you need. They have many more men than you," Jose said. "And they are not far away."

"Well, we have 1,500 more coming," I said. "If you're so worried about him, just tell him we came inquiring about some horses, like maybe those there in your corral with the U.S. Army brand on them."

"In my corral? Why that's impossible," said Tafoya.

"Stealing horses from a hard-fixed cavalry patrol could really bring on the wrath of the Federal government," I said. "Stiff rope and a short drop."

"I mean, I suppose it's possible my men may have overlooked brands on a horse or two, mixed in somehow with the hundred or so the Comanche brought us last month," he said. "I ain't got no recent horses."

"Is that right? Because one of them is the pony I rode out of Ft. Sumner a few weeks ago," I said. "Him and some others were stolen from our night camp just three nights ago."

"You don't say?" said Tafoya. "Why, that's incredible. Maybe he escaped from the Comanche and smelled the other horses and come in to soothe his loneliness."

"Sure," I said. "Somebody is going to be soothing your widow's loneliness if you don't stop the nonsense."

"You want to kill me over some cavalry horses?"

"No, I've wanted to kill you for a very long time, that ain't no secret," I said. "This would just be squaring old accounts. I'll shoot you if you don't tell me where Porter Higbee is. You think I won't?"

"No, I know very much that it would please you to do so," he said. "Why must life be so full of such hard choices? It is against my principles to inform to the law or the Army. You understand that, certainly."

"Right. Except those times you wanted the Army or Rangers to get rid of a competitor for you," I said.

"Yes, there have been those few times," said Tafoya. "But furtherance of my own interests is not really informing, per se. It's more a business practice. So my principles haven't really been broken, you see."

"I don't care to parse the fine points out at this time," I said.

"To keep the peace," said Tafoya. "I would say, if I was trying to avoid him, I would not go to Cañón del Rescate. You could avoid him other places, but probably not there."

"Ransom Canyon?" I said. "We've been through there."

"Perhaps so, but if I was trying avoid him, like I said, that is not where I would go," he said. "My men have not avoided him there."

"He wasn't in the main canyon," I said. "And there are no side canyons there large enough to conceal a group as large as Higbee is said to have."

"No, not one campsite, not from what I hear," Tafoya said. "And I am not informing on Higbee. His presence here has had adverse effects on my business, so I'd not be breaking my code."

"Sure," I said. "However you want it."

"The Yellow House has several side canyons which could possibly hold many smaller groups until all is ready. The main camp is Valle de Rescata. The others are split up, small groups led by his capitanos, many connected by back trails. They are widely dispersed, but laid out so if one camp is ever threatened, the others can respond quickly. Or so rumor has it. That is the last I know of the subject."

"Good enough," I said. "Now, you just stay out of it and we won't have a problem. You take sides with Higbee you'll wish you hadn't."

"Why would I side with him? He's been selling guns to the Indians for much less than I can, practically giving them away," Tafoya said. "I got guns I can't sell, and I can't move those horses out there. All I'm getting is a few at a time, like those stole from you. That was just a couple boys, out on a lark. The warriors deal directly with Higbee. When they do that, there is no business, no profit, for an honest trader such as myself. Take them cavalry horses when you leave, and take some more, too, if you need them. I can't do nothing with 'em. I ain't looking for no problemo with the blue coats."

"And the others?"

"What others?"

"The other Comanchero leaders," I said.

"What would I know of them?"

"Plenty," I said. "Quit playing games."

"Quien sabe? Some have joined Higbee, a few have joined Luther Walsh. Them two is very possibly at odds," Tafoya said. "Right now the prairie is aflood with rifles, and everybody is blaming everybody for a bunch that got stole by Comanche."

"No honor among thieves, right?" I said.

"I won't be getting no horses now," said Tafoya.

"Look at it this way, if we take out Higbee, you're back in business," I said.

"Yes, but if you don't?"

"If we don' run Porter out of the canyons he'll probably just shoot you anyway," I said. "This is a big place, but not big enough for two outfits as big as yours."

"Yes, I expect that is so," Tafoya said.

176

We rode to the very southern tip of Yellow House canyon, a green thirty-mile-long valley along the Double Mountain Fork of the Brazos River. It was several day's ride from the Palo Duro in one of the most remote, and rugged, canyons.

"Down here, there is a real good chance the Army will never find us," I told Hardy. "That's the reason for the canyon's name, after all. They could sell people with little chance of getting interrupted. Not only that, if they're split up in all these side canyons, they could ride down and cut us off from a dozen different direction."

"All we need to do is find evidence they are here, something to show to the Colonel as proof," said Hardy. "I'm no more eager to ride in there than you are."

"Fine," I said, and we kept going.

It wasn't long until I found the dead horse and knew we were in the right place. It hadn't been picked apart by the buzzards, and it wasn't just any dead horse. It was twice the size of any 800-pound mustang. This was a solid black, 1,600-pound draft horse of the sort used to draw the big wagons Porter Higbee was said to have. I got down and poked through the brush for an hour, until I had found some tracks left by an iron wheel during a recent rain. More searching revealed more wagon tracks, a fresh cork from a whiskey bottle and a packet of needles and thread."

"Well, up there is where they are," I pointed to a wooded ridge. "Beyond that ridge lies a box canyon. That's where they are."

"Porter?"

"I don't know about Porter, but a big bunch of them, by my guess," I said.

"I'd sure like to know for sure," he said.

"This is where they are. If we go further you may find your answer, but we'll be surrounded with no way out when you do," I said. "It'll be like a hornet's nest if you poke it. With this few men, we go to poking, we're going get swarmed. Time to go find the Colonel."

"I expect so," said Hardy. "But they could disappear before Col. Carleton gets here. If we entrench at the canyon mouth, maybe we can keep them in place."

"Sure," I said. "As long as we know who is keeping who in place."

We were riding away when the first sniper hit us, just as we crested a scrubby, sage splotched hill. The canyon had narrowed to a mile across, and sharp ridges protruded from the rim rock above us.

"Down the ravine," the Captain yelled, and we made a mad, cursing dash down a shrub lined arroyo.

"Who's hit?" asked the Captain as another shot cracked through a dry branch above our heads.

"Sgt. McGuire," Payton said.

"Bad?"

"Dead."

"That's a Whitworth rifle up there," I said after another shot passed harmlessly. "Confederate sniper rifle. I can recognize that sound in my sleep. That's no Winchester."

"Yes, I saw a lot of men fall to Whitworths during the Petersburg siege," said Captain Hardy.

"What difference does it make?" said Payton.

"Comanches ain't long distance sharpshooters," Bigfoot said. "They'd have no use for a Whitworth."

"We found Porter," I said. "And if they start shooting at us with long-range rifles we'll be in real trouble."

We waited in the ravine for two hours while the Tonk scouts searched the surrounding hills. Satisfied the snipers were gone we mounted up and rode for open prairie. We were almost out of the Yellow House when another shot rang out. Captain Hardy groaned and slid off the side of his horse. Another shot came from the other side, from the flat top of a mesa five hundred yards away. Then a flurry of shots rang out. Not Whitworths, but short and wild shots, from light Henrys and Spencers.

We charged for the dry creek bed. Bigfoot leaned over from his saddle and snatched the Captain's shirt collar, dragging him down the embankment. It was narrow, but deep enough to hide us from any snipers.

The Captain's breathing was ragged, and the front of his shirt was covered with blood. The bullet had hit him directly in his right collar bone, shattering it. He'd completely lost the use of that arm, at least for now. It was painful and very bloody, but not immediately fatal.

"Good lord, that hurts," groaned the Captain.

"Shattered that bone," said the surgeon. "I need to clean it good, and set it."

"How many men have we lost?" said the Captain to Payton.

"Two were killed," said Lt. Hopkins. "Sutter and Maynard were hit, but just scraped. A couple more are injured, got flipped off their mounts. The air knocked out of them."

"And we lost five more horses," said Bigfoot.

"This is a bad spot," I said. "Maybe they can't hit us from the rim rock, but they could bring 500 men out from behind those ridges and we'd never know it until they were on us."

"We have to move fast or they really will kill all our horses," said Bigfoot.

"And moving fast will kill the Captain," said the surgeon.

"I can ride," groaned the Captain.

"You can't move. You bounce around, all those little splinters in there will get in your blood and go straight to your heart," said the surgeon. "That is if they don't get infected and kill you first."

"What now?" said Bigfoot.

"We found the Higbees," I said. "That's what we set out to do."

"We don't know their exact location. We don't know how many they are," said the Captain.

"No, but they sure know ours," I said. "I thought that was the point. We've drawn them out."

"Yes, but they could still sneak away if we pull out completely," said the Captain. "They could still get away."

"Yes, and we may not," I said.

"They kill the horses we're as good as dead," Bigfoot said. "Maybe better than dead. If we get unhorsed out here, they could toy with us as long as they wanted."

"We need to hang on," said the Captain through gritted teeth as the surgeon packed his wound.

"Captain, I won't be party to no suicide, especially one over vanity and pride. We know where they are, you done your job," I said. "You know you can't stay here. That would endanger this mission you are so intent on completing."

"Only until the cavalry shows up," he grunted.

"If the cavalry shows up. This is a big place," I said.

"I will lead the column," said Lt. Payton.

"Lord help us," said Bigfoot, plenty loud enough for Payton and all the men to hear.

"Mr. Wallace," said Hardy. "Please...."

"All right, Captain, look. If we all try to ride out, they'll be on us like wolves on a straggling calf. It'll be dark soon. You and the other wounded men can follow this creek bed out of here. Even going slow, you can be five miles away from here by morning. They're unlikely to risk any great frontal attack. We can hold on out here for two days and keep them off you. Then we head back," I said. "Otherwise, me and my boys are heading for the Llano. I told Carleton I wouldn't obey idiotic or suicidal orders and I won't. Two days, and then we're done."

"I can carry on without these men," said Payton. "I have the Tonks to scout. I'm not sure why the Colonel wanted these vulgarians anyway."

"Just keep thinking that way, sonny," said Bigfoot. "Me and Pete leave, them Tonks won't be far behind. They ain't stupid."

"You need to get back to the fort," I said. "I think you can tell Col. Carleton we found the bad guys, and for him to hurry up and get here."

"I can't leave my men," said Captain Hardy.

"You'll just slow us all down and get us killed. If you don't get back, you'll die," I said. "You've done your job. We'll keep them off you for two days. That's it."

"I'll not let these men decide our mission," snapped Payton.

"I'll decide our mission, Lieutenant. You listen up. I know you're eager, but this is a powerful and wily foe," said the Captain. "You'll take the council of these men, you understand. This is not the time for rashness."

"I know my duty, Captain," said Lt. Payton.

"I sure to God hope so," Captain Hardy said. "We have a large force on the way. It is their job to destroy Higbee. Do not get distracted. This is no time for heroics. It is your duty to make sure they can complete their mission, understand?"

"We will finish the mission. We will stay in the field until the other columns reach us," said Lt. Payton.

"You'll do as ordered," said Hardy.

The ravine protected us from the snipers, and we followed it back a few hundred yards to a barely-moving trickle of a creek with grass enough for the horses. The troopers spent the day cobbling together travois for the wounded out of saplings, harness straps and rain slickers. When darkness fell, the four wounded and an escort of five rode away.

Bigfoot and I ventured out, slithering across the cooling earth until we were well away from the ravine. Then we sprinted from sage bush to sandhill up the ridge where the snipers had been. They were long gone.

"No one's up on that ridge anymore," I told Payton when we returned.

"All right," said Payton. "We'll push on in the morning."

"Push on?" I said. "No, the orders are to back out gracefully. Seems pretty clear where they are holed up."

"I'm not going to just let them disappear," Payton said.

"Then we will," I said. "We're staying put like the Captain said we would, and we're watching his back until him and the wounded get clear. Anything else, you're on your own."

Two days in the ravine passed without incident. Despite Payton's gasconades that he and his company could whip every Indian and outlaw gang in Texas, we headed back. I reminded him of his orders, as did the surgeon and Bigfoot. Especially Bigfoot, and the Lieutenant was seething mad. The men in uniform were happy to be going back, and the Tonk scouts were somewhere in between. They didn't say much.

We started out on foot after midnight, leading our horses down a buffalo trail where the canyon spread out to its widest. We stayed on flat ground that wouldn't likely lame our horses in the dark. At dawn we mounted up and rode through the day and night until we reached the Palo Duro. The next day, at midmorning, we saw smoke off in the distance. The Tonk scouts reported back there were three Indians and three horses up ahead. The men looked like Apache and were cooking some meat over a campfire.

"This is not Apache land. We're hundreds of miles from it. There's no good reason for them to be in the Palo except for trouble," I said. "The only Apache in this part of Texas is those with Luther Walsh. Unless they switched allegiances to Higbee. It's not likely they're just passing through."

"Yes, precisely. That's why I'm sending a patrol forward," said Payton.

"They could have an army waiting on the other side of that ridge. Wait here while we get up on that rim rock where I can get a better look," I said. "I don't know of an Apache, a Comanche, or any other Indian that would have a big fire like that, especially right out in the open in the middle of the day."

"All your scouting has done so far is get the Captain and some good men shot," he said.

"Is that right?" I said. "If you're unhappy with my job, send me on home."

"Sonny, it's his guiding so far that has kept this patrol from getting wiped out half a dozen times," Bigfoot said.

"They might have knowledge of Higbee's whereabouts," Payton said. "Perhaps they're friendly."

"And probably they ain't," I said.

"I appreciate your opinion, but I'll handle this. I can read terrain as well as anyone. I studied my maps at the Point," said Payton. "There could be any number of reasons why they're out there. Perhaps they have injuries. Perhaps their horses are spent."

"That's not likely. At least let us go up the rim rock where we can look around first. You can send some men forward, but wait for our signal."

"Hurry up about it. I'm not going to wait around and get these men killed day after day," said Payton. "I was ordered to engage if we had no recourse. I see no recourse."

"We have plenty of recourse," I said. "Engaging those Apache is no part of recourse."

"None other than backing away, and that's no longer a recourse. We are already retreating in shame," he said. "I'll not let a few raggedy redskins hinder me."

"I don't think so," I said.

"We will take the fight to the enemy," said Payton. "If, in fact, that is the enemy."

"You can count on it," said I. "Just wait until we can get to the top of that ridge over there and give it a good look see."

"Very well, get going," snapped the Lieutenant. "But I'm sending that patrol forward to the halfway point. If there is more provocation from those murderers out there..."

"Pierpont, Andy, Zach. You all come on with us," I said. "We'll head down those far side canyons if things go awry here."

"Let's go," said Andy, and Zach nodded along.

"Coming?" I said to Bigfoot.

"I reckon I will," said Bigfoot. "This boy plans to get those soldiers killed."

At the ridge top I pulled my field glasses out and watched the Apache sitting cross-legged around the fire. They weren't just lounging. I could see their faces clearly. Two had their back to a fallen tree trunk, bleached ash gray from years in the sun. They watched the cavalry column intently. All three had new Spencer carbines across their laps.

The Apache made a show of leaning their rifles against the tree and raising their hands. But they hadn't stepped away from the guns. The land between the Indians and soldiers looked flat from down below. From up here it was easy to see the little dip in the ground, just deep enough to shield the men at the fire from cavalry bullets.

I cursed as the corporal led his squad closer, just a hundred yards from the Indians and a thousand yards from the column. I could hear the corporal and the men at the fire hollering back and forth, but could not make out the words.

The Apache grinned and shrugged and made a few servile gestures. Things I'd never seen a free Indian do for a white man in twenty-five years of fighting them. The soldiers seemed to relax some, but not much. They rode closer, their pistols all still aimed at the Apache at the fire. The answers the Apache gave, interpreted by the Tonks, didn't seem to satisfy the young corporal and I heard the anger rising in his voice.

With an explosion of gunfire and banshee screams, six Apache on horseback charged out from behind a blade-like red-rock ridge five hundred yards away. They jerked their horses to a sliding stop, unleashed a wild volley at the patrol, then wheeled around and galloped back into the hidden gorge. The Apache at the fire grabbed their guns and dove for cover.

The patrol charged off after the attackers. Hopkins screamed and the column raced forward, thundering flat out after the ambushers. The cavalrymen raced around the wall of rock, hidden from view for a moment. Then they were flashing past sharp, jutting ridges, the horses' neck stretched out, ears back, legs ablur, eating ground like they were at a racetrack. The hooting troopers leaned forward, pistols in hand, horses straining in the chase.

It was a thrilling chase to watch until the first four cavalry horses hit the heavy cable yanked up in their path. The horses crashed forward, flipping and flopping end over end, crushing the screaming riders still caught in the saddles. A ball of dust erupted as the other cavalry horses skidded to a stop, but it was too late. Dozens of rifles from both sides of the pass blasted a crossfire of hot lead into the chaotic column. A roiling cloud of red dust shrouded the ravine as the troopers wrenched at their reins, yanking their horses in one direction and then the other as bullets ripped into them.

Apaches in red head bands and belted calico shirts leapt out from behind every boulder and sage bush on the slopes of jumbled rock. They charged into the mounted cavalry men with pistols and hatchets and knives, dragging them from their bucking horses, screeching and shrieking like demons, five to every horseman. The horses reared and plunged, colliding as the Apaches swung their stone clubs and war axes in heavy blows. It didn't last three minutes. Kill shots ended the moans of the wounded troopers.

"What are we going to do?" asked Andy after a few stunned seconds.

"We can't be no help to them down there," I said. "I think its best we go find a cave and hole up for a while. Once the shooting's over they will realize we're not among the dead and come looking."

We were heading down the side of a ridge when rifle shots rang out and bullets started chipping and zipping off the rocky outcroppings around us. My sure-footed mustang took off, skimming over those rocky slopes like a mountain goat. I looked behind and saw a group of six or seven men galloping out of the gulch, shooting at us wildly. The fat Apache in the lead shouted, and the rest of them let out a whoop and spurred their horses across the canyon floor toward us.

We galloped over the scrubby hills for a good three miles, then slowed our lathered horses to a tired jog for another five. The rugged country didn't allow us to gain much distance on our pursuers. The escaped Higbee boy wasn't much of a rider, and neither was Pierpont, for that kind of circumstance. From time to time we could hear the yips of the men chasing us. The five Apache braves in castoff Union Army coats had been joined by two white men in range clothes and Confederate cavalry trousers.

Several times we thought we'd lost them but after a while they'd come back into view. I figured we could easily take that group by ambush, but stopping to fight was what they wanted. Finally, as dusk neared, we had not seen the pursuers in an hour and I saw a crack in the wall that led to a hiding hole I'd camped in years before.

"Up into those rocks up there," I said. We galloped down a narrow side canyon hidden behind a pastel striped, fan-shaped red-rock formation called the Spanish Skirts. The red sandstone cascaded out, ribboned by layers of crimson and amber and pearl that looked like the bright swishing skirts of a Jarabe dancer. Fifty feet in, the crevice narrowed more. We dismounted and led our horses another five hundred feet to a small green valley. The only entrance was the small gap we'd just come through. It had plenty of good grass and a spring with a few inches of clear water.

"Getting dark soon," I said. "Looks like a good spot."

"Yes, sir, nice and snug," Bigfoot said. "I'll take first watch."

"Should we try to get up onto the Llano?" Andy said the next morning.

"Not yet, better not try it. We'd be out in the open, completely exposed," I said. "Our horses are spent. With no cover out there, we'd be easy prey. We can stay put in here a few days. Let the horses rest up and get some good graze. No reason to rush anything."

"You could ask Lt. Payton about rashness, 'cept he ain't no longer with us," said Bigfoot.

"Getting hungry, is all," said Andy. The trail rations we had in our saddle bags were running thin, and risking a hunting shot or campfire was not an option. "This jerky and hardtack is getting purty stale. And there ain't much left, neither."

Bigfoot and I took turns watching for hostiles from the mouth of the slot. We saw no sign of any enemy, but one afternoon we did see some movement a few hundred yards below us. Down on a sandbar of the Prairie Dog, like they were waiting for us, were two of the Army pack mules. They had full saddle bags and panniers still strapped to their backs.

"Let's go get them mules," Bigfoot said.

"They'll just slow us down," I said.

186

"If pursued, we'll cut them loose," Bigfoot said. "But there might be some food in them saddlebags. And if it comes to it, I've et worse than raw mule."

"It ain't bad eating," I said. We started inching ourselves down the slope, scooting bush to rock, constantly scanning the canyon. The mules seemed almost glad to see us, apparently not understanding they might be a meal soon. They were only slightly stubborn as we lead them back to our hiding place and they provided a bounty. One set of panniers carried a crate of Walker Colt pistols and near fifty boxes of cartridges. There were some canned beans and salty sardines and a half wheel of cheese. Someone had been hoarding Arbuckles coffee and a few packets of Gayetty's Medicated Paper hidden in a hardtack crate. We couldn't use the coffee right away, but the Gayetty's was a relief.

On the fourth day we decided it was time to find our way out of the canyon. Going straight over the Caprock to the Llano would still leave us too exposed. Instead we followed an old Comanche trail toward the north end of the canyon. I was feeling pretty confident until we came over a rise and saw three Comanche braves spread out, staring directly at us. We turned around and retreated slowly over the hill, then broke into a trot. We hadn't gone far when an arrow thunked into a mesquite tree an inch from my head. Then the air filled with shrieks and war whoops as a dozen Comanche charged across the canyon floor toward us.

"Go! Go! Head for the skirts! Back the way we came!" I shouted. We cut loose the pack mules and galloped hellbent back over that game trail as fast as our horses would carry us. We came around a scrubby hill near our hiding spot but more Comanche had it blocked. Five hundred yards away was another narrow slot and we thundered toward it. We reached it just ahead of our pursuers and darted inside. The passage was clear of brush and choke-stones as we trotted our horses with no sound of pursuit. The trail widened until we came around a turn and, on the canyon rim fifty foot above us, was a line of mounted Comanche braves. They stared down through the sights of Spencer carbines with the midmorning sun bright behind them.

"Well, ain't this just a precious piece of pudding," said Bigfoot.

"Best reach for the sky, fellows," I said, as more Comanche rode in behind us. "We ain't winning this one."

"Hola," said the young Comanche brave, astride his horse at the center of the mounted warriors. He was an exceptionally handsome man in any society, with dark copper skin, high cheekbones and straight European nose. Young, maybe twenty, tight-jawed, dignified and solemn, his bronze body rippled with muscle. A single feather fluttered in a long, black braid of hair. He rode a big silver stallion with a double rig Texas saddle.

The other Comanche, more short and thick muscled, glared at us from their ponies. Like their spokesman they wore only breech cloths and buckskin leggings. I recognized them as the same group that had been dogging us, and I let out a slight sigh of relief that they still weren't painted for war.

The frowning warrior in charge barked a harsh, guttural command and rough red hands relieved us of our guns. The leader barked again and the Comanches on the rim lowered their rifles.

"Hola," I said. Most Comanche spoke at least a little Spanish. "Cómo se llama?"

"I am Quanah," said the Indian in Spanish. His intense gray eyes stared hard at me. Gave me a jolt for some reason.

"We have not come to fight the Comanche. We do not seek you. My name is Pete Horse," I said. "This is ..."

"I know who you are, Buffalo Man. I know who you seek," snapped the young brave. "I have known thus for three months...You come for the man with the visions who carries the holy sword."

"Yes," I said. "And he comes for you."

"That's what I am told," Quanah said.

# THE COMANCHE CAMP
## SEPTEMBER 1866

We left the canyon in single file, riding through a maze of hidden valleys and narrow gulches squeezed between rock walls. As dusk neared, we crossed the canyon floor and entered the open end of a horseshoe-shaped meadow. Steep rocky ridges curved around from the sides and the closed end was a thick juniper and hackberry forest on a slope with tall cliffs behind. Comanche braves with new rifles watched from rock ledges above as we rode through the dense trees. The trail dipped and hidden by the foliage was a crack in the rock just wide enough to let a single rider pass.

Quanah led the column through the narrow passage. After a few hundred yards the trail opened into a lush box canyon and Comanche encampment. The camp had a circle of buffalo-hide tipis and two women tended cooking fires. Another dressed a deer that hung from a tree. The rest of this band were all young braves, maybe twenty in all now.

"You will stay here," Quanah said, directing us to a pallet of buffalo robes under a canopy of tree branches. "Do not attempt to leave."

"What are your plans for us?"

"Are you men of honor?

"Yes."

"I'm told you are," he said. "Will you promise not to escape?"

"For how long?"

"For now."

"Can we talk it over?"

"It would seem to be a reasonable thing to allow," he said. I watched him walk away, across the campground. He stopped and spoke to the women at a cooking pot, and I could see him tilt his head our way.

"What do you think are their plans?" asked Pierpont.

"I don't know. I already told you. If they wanted to kill us, they could have trussed us up and cut out our giblets long before now," I said.

"Unless they just want to torture us," Andy said.

"They could have done that at any time, too," I said. "No reason for any duplicity."

"There ain't that many of them," said Bigfoot. "If we could just get at a few of them pistols, we'd have a fair fighting chance."

"No, I think we're safe," I said. "At least for now. Let's see how this plays out. Anyway, the longer we behave, maybe they'll let their guard down. Should we ever decide to make a run for the guns."

"As long as you trust him," said Bigfoot. "But lulling a Comanche to sleep is a rare thing."

"Well, there's no good reason or need for him to be tricky," I said.

"He's their chief? That young?" Pierpont said.

"Comanches have no permanent chiefs, but I guess he's boss of this particular crew," I said. "He seems to want something other than our scalps. I say we just sit back and see what it is that's had them dogging our trail like they have been."

"I don't see much choice," said Bigfoot. "I guess we can tell Quanah he has some lodgers."

I waved at Quanah and he walked back over to us.

"You have our word," I said. "We will not try to escape."

"Bueno. I will tell you if I plan to kill you. It will not be tonight," Quanah said. "If you need to make water, walk down below the trees. If you go to make water and do not return, your friends will die a very painful, slow death."

I watched the two women tending the nearby cooking pots. One had a weathered face and wide streaks of gray in her hair. The other was a young woman, not yet twenty, taller than the stubby little Comanche women. Her long black hair was thick and full and wavy down her back, tied by a single rawhide string. She wore a simple deer hide dress, greasy and ash smudged.

The old woman huffed with irritation as she brought us clay bowls of boiled turnips and radishes and charred deer steaks. Andy smiled and gave a friendly hello to the girl. The older woman glared with hate. The young woman's eyes stared straight down at the ground as she handed me the water bladder. If she understood what Andy said she gave no reaction.

"That's Coralee," said Andy after they walked away. "She's the purtiest darn gal I've ever seen."

"Maybe," I said. Even in the dust and harsh conditions of an Indian camp it was obvious the girl was a stunning beauty.

"Simon pure, she's pretty as a peach," said Bigfoot.

"Think she's scared to say anything?" asked Andy.

"If it's her, maybe," I said. "Also, if it's her, she's been a Comanche for twelve years, since she was six. She may not remember any English. She wouldn't be the only black girl living among the Comanche."

"Well, if it is her, what are we going to do?"

"Our options are limited at the moment," I said. "I suppose it will all become a little clearer in a day or two."

"Well, fellers, since they don't plan on taking our scalps, or roasting us over one of them fires, I suggest we get some shut eye," Bigfoot said after we ate. "Sure could go for a plate of eggs about now."

I laid back on my buffalo hide mattress with my saddle for a pillow and was soon sound asleep.

For the next few days we mostly stayed beneath the shade of the willow and cottonwood trees along the timbered creek bottom. The meadow was evenly split between cool shade and warm sunshine most of the day, and the bluestem grass was green and belly-high on the horses. The creek had a pool in the shade, beside dense thickets of plum trees and blackberry bushes.

On the far side of the creek, the canyon ended with a towering red cliff about two hundred feet up with barely a bush or weed growing on it. Behind the cliff was a straight drop off, too steep for anyone to come up other than with a grappling hook. We were allowed the freedom to walk around or bathe in the stream. Raw game meat and corn meal was given to us to prepare over our own fire.

Quanah came by a time or two and asked us questions in Spanish, mostly about the Army's movements, what their strength was, what their plan was. I answered mostly honestly that I didn't know. The young leader was a careful thinker, neither fast nor slow, but serious, seeming to give every option and possible outcome its due gravity. He would seem to study on it for a minute, grunt that he would return, and then walk off into the trees alone.

"Hello, my friends," said Quanah on the afternoon of the seventh day. He sat down beside us holding a big slab of buffalo roast wrapped in deer hide. "Eat. Fresh tasiwóo. Buffalo.

"You speak English?" I said.

"Some, maybe," he said.

"I suspected as much," I said.

"I had to see if you were plotting or lying," said Quanah. "It is good you did not. Otherwise it would be you roasting over the fire."

"Did we pass?"

"You still have your hair, don't you? Do you not remember me buffalo man? I recognized you on first day you led the spotted buffalo. I remember you. I have dreamed many times of the day I would find you," said Quanah. "You took my mother."

I stared at the boy. I remembered him. I had remembered him for years. Those light eyes that reflected fire at me in the burning Comanche camp on the Pease River. I had dreams about him, too. They hadn't been pleasant.

"I am Quanah, son of the great Quahadi war chiefs. I am grandson of Iron Jacket. My father is Peta Nocona. My mother is Nadua. You captured and stole her, and my sister Prairie Flower," said Quanah. "You and Charles Goodnight and Sul Ross. When I was twelve summers. On the Pease, the River of Tongues. I saw you. Woman killer, twice over."

"What is he talking about?" Bigfoot said. "You two know each other?"

"He doesn't know me, but I know him," said the young Comanche, his gray eyes aflame. Like before. The eyes that haunted me. "He took my mother, and now they hold her captive."

"Me and Charlie was guides for Sul Ross and a company of Rangers and Militia, back in '60," I said, staring hard at the young warrior. "We attacked a Comanche village. His mother is Cynthia Ann Parker. Me and Charlie caught her trying to run away."

"The White Squaw is his mother?" gasped Pierpont. Quanah's mother had become the object of enormous curiosity and attention after her rescue. She was discussed in parlors and saloons world-wide as a source of wonder. Captured at the age of eleven, she had spent more than twenty years living as a Comanche, wife to the fearsome war chief, Nocona.

"You say we took her. Some say we rescued her. I say me and Charlie saved her life," I said. "If you remember it, then you remember the soldiers were shooting everyone, old women, children."

"Especially old women and children," said the stern young warrior.

"Yes, there's some truth to that," I said.

"Much truth," Quanah said.

"Cynthia Ann taught you English? Your mother seemed not to remember any English when I caught up to her," I said. "The way I heard it, once she got back home, she had a real hard time remembering any."

"I think maybe that is true not so much," said Quanah. "I think maybe she keeps many secrets as she tries to escape her freedom with the white man."

"I guess so," I said.

"Why will they just not let her go?" said Quanah.

"I can't answer that," I said.

"Is it true they sell tickets for people to look at her?" he said.

"I don't think it's like that exactly," I said, knowing it was just about exactly like that. Or was for a while, anyway. For the first months after we'd found her. The actual story was not a happy one for Cynthia Ann. The last time I'd seen her I was riding through Fort Worth. Cynthia

Ann was part of a carnival, bound with rope and set out on a platform as her Uncle Isaac Parker sold tickets to large crowds that came to gawk at "The White Squaw." She hadn't been facially tattooed or disfigured like some Comanche captives I'd seen, but she was still a pathetic sight. Tears streamed down her face and she was muttering in the Indian language. Her face was drawn and scared, filled with sadness and misery. Her hair was cut short, a Comanche sign of mourning. The whole thing was hard to look at.

Last I'd heard, the Parker family still kept her locked in at night, and under guard during the day. She had made so many attempts to escape, to return to her life with the Comanche, that they started putting the dogs on her. Like Charlie moving his cows away from their home ground, the Parkers did the same with Cynthia Ann, moving her farther and farther away from the frontier with each escape attempt.

I didn't know the whole story, but I did know the Texas legislature had granted her a 4,400-acre parcel of land and an annual pension of $100. Her cousins, Isaac Duke Parker and Benjamin F. Parker, already two of the largest landowners in Texas, were appointed as her legal guardians. Since the stories I'd heard said she was usually locked in the house, I wasn't sure how she worked it.

"Ross says he killed my father," said Quanah.

"I've heard him make that claim," I said.

"It is a lie," said Quanah. "At least he did not kill him with bullets. He died of a broken heart. A broken spirit, from many years of mourning after you took his wife away. Now she dies a slow death, a slow torture of her spirit. And you say Comanche are cruel."

"How do you know this?"

"I get word from reservation Indians at the fort near where she is kept," he said. "Locked in a jail room at night, always being watched so she doesn't escape. They tell me these things. My people see many things at forts."

"She's 400 miles away in Van Zandt County, last I heard," I said. "You got some good eyes out there."

"That is true," Quanah said. "But what I say is true, too, yes?"

"Yes, sadly, I've heard the same thing," I said. "Like what else do your people see? Like you knew me and Charlie were coming?"

"Yes. I thought in the beginning maybe you came to kill us," Quanah said

"You knew who we were? That's why you've been riding beside us practically the whole way."

"We knew who you were."

"So, what now?" said I. "What do you plan to do with us?"

"I do not know. I have great hardness in my heart toward you, but this Higbee is maybe even worse."

"He's a sight more dangerous than me," I said. "You know why he is coming after you now?"

"The rifles," Quanah said. "He believes we have many that were meant for him."

"Do you?"

"We do not," said Quanah. "That was Tosahwi. White Knife's raid. He is generous and gave us each one rifle and pistol and many bullets. But the rest are far away from here."

"Besides the rifles, do you know why else?" I said. "He wants you to bend the knee to his sky god."

"That's what we have heard also," said Quanah. "Why?"

"To be saved."

"Even me?"

"Everybody."

"From what?"

"I'm not sure."

"Hunh," said Quanah. "I never asked anyone to save me. I never even knew I needed saving."

"That's a common complaint," I said.

"That will never be the Comanche way," Quanah said. "He is your enemy?"

"He is. I killed his son," I said. "Shot up some of his fellers. They were in the wrong, but Higbee doesn't see it that way. They're coming for me, too. Not with saving on their mind."

"Will you help us kill him?"

"Probably. I'd been thinking of discussing that matter with you. He's a bad one," I said. "If we don't, will you kill us?"

"Maybe," Quanah said, getting up to leave. "Very maybe, buffalo man. You have many blue coats coming, is that right? Many blue coats from many forts and you were sent to find Higbee."

"Well, that was the plan," said I. "After the massacre of the column, I do not know."

"It will be bad if the soldiers come to the Palo Duro," said Quanah.

"Yes," I said. "I know that is true. Bad for everybody."

"Yes."

"Just so you know, we thought we were doing the right thing when we returned your mother to the whites," I said.

"Yes, I understand why you took her. I do not understand why they keep her," Quanah said. "This war the blue coats had with the gray coats over freedom. Where is it for my mother? I think I don't want that kind of freedom."

"And now?" I said.

"And now we wait," said Quanah.

"And later?"

"We'll see when later comes," said Quanah. "I believe I can trust you. You may walk anywhere in this valley, but you must not try to escape. That would be very bad."

"You have our word," I said. "I appreciate your trust. It won't be betrayed."

"You speak the language well," I said when Quanah returned later that day. We'd walked back into the meadow and were watching the pony herd graze. "How did you come to know it so well? Your mother has been gone from here a long time."

"Missionaries. Buffalo hunters. Traders. Others."

"Captive women and children?"

"Some."

"Some that are here now?"

"Yes."

"The girl?"

"Yes. I had Sparrow listen, to see if you spoke in riddles, or planned an escape," said Quanah.

"Sparrow?"

"Sparrow-in-the-Morning," said Quanah. "The girl that brings you food. When she first came to us, she sang to the trees and the birds, like she was already a Comanche. It was not painful on the ears like I have heard white men sing, but so beautiful even the birds stop to listen."

"I see."

"I know very young I must learn the language," Quanah said. "Peta Nocona and my mother taught me that the great confrontation will be between Comanche and white man. It is best to try to know your enemy. So you can better understand the lies he is telling you."

"I've heard that," I said.

"Since Sparrow has been with us, she has always asked traders for white man's talking leaf books. I want to know the white man's language too, and how his brain works, and his spirit, to better fight him. So we read together," said Quanah. "She is like my little sister."

"I see."

"Sparrow is my translator when we meet the whites," he said.

"But you know English...and Spanish," I said.

"My enemies do not know this," he said. "I can hear the lies as they are spoken. I will know the promises they don't intend to keep."

"Your secret is safe with me," I said. "That is Coralee Tucker, isn't it?"

"Maybe. Once a long time ago," he said.

"Men come for that girl. You know that?" I said.

"Men I need concerned with?" asked Quanah.

"Two men. Britt Johnson and Bass Reeves."

"This Johnson I know, this other not, this Bass Reeves," said Quanah.

"Well, I reckon you will soon enough," I said. "He seems destined to get his name known."

"A good man?"

"One of the best," I said. "If you know Johnson, then you know."

"Johnson is a hard man," Quanah said. "His woman and children were in our big camp when he found them, and the white women, too. I hope Britt Johnson does not want to fight."

"He wants the girl," I said. "Not a fight."

"Why have they not come before now?"

"Her mother and father were slaves. They were sold across the country shortly after the raid that took Coralee," I said. "And then the big white man's war came. They had no way to come get her. No ransom to pay. Until now."

"Why were they sold as slaves?"

"Their owners were losing money," I said. "Slaves are expensive. The Comanche kept stealing them."

"Hunh," said Quanah. "So Comanche did a good thing."

"Sure," I said. "Sure. I guess."

"You know they will come?"

"Eventually. They probably don't want to shoot it out with a bunch of Higbees to get her, but they won't be deterred forever."

"She has been here a long time. What if she doesn't want to go?"

"What if she does?"

"She doesn't belong to me. She is not mine to trade," said Quanah. "She belongs to that old woman there, Stone Pony, and that woman's husband Red Otter. She will be expensive. Many horses. Red Otter has promised Sparrow to Screaming Hawk, to take her as his wife. Screaming Hawk is right now raiding in Mexico. He said he will bring back one hundred horses to pay for her. Does Johnson have a hundred horses?"

"Unlikely. What if she doesn't want sold for horses?"

"What's all that racket?" said Bigfoot, sitting up quickly from his afternoon nap. There was hooting and hollering coming from the trail, with happy answering shouts from the Comanche in the camp. Three Comanche came trotting into camp on horseback, leading the two Army mules we'd left behind. A Comanche was excitedly waving a bright blue package of Arbuckles Roast Ariosa over his head, and another held up a five-pound sack of good smoking tobacco. The only thing missing from the Comanche's most favored trade treats was a cone of sugar. I remembered I had a chunk of white in my saddle bags, and so far it hadn't been discovered. I'd make sure to let Quanah know. A little goodwill goes a long way with an Indian.

There was a lot of celebration as the Indians emptied the panniers of more pistols and ammunition, the coffee and tobacco. Out tumbled a pack of Gayetty's Medicated Paper. One Indian had opened a package of the moistened therapeutic paper and had filled a sheet with loose tobacco, rolling a very large cigarette. The other Indians were gathered around, watching and waiting anxiously for a puff.

"Hold up, Quanah," I said. "Tell your man there that paper he's using won't light. It ain't for rolling and smoking. It's got something called aloe in it. But if you think coffee is grand, wait until you try this. The Greatest Necessity of the Ages."

"What is necessity?" Quanah said.

"Sometimes it's hard to explain," I said. "Just come see me sometime after dinner. I'll show you. It's to use instead of leaves and such for things of a personal nature."

"No trick?"

"Nope, no trick," I said.

The days were passing easily. We'd been in the camp for a week and a half, lounging about mostly. Quanah didn't seem in a hurry to go anywhere. Messengers and fresh faces came and went, young boys at the cusp of warrior-hood mostly. The time of the Comanche Moon was coming fast, which meant there was probably no safer place in Texas than in a friendly Comanche camp. We mingled with the Comanche freely. Bigfoot had been a voracious killer of Mexicans for decades, but there was little entrenched ill will between him and the Comanche. Pierpont and Zach got over their case of the frights, and Pierpont scribbled furiously in the notebooks he carried in his saddlebags. He said he had a story of the ages, a story of the Comanche nobody else ever had and he was probably right. Few outsiders ever lived long enough to write it all down. Andy and Coralee acted as his interpreters as he interviewed Quanah and some of the braves. They all seemed to be getting along just fine.

"Why did you come for the Comanche before?" asked Quanah.

"The Comanche raided my people," I said. "The Comanche took many slaves for bounty. They took my mother and sisters. They took many Black Seminole scalps, too."

"You are Seminole?"

"I am Maroon. A Black Seminole. An Estelusti. My mother was a full Negro, the daughter of a slave that was brought here from Africa," I said. "My father was Spanish and Seminole mixed. He owned my mother. I was born a slave, as was my brother".

"When did the Comanche take your women?" Quanah said.

"It has been many years ago now. I was a young man. We lived on the Seminole Reservation in the Oklahoma Territory. The white man's generals forced us there on the Trail of Tears. They promised peace and freedom and a happy life. They put us on land controlled by the Creeks, who owned slaves just like the white man did," I said. "The Army lied. They did not protect us as they promised. Creeks and Comanches raided the new Seminole reservations to capture slaves. They also captured free blacks and sold them into Mexico. That's what happened to the boy Andy's mother. My women also."

"And that is when you joined Bravo-Too-Much, Captain Hays, and killed many Comanche?"

"I did. Yes," I said. "You seem to know many things."

"Yes, I know many things," said Quanah. "I know if you are lying."

"I'm not."

"Yes, I know."

"You killed many Comanche after that battle, too," Quanah said.

"Some," I said. "They was generally trying to kill me."

"Why do you care about the whites?" Quanah said.

"I try to help out the good ones if they need it," I said. "Just being neighborly."

"But you don't hate the white man?" asked Quanah.

"No, not the majority of them. Why should I do that?" I said. "Half a million of them just died trying to free people that look like me from bondage. It's good ones versus bad ones right now. Less worse, maybe. Like all people. Of all ages."

"And that many died fighting to keep you in chains, also?" said Quanah.

"Yes, like I said. Good men versus bad men. And too many times bad men deceive good men into doing bad things. That's the way of the world," I said. "My mother was from far across one ocean, and my father from far across the other. There's powerful men everywhere. Some are very good. Some are very bad. Most are in between. Good men must stop bad men. Otherwise we are not good men."

"This is true," said Quanah.

"You best be careful of the chief if you're sparking that gal," I said to Andy that afternoon. Earlier I'd caught Andy and Coralee slinking out of the bushes by the creek, with matching purple berry stains on their lips. I'd cautioned them then, too.

I'd also noticed Coralee had put on a fresh deerskin dress, very light with lots of bead work, and with none of the grease stains and rips and tears of her old one. She'd scrubbed her face to a shine and it looked like the old woman had spent considerable time brushing her thick black hair out to a glimmering fullness. She was striking. More than once I'd woken up in the night and noticed Andy wasn't on his pallet of buffalo robes.

"Maybe that chief best be careful of me," Andy said.

"You got it bad like that?" I said.

"I reckon I do," he said. He straightened up and stuck his chest out a little when he said it. I hoped I'd taught him better common sense than to try to back that up.

"Calm down. If it's as serious as all that, let me run it by Quanah before you get yourself kilt," I said.

"We must get her out of here," he said. "She's a Negro, not a Comanche. That's clear enough."

"Are you mooning, or lusting?" I said to Andy.

"I ain't just lusting," Andy said. It sounded like he meant it. We were sitting on our pallet of buffalo robes in the shade of our cottonwood branch canopy. Coralee was doing chores near a tipi at the edge of camp. He was keeping a close eye on her. There was more than the look of lust to him.

"As long as you don't pass along any regrets you might have got back at the fort," I said.

"Never did nothing to have no regrets," said Andy.

"So, all you and that pretty girl Eunice did was talk?" I said.

"Well, we didn't do that exactly neither," Andy said, slightly annoyed, like maybe I shouldn't be talking about Eunice when he was thinking about Coralee. Eunice was the past. I liked it like that. "Let's just say it left me feeling better about things."

"Just a handshake then," I said.

"Something like that," Andy said.

"As far as saving Coralee, its best to find out if someone wants saving before getting to it," I said.

"I'd want someone to do it for me," Andy said. "I sure wish someone had done that for my mama."

"Hard to argue with that," I said.

"I know well what you fear," I said to Quanah at dusk. "I lived many years on a reservation. It is bad living."

We had climbed to a flat rock at the top of the cliff that protected our meadow and looked out upon the vastness of the canyon. A pinkish half-moon rose above the horizon over the land of the free.

"It is sad you were on a reservation," Quanah said. "I do not want to be on a reservation."

"Yes, I hope you never have to," I said.

"You may go whenever you wish," said Quanah after a long silence.

"We will stay and fight Higbee if he comes," I said. "All of us. We talked it over."

"That is good, and I welcome you," he said. "But the Comanche don't need your help."

"No. I reckon not. But I need the help of the Comanche," I said. "It is not only for the Comanche. The Higbees and Walshes might be hoping to enslave my people eventually. He brings darkness to many people. I will fight him. Now. Later. More than once, I figure. Until it's done."

"And the Comanche will fight him more than once?" Quanah asked.

"I'd count on it," I said.

Quanah was quiet for a few seconds. His face was serious in concentration, though I couldn't tell if he was pondering Higbee or just focused on the cigarette he was rolling from the captured Durham tobacco.

"Is he a worthy adversary?" he said after construction was complete and he'd exhaled a deep lungful of blue smoke.

"More than capable, I'd say," I said. "If he gets his hands on all those guns, there could be pure hell to pay. Be wise and careful with those rifles. That's a war coming."

"It was coming anyway," said Quanah. It was a fact, spoken plainly.

"Yes," I said.

"What will happen once we vanquish the great white prophet?" said Quanah. "Will you return?"

"I will never return to make war. I will never return beyond the current line of forts to live. If I cross the Comancheria with cattle, I will pay all Comanche through whose lands I travel. Cattle or gold," I said. "I will find Quanah and pay him his tribute in addition to the others."

"And not to save us neither?" said Quanah.

"I don't see why I would," I said. "I have enough to worry about saving myself."

"Bigfoot, he doesn't fight the Comanche," said Quanah. "He rarely even fights the Mexicans anymore. He was a mighty killer of Mexicans."

"They killed his brother, who had surrendered. He took out his pay," I said. "He may have slowed some, but he ain't forgot. He's still not one to cross."

"No, I think not," said Quanah, drawing deep on his cigarette, the tip glowing red in the dusk. An owl hooted somewhere near the stream and off in the distance a wolf howled.

"There is something else," he said. "I want to talk to you about my mother."

"Shoot," I said.

"Will you bring her to me, after all this is done?" said Quanah. In the dimming light I could still see the shapes and shadows of the ridges and mesas in the canyon before us. I could see why Cynthia Ann so desperately wanted to return. When it was peaceful, there were few equals to the wonder of the Palo Duro.

"If that is what you want, I will try. I make you that promise," I said. "It may not be easy."

"No. I know it is not an easy thing I ask," said Quanah.

"I also have something else," I said. "I want to talk to you about the girl, Coralee. Sparrow."

"Yes?"

"Andy, that boy I'm with, is smitten with Coralee. She also is smitten with him," I said. "I think she wants to go home. She wants to live as a free Americano. Andy fears she will receive a beating from Red Otter. Or worse, from you."

Quanah's face was stern, but I thought I saw just the slightest hint of a smile behind the orange glow of his cigarette. I'd rolled us a couple more and lit his just before I'd mentioned Coralee. A peace offering, of sorts.

"Yes, I have eyes. I have been expecting this," said Quanah. "The others call him purple-faced-black-white-man-who-thinks-he-is-invisible. The berries by the shaded creek stay juicy."

"So you noticed," I said.

"I noticed. Everyone noticed," Quanah said.

"I see," I said. "They call him purple-faced-black-white man...what do you call him?"

"I call him silly indeed if he thinks he can canoodle unnoticed with a Comanche woman in a Comanche camp," Quanah said.

"Canoodle?"

"That is the word, yes?" Quanah said.

"Sure, I guess," I said. "You are not much older than he. You know how it is."

"I know how it is. That is why he is not dead," Quanah said. "Red Otter, maybe not so much. It is good he remained at the other camp. There would be trouble if he knew. He would not want to lose a hundred ponies."

"I'm sure he wouldn't," I said. "Maybe, when we are done, we can bring Red Otter a hundred ponies. Maybe two hundred."

Trading horses for women probably wasn't the best method. On the other hand, rounding up a hundred wild mustangs was no easy task. It took determination, initiative and a fair amount of smarts. Not bad traits for a husband. Andy had those traits, but since I'd volunteered him for two hundred ponies, I figured I would end up helping. But only so much.

"That would please the old man," said Quanah. "For the rest, Andy has no reason to fear. All in camp like Sparrow. She is a sister to many. Few like Screaming Hawk. He is a bully and a loudmouth. No one but Isatai'i."

"Good. I'll get Andy and we'll set down on the trading blanket with Red Otter when this situation untangles itself," I said.

"I am not her chief to stop her anyway, and she will receive no beating from me. But it would be worse than a beating for her if Screaming Hawk returns and thinks she has been with another man. Also, Red Otter will be very angry if he loses out on all those ponies," Quanah said. "It will be bad for me for such disputes to occur in my camp."

"I see."

"But I saw her look at him, too," said Quanah. "She is a nice girl who deserves better than Screaming Hawk. What of that boy?"

"Andy is rock solid," I said.

"Why has he not come to me himself?" Quanah said.

"He wanted to. I told him no. He does not understand the Comanche to come to you with such matters," I said.

"And you do?"

"Maybe more so than him," I said. "If you know me, you know that is true."

"Yes, I reckon so," said Quanah. "But if Red Otter objects, or Screaming Hawk shows up, that's between them. Screaming Hawk is a loud-mouth, but that does not mean he is not dangerous. Isatai'i will be pleased to cause trouble."

"That is Isatai'i? The fat guy always staring at us?" I said. A fat Comanche, a very rare thing, waddled around the camp, scowling at us and acting preachy to all the young braves. Some of the braves in the camp still watched us warily, but most had become friendly, or curious, and came and sat with us. We shared stories of hunts and battles, allies and enemies. All but one, and I'd noticed the hateful glares of the obese Indian.

"That is Isatai'i," said Quanah. "Whites killed his family, but he is a fool, and coward. I did not want him with us, but I could not stop it. He tries to sell the young ones dreams."

"A couple of them seem to believe what he's selling," I said as Bigfoot climbed up beside us. He brought a sack of tobacco and some rolling papers.

"They are foolish and impressionable," Quanah said. "He tells them the old ones talk to him, that they have given him special powers. That he can make them harmless from bullets. He claims that he has ascended far above the earth, into the clouds. He claims he conversed with the Great Spirit, who granted him these powers. He talked to your god book men too much, and then a horse kicked him in the head. But it is not my place to tell them."

"But you don't believe him," I said.

"He is the one that got kicked in the head, not me," said Quanah.

"You don't believe in the spirits?"

"I believe in the spirit of Sam Colt," Quanah grinned, patting the pistol on his hip. "That is what the Texians say, yes? Right now Isatai'i may be useful. He is vain and easily fooled, perhaps to suit my purpose. If need be."

"Why does he glare at us?"

"You have big medicine," said Quanah. "That worries him a little."

"His name..." Bigfoot said. "Ain't it..."

"Yes. Coyote, how do you say..." he said, making a V with his hands and slapping his groin.

"Cooter," I said. "I reckon,"

"Cooter," Quanah said, and broke into a big grin. "Hmm, Cooter. Yes."

"Dang, Coyote Cooter," said Bigfoot. "No wonder he's salty."

"You know, Buffalo Man, we didn't really even want the cows you allowed us to steal," said Quanah after we'd built our smokes and started puffing. "They just slowed us up. We left most in the plains."

"If you didn't want them, what did you want?"

"Just to see, would you kill us over fifty sick cows," said Quanah.

"You took quite a risk. You could have got a bunch of your braves killed finding out who we were," I said.

"Don't flatter yourself," Quanah laughed. "You would be lucky indeed to shoot a Comanche on a running horse at night in a storm."

"Yes," I said. "You're right there, but still you take a lot of chances."

"Maybe. But otherwise, what would be the point?" he said.

"I suppose," I said. "But why'd you have to whack me so hard in the head with that coup stick? I had a goose-egg for days."

"Just needed to get your attention," Quanah said.

"You got it, all right," I said.

Early the next morning I heard a commotion coming from down the hill, and then one of the sentries came running into camp. He spoke to Quanah in urgent tones while they both looked our way.

"We have intruders," said Quanah, walking toward us. "There are men down there in the trees. They say they want to talk to you."

"To me? What men are these?"

"I do not know, only that our scout said they made themselves known, and said they wanted to talk to you."

"Why me?"

"Don't know," said Quanah.

"Hallooooooooo up there," said a deep voice. "This is Bass Reeves. Is that you, Pete?"

"It's me," I shouted.

"It's me and Britt Johnson. And we found Clay Allison out there, too."

"These are the men that come for Coralee," I said.

"They are the good men you speak of?"

"The best. Deadly fearless," I said. "But they want the girl, not a fight. I give you my word on that."

"Then they may come in," Quanah said.

"Where you been?" I said when Britt and Bass had joined us near the entrance to our hideout. Their clothes and hair were flecked with bits of grass and leaves, and in some places caked with dirt. It looked like they'd done some serious sneaking to get here.

"Hither and yon, looking for little Coralee," Britt said. "She's here, ain't she?"

"She is, but she ain't so little," I said. "The chief says she can leave if she wants. Someone's going to need to come up with a hundred horses, though."

"You already spoke to him about it?"

"It came up in conversation," I said.

"Well, that's dandy, and I thank him," said Britt.

"Where'd you find this one?" I said, nodding at Clay.

"On a near-dead horse about a good rock throw ahead of a dozen painted Comanche," said Bass. "Not far from where I reckon you seen Barney Olmsby and them. What was left of them."

"We seen them," I said. "They were some decent fellows. Looked like they'd made a fight of it."

"They was and they did. Now we'll just need to figure a way out of here," said Britt. "There's a sizable contingent of Higbees coming this way. They are well provisioned, and heavily armed. Looks like they're planning on settling in. Maybe laying siege to you?"

"Maybe. We've halfway been expecting them. We knew there were some out there looking for us," I said. "How many is in a sizable contingent?"

"About seventy-five, maybe more," Bass said. "They don't seem to be in no big rush, but they're not far behind."

"How did you find us?"

"Ran into a couple Comanche I've had dealings with in the past," Britt said. "Friendly dealings. They're more than a little concerned about all those Higbees. They know Porter's past."

"I sure appreciate you risking your neck to tell us," I said.

"Getting that little girl shot in all this ain't going to help no one," said Britt. "If you all want out without a fight, we'll have to go now."

"This is not possible," said Quanah, who had been silently studying the men. "Our braves must return from the hunt first."

"Are you the chief around here?" asked Britt.

"Close enough," said Quanah. I was surprised to hear him speaking English. I took it to mean he trusted Britt.

"I've seen you before a few times," said Britt, looking at him hard.

"Yes, I am in camps where you searched for your family," Quanah said.

# THE ULTIMATUM

Our vantage point on the rocks above our sanctuary had a good view of the canyon floor below. We saw the riders coming from a long distance off. The big man leading the group was unmistakable. Porter Higbee's golden hair flowed over his shoulders and his beard swayed with the movement of his horse. Befitting a man of Porter's stature, his mount was a coal black, thick-chested stallion a good eighteen hands high.

Purnell Higbee rode on one side of Porter and a hawk-faced man with white hair and a white rag on a stick rode on the other. Five more men followed close behind. We allowed them to get within shouting distance before I fired a warning shot into the ground in front of Porter's horse.

"That's far enough," I shouted.

"Who's in charge here?" bellowed Porter Higbee.

"Hold on, we're coming down," I hollered back.

"I want to talk to the sinner that shot my son," said Porter, after we'd made our way down the hill. At the edge of the trees we'd made a small fortification of jumbled rocks and dead logs.

"I reckon that would be me," I said. "After him and his gang tried to dry gulch me and steal my horse."

"They say you shot him in the back," said Porter.

"He was in heavy brush when he was hit," I said. "Maybe he had his back turned, but I couldn't have seen his back if I'd been looking for it."

"You accusing my boy of cowardice?" said Porter.

"Cowardice? No. We have to go through this again?" I said. "Stupid, maybe. I didn't murder your son and you know it. He was trying to steal my horse. At gunpoint."

"He needed that horse in the furtherance of the lord's work," said Porter.

"If the lord would have asked, I might have give it to him," I said.

"Blasphemy. You'll answer in blood for that."

"You want a shooting war over something you know good and well your son and them other dimwits brought upon themselves?"

"That, and kindred matters," said Porter.

"Such like?" I said.

"You'll answer for the murder of my son. And I'm told the murderer of Myron Hoagland and Jeziah Haight has slunk into your camp like the dirty, stinking wet dog he is," roared Porter in his best thunderation tent-meeting voice. "Also, we come for the apostate Zachary. You'll give him up, or burn in Hell with him."

I hoped Clay hadn't heard the insults hurled his way. He was already acting halfway agitated.

"Ain't likely," I said. "Rumor is, you're here to get your hands on near a thousand rifles so you can start a shooting war. Trying to disarm these Comanche so you can fill their heads with your hogwash. Place them under your dominion. That's unlikely, too."

"I have been anointed to fulfill the Scriptural command that we bring the red man to Christ. Getting them rifles back would make my task easier, obviously," he said. "Since my interests and yours are clearly divergent, I want to speak to that chief directly. I don't suppose he speaks English?"

"Other than terbacky and coffee, nope," I said. "He's got a little interpreter gal. You and him can talk all you want. Sounds like me and you will come to triggers, regardless."

"I reckon its ordained. Go get them," he shouted. "And tell that chief he'll lose a lot of braves if he don't want to be reasonable about this."

"He ain't a chief, and I already told him that," I said. "The rifles ain't here, anyhow. The band that stole them is somewhere out on the Llano, and I think the Comanche intend on hanging on to them."

"I don't believe you. I paid good money for those rifles. I can leave the Comanche a few, certainly, as a gesture of good will. I'm willing to trade plenty, as had always been my plan. But I got to have the most of them guns," said Porter. "After we get them rifles back, we'll have a set down with the red heathen and discuss salvation."

"There's few of them rifles here," I repeated. "But there's enough that you'll lose a lot of boys trying to find out."

"My sons don't mind flying off to their heavenly reward in their pursuit to glorify the kingdom," Porter said.

"Then why in the Hell do you get so peeved when I send them there?" I shouted.

"That's between me and the Lord," said Porter.

"I think you and the Lord need to discuss that a little further," I said. "Seems like an awful high price to pay. Anyway, the Cavalry will be here soon, Porter."

"I doubt that. They would be here if they were coming. I don't care about no cavalry anyhow," Porter said.

"Maybe not, but the cavalry cares about you," I said. "I reckon by now there's warrants out to hang every Higbee and Smoot that can be found in Texas. They have finally issued the Federal writs for Mountain Meadows, and territorial paper for horse thieving, selling whiskey to Indians, armed robbery, insurrection and bribery of a state official."

"I'll not leave while you draw breath," shouted Porter. "You will answer for Ezra and Reuben. Whosoever sheds man's blood, by man shall his blood be shed. Vengeance sleepeth not, neither does it slumber. It will overtake you at an hour when you do not expect it, and at a day when you do not look for it. For you there shall be no escape. Ye shall be pitched into the lake that burns with fire and brimstone, which is the second death."

"Might be the third, after listening to you jawboning all damn day. Gol dawg, you're boresome," hollered Bigfoot. "You Brighamites sure talk a ton of smite. If you all smited as much as you talk smite, the whole world would be wearing magic underwear and being brow beat by half a dozen wives. Shoot Porter, or get off the pot."

"Blasphemer. Drunkards, whoremongers, idolaters and sodomites," thundered Porter.

"Sounds like someone follered me on my last trip to town," said Bigfoot. "Who's the blabbermouth that spilt the beans?"

"You'll not jest in the fiery pit," said Porter. "And it is nigh at hand."

"Why are you bothering folks around here anyway, Porter?" I said. "These Comanches don't want nothing you're peddling."

"The Holy Book says we are to bring salvation to the savages, so we're bringing it to them," said Porter. "After we attend to these immediate matters."

"Yeah, didn't your salvation kill about 400 Shoshone just a few years back?"

"The garden must be weeded from time to time for new flowers to thrive," said Porter. "I pray that will not be the case with the Comanche."

"You seem to find an awful lot of weeds."

"The garden has been left untended for quite some time."

"The Federal Government ain't going to be happy, you trying to start some big shooting war," I said. "Especially if it's meant to bring on Armageddon."

"You might be surprised, what actually pleases the Federal Government," he said.

"You may have a point there, Porter," I said. "I'll send for the man you want to talk to. His name's Quanah, and he's not dumb. He already told me he won't talk to you until you prove you're real. He wants to see all this magical armor you have. Wants to see if you really have big medicine."

"The lord doesn't need to put on frivolous displays to prove his power," Porter said.

"I don't think he's talking about the lord. Just you," I said. "He's come across a dishonest white man a time or two. He likes to be careful. He's not as sophisticated as your disciples. He actually wants to see some evidence. I suggest you play it straight up with him or you'll lose all that hair."

"I'll parley with the chief, but my patience is not infinite," said Porter.

"Alrighty then," I said. "You go get ragged out proper and we'll meet back here in two days, mid-day."

"Why wait two days?" said Higbee."

"Cause that's what the chief said."

Two mornings later, Quanah, Coralee, Bigfoot, a few Comanche warriors and I watched from behind the logs and sharp-edged limestone slabs as Porter arrived for the parley. Britt and Bass watched from the rock-tops, with their rifles aimed at Porter who was in full regalia atop his monstrously muscled black horse. A dozen men were spread out behind him.

"Is that the magic armor?" I said. I'd seen the armor of the Spanish explorers in museums and paintings when I'd visited Washington and St. Augustine. He was wearing a Conquistador chest plate. It was steel with copper plating and I could see a faded inscription chiseled in Latin across the bottom. He wore some short gold and purple robes beneath it, and it was edged with twelve stones of ruby, jade, turquoise and topaz. I'd never seen any such gaudy display of jewels in any conquistador painting, so I figured those must be his added seer stones.

"It is," Porter said. "The Breastplate of Aaron, brother of Moses. The Breastplate of Judgement."

"If you say so," I said. "And that's the sword, I reckon."

"It is," he said. "The Sword of Laban."

"Looks heavy," I said. The long blade was Toledo steel, and the hilt was gold plated with more precious stones.

"You're about to find out," Porter said.

Quanah and Coralee spoke back and forth briefly in Comanche, then Quanah spoke to me in Comanche.

"What's he saying?" said Porter.

"He said he doesn't want the girl to translate. He wants me," I said. "She'll just listen to make sure I'm quoting you right."

"How do I know that's what he said?"

"You don't," I said. "Deal with it.

"Hola, amigo," Porter said to Quanah. "I am your friend. I will bring great things to your people."

"Hola," Quanah grunted, a scowl on his face. He again spoke to me in Comanche, grimacing and moving his hands across his face in hard, sharp movements. It brought stoic nods and grunts of approval from his warriors.

"What's he saying?" said Porter.

"He says touch your nose," I said.

"What is that supposed to mean?" he said.

"I don't know. Indian stuff, I reckon," I said. "Touch your nose."

He touched his nose, and glared at me when Quanah's braves hooted in laughter.

"What's so funny?" Higbee said, with his finger on his nose as Quanah spoke again. "What's he say now?"

"Simon says touch your nose," I said.

"Oh, you think that's funny?" snarled Porter, face glowing red behind his beard.

"I'm just the messenger. But, yes, I got me a chuckle," I said, glancing at all the grinning Comanches, a rare sight. "Quanah wants to know why you came here, how you came to find that magic armor."

"I had a vision to come here," he said. "The angle Moroni gave me vision and sent me into the Palo Duro where I found the Sword of Laban, the breastplate, and the Golden Plates."

"Sounds a little fantastical," I said, repeating it in Comanche to Quanah.

"You resemble a Lamanite yourself," said Porter.

"Pretty sure I'm not," I said. "I'm not even exactly clear on what a Lamanite is."

"A Lamanite," said Higbee. "The Indian. The noble red savage."

"I reckon I'm about one quarter Lamanite," I said. "Does that mean I get one quarter salvation?"

"Don't be impious," he said. "It is disrespectful to the lord, and I won't stand for it."

"I am about a quarter Spaniard, too," I said. "I think that armor you found was left here by the Conquistadors. Not any chosen people, nor angels, nor macaronis."

"It may have been through them that it was left for me. It's hard to speculate," said Porter. "The facts remain."

"Chief wants to know what have the rocks told you today," I said after Quanah spoke again.

"Mockery will only make your eternal fire hotter. The stones say I am to destroy you, and those that ride with you. The Comanche that have given you sanctuary must be destroyed, in a giant ball of fire," Porter said. "Then we'll find the others and show them what great things the Lord has done for their fathers."

"Hunh," I said. "Well, I won't pretend to be surprised. What if me and my men just ride on out here and meet you on the battlefield. You still gonna bother these folks up here?"

"If ye are not the sheep of the good shepherd, the devil is your shepherd," said Porter.

"He wants you to be a sheep," I said to Quanah.

"I will make him a ewe," said Quanah.

"They haven't done anything to you," I said to Porter. "You got a beef, it's with me."

"They have provided succor to an apostate, a whore of Babylon," Porter roared loudly. "They are to be destroyed and cast into the eternal fire."

"That seems excessively harsh," I said. "You're just sore because he hoorawed you at Simon Says."

"Judgement has been passed. It is out of my hands."

"You're insane, you know that?"

"There will be no more words between us," said Porter. "Prepare for the vengeance of the lord to land on your head with fury."

"I don't think it needs to be like that," I said. "But if it is, when should we expect you?"

"Your end draws nigh," Porter said.

"So, this week sometime?"

"There's no way out for you. We can be patient."

By morning the Higbees had formed a siege line across the valley, a half-mile away. Their 300-yard-long line along the near edge of a shallow red-dirt ravine blocked our way to the open canyon floor. They'd piled tree limbs and brush in front of it, forming a flimsy barricade. I counted roughly seventy Higbees milling around behind their fortifications. A remuda of more than a hundred horses was being tended by some youngsters beyond the ravine. There were only a few saddled horses among the men facing us.

"Doesn't look like he plans to let us go any time soon," I said to Quanah as we watched from the rim of our fortress.

"We couldn't be in a safer place," said Bigfoot. "They can't get in, either."

"We can wait, only a few days. Our hunters returned last night and our raiding season is here. My men will not want to be prisoners," Quanah said.

"I don't think we can bust through there, not without taking heavy losses," I said. "Is there another way out you haven't shown us?"

"There is one, but even more narrow than the one we came in on," Quanah said. "Wide enough only for one person to squeeze through it at a time. And then only on foot and with great care. Horses cannot pass through it and in many places it is too deep for sunlight to reach."

"I have visited this site before," said Britt. "It's more a tunnel than a canyon. It's a drop of close to a hundred feet down and only a couple feet wide. It branches off and twists around like a maze. There's places that is knee deep in the bones of people and critters that took the wrong turn."

"Where does it lead when it does take you out?"

"Several places. The shortest branch comes out just on the other side of the Higbee's remuda. Others come out for miles."

"Well, if we had to," I said.

"If we had to, we'd come out into the open, on foot, and with nowhere to hide," Britt said.

"But to get a messenger out?" I said. "Quanah, what are your thoughts?"

"We have a pony herd hidden in a box canyon, north of here. Following the hidden trail, a brave could reach them in three hours if he ran hard the whole way."

"Do you have ropes?" I said.

"We have ropes. But little help is close by. Only the old, and the women and children remain in the Palo Duro now," said Quanah. "It is raiding season. The warriors will be along the Texas settlements. Or down in Mexico. Many days away, and on the move."

The waiting was hard on Quanah and the Comanche. These young warriors wouldn't be satisfied hiding from a fight for long, especially not during the season of the Comanche Moon. It was the time that every Comanche man lived for. The only thing holding them together was a temporary allegiance to Quanah, and any brave was free to go. It would not help Quanah in the future if his men left now because we were avoiding a fight. That was just not the Comanche way. Clay was never one on waiting, either, and was getting discomposed enough that Bigfoot put him to work digging holes with a spade from the pack mules.

"Why is that white man digging holes?" said Quanah as we walked through the camp. Clay was just beyond the ring of tipis, neck deep in a ditch ten feet long.

"He gets real fidgety sometimes, and digging holes is what he does," I said. "I'm not clear on it myself."

Clay had been out on a scout when the Comanche had wiped out Barney Olmsby, One-Eyed Bill Hoover and that gang. He was greatly disturbed that he had missed a chance at such a ferocious shooting fight, and claimed to harbor a grudge even though he barely knew the dead men. He lost a fair amount of supplies and personal items in the attack, including his slick pistoleer outfit. He was pretty unhappy about that, but the Comanche had no interest in trading it back to him. He was kept from causing disaster only by pointing out that he was, in fact, alive, and with that pugnacious and ill-tempered crew of frontiersmen, it was hard to say who provoked the incident.

"That's all he does, walk the earth and dig holes?"

"And shoots folks, apparently," I said.

"What folks?"

"Them that rile him," I said. "So far, it has always been bad folks."

"I thought maybe he was trying to escape," Quanah said. "If he can escape by digging a hole in the earth, I will allow it."

"No, it's not that," I said. "Just a nervous condition."

"It seems common in the Americanos," said Quanah.

"Some of 'em do seem to get more overwrought about things than situations merit," I said. "I think fellows like Pierpont there have some responsibility for a lot of that."

Two mornings later, just before dawn, a young Penateka Comanche boy arrived in camp. His name was Sits-in-the-Sun and he had slipped through the Higbee line. He said it had not been difficult since the Shizzites were spread out and slept soundly. He said there were lookouts but they snored the loudest of all. The message he brought alarmed Quanah.

"There is a group of men, Apaches and Anglos, that have left those men down there. They are riding toward our village three days north, at Yellow Spring," said Sits-in-the-Sun. I was examining the boy's ankle. He had badly sprained it hurrying to get here in the dark. "They are in great danger. The men are all out raiding. It is only women and children in the camp."

"How many riders are headed for the camp?" Quanah said.

"Twenty," said the boy. "More than enough to kill everyone."

"I don't figure that's it," I said. "Now, taking them hostage to get those rifles would be something Porter would do."

"Yes, this is what I would expect," said Quanah.

"That still leaves a good sixty men down there. They still outnumber us," I said. "But I suppose three to one is better than four to one. If we break out through the line, is there time to reach the other tribe before Higbee's men get there? That's a long time with their head start."

"Higbees follow the river. The path they follow is much longer," said Sits-in-the-Sun. "They leave many liquor bottles. They argue often and are careless. I was able to get close and listen. They brag about what they will do to the women when they reach camp."

"If we can get through the line, we can get there first," Quanah said. "There is a good trail that cuts through the hills. But someone must get out to warn them. Should we fail."

"We can't waltz down there in broad day light," said Bigfoot. "They'd see us coming and blow us out of the saddle the moment we cleared the trees."

"But maybe we could walk our horses to the edge of the trees after dark fall" I said. "Hit them just as the sun comes up."

"They are facing due east," said Bigfoot. "That helps. Some."

"That is the only way. We must send a messenger out immediately," said Quanah. He called for Coralee to come over.

"She can run for three solid hours in the dark over this rough ground, and ride for another twenty-four?" I said.

"Yes, she is Comanche," he said. "She is light and rides as well as any warrior. She can run longer and faster than many braves."

"Fair enough," I said.

"Do you know the way?" Quanah asked her.

"Yes, I have been that way before. Many times," she said. "I know how to reach the ponies, and find the Penateka."

"Good," said Quanah. "Make your preparations and meet us at the edge."

"I should go with her," said Andy.

"You'd just slow her down, or get yourself lost down there in them narrow slots. Didn't you hear him say she'd have to run three hours? And ride for twenty-four, without pause? Do you really think you can do that?" I said. "Honestly now."

"No, I don't reckon I could."

"All right then, let's get back to planning this fight," I said.

"Yep, you're right. Hit 'em before they have time to think. When they still got sleep boogers in their eyes and they're taking their morning squats," said Bigfoot. "That'll knock the sparks out of them."

"We'll have the surprise with us," I said. "But that's still long odds."

"Maybe I can improve them," said Britt. "That first trail we talked about, that comes out behind their remuda? I think, if we could get in there and scatter their horses, they might be a tad disconcerted by that. Me and maybe two braves could stampede the whole herd. They might think there's a bunch of us if we're loud enough and get them ponies running in all directions."

"You think so?" I asked Quanah.

"Yes," Quanah said. "That is what I would do. There will be moonlight to see the way."

Within five minutes Coralee had returned wearing her old torn rawhide dress and thick moccasins. Quanah called the others together and told them our plan. Then I watched as they lowered Coralee down the deep, dark crevice between the rock walls.

# THE CONFRONTATION

"Those fellows familiar on how to use those guns?" I said to Quanah as I watched the young braves gird for battle.

"They know," said Quanah.

"How many of these men have been in a shooting fight before?" I said.

"Few. But they will fight."

"Tell your boys not to shoot until we're on them, and then get in close with those pistols," I said. "Powder burn 'em. The Jack Hays way. Stick the barrels in their ribs, and thumb them hammers. Hard to miss that way, no matter the rough ride."

"Comanche know how to fight Hays way," Quanah said. "We know well how Bravo-Too-Much fought. Hays fought the Comanche way. You just had better guns."

"Can't argue that," I said. "Just tell your fellows not to shoot until we can reach out and touch them. Shooting pistols from a galloping horse is no more likely to injure a Higbee than throwing paper wads."

"What is paper wad?" Quanah said.

"It'll turn into a knife and club fight real quick, I imagine." said Bigfoot.

"Knife and club fight is good for Comanche," said Quanah. "Bad for Higbee."

"Yes, but they still got us three to one, maybe more," I said. "It won't be no picnic."

"Comanches no picnic," Quanah said.

"I'm not questioning," I said. "But you know it's never what you expect. It can be a real shock to the system, even to the bravest men.

Those boys are young."

"Not so young," said Quanah. "Did it happen to you?"

"It still happens to me," I said. "So, I try not to think about it. Just checking is all."

"And those boys with you?"

"I don't know," I said. "Andy, I figure will be fine. The other? Going against his own kin? I'm going to stay close to him."

"That is good."

Throughout the camp the young warriors went about their solitary preparations for war. Sitting cross-legged in the grass, they held small mirrors in one hand and dabbed war paint on their faces with the precision of a barber. On their chests and arms they made bold strokes and stripes and slashes of white or red or yellow against a thick layer of black. They made their own designs, and had their own medicine. Quanah painted himself completely black from the waist up. He added a stripe of bright red across his eyes and nose, with two slashes of red down his chest. Once their paint was just right the warriors applied a generous slathering of bear grease to make it shine. The young Comanche wore long-bladed knives around the waist. Some wore necklaces of grizzly teeth or breastplates of hair-pipe beads. Each carried at least one Colt, a new Spencer carbine, and more ammunition than most Comanche warriors held in a lifetime. The boys that yesterday could have passed for ornery schoolboys pulling girls' pigtails had become the demonic killers whose image struck fear across all Texas and beyond.

Back by our fire, Bass was oiling his pistols. Beside him was his double holster gun belt and a slick shoulder contraption for two more. Britt polished a buck knife and his gleaming Yellow Boy carbine stood against a tree. Zach and Andy were likewise tending to their weapons. Bigfoot was eating a plate of prairie hen eggs that Coralee had brought him special.

"You two don't have to fight the Higbees," I said to Bass and Britt.

"I reckon I'm in it 'til the finish," said Bass. "I've been wanting me a piece of Mr. Higbee ever since we left Belknap. I'll take that sword of his and give it back to him in a manner he'll find unnatural."

"We come to get that girl safe back to her mama," Britt said. "We didn't ask no questions about who we'd have to fight get her. It ain't a material issue."

"If we get through this and mama gets her girl back, she'll likely have a son-in-law as well," I said. "Her and Andy is quite taken with one another."

"That ain't exactly no hushed-up secret," said Britt. "She's free to do as she pleases. But her mama sure wants her back."

"Yes, and she wants to see her mother," Andy said.

"She remembers her?"

"Some," Andy said. "I am worried about her out there all alone."

"I figure Coralee will be just fine," Britt said. "She's been running through these canyons for the past ten years. This is her world. Her land. Something else to keep in mind once we whip these Higbees."

"What do you mean?"

"She's lived with Comanche for a long time," Bigfoot said. "Moving back into civilized society ain't going to be an easy thing for her."

"We know," Andy said. "But that is why she always got books and newspapers from white visitors to their camp. To get some understanding."

"Still ain't the same," Bigfoot said.

"You'll not discourage me," said Andy. "We'll live on the Seminole Reservation, where she can adjust more gradual."

"It's going to get mighty hot down there," I said to Zach and Andy. "Charging men that are dug in like that. They did a poor job of building their barricade, but it's still going to be rough."

"Ah, you was in plenty of them," said Andy.

"Not like this. Those Indians had old muskets and arrows," I said. "Most of these boys have repeating rifles themselves. Big difference."

"I reckon," he said.

"You know how many bullets they can put in the air in thirty seconds?" I said. "A lot more than you'd think, and it'll feel like a hundred times more than that."

"I just hope Britt and his Comanche sneakers get around behind them," he said.

"If any man can, Britt can," I said. "Zach, you really don't need to do this. Those are your people and all."

"They ain't my people, I been telling you that," said Zach. "I don't have no kin among 'em. Not in my mind. If I can get me a shot, there's one or two I'll be looking to plug special."

"So, what do you think of all this, Mr. Pierpont?" I said. "Reckon you'll have a story your readers will like?"

"I already have enough stories to keep my readers riveted for the next five years," he said. "This one will be a fine story too, if we just ride on out of here. Can't you talk sense to them, come to some sort of a resolution?"

"Unlikely. And even less likely to be anything Higbee will honor for long," I said. "He claims to be sent by the Lord. I expect another vision would come to him soon. That seems to be generally how them things work."

"Them reformers is always the hardest to dissuade," said Bigfoot.

"Those men intend to kill us, all of us. If not this time, it will be another," I said. "But since you've written them flattering stories about Carleton, they're likely to save you for last. And let the Apache play with you for a few days."

Pierpont swallowed and looked a little peaked. It didn't help when Bigfoot pointed to Pierpont's Colt and told him to always save a bullet for himself.

The red Comanche moon was in the sky when we lowered Britt and two braves into the deep slot canyon behind our camp. I had every bit of faith in Britt and those with him, but navigating through those dark, twisting gorges in the dark would require every ounce of their abilities.

As soon as the ropes went slack we gathered up and headed out to meet the Higbees.

We rode single file down the narrow, rock-walled passage toward the open meadow, silent but for the muffled footfalls of our horses. The space was tight, and I smelled bear grease and horse dung and my own nervous sweat. At the entrance we dismounted and spread out through the trees, using the moonlight to move cautiously down the slope. We stopped often to listen to the hum of the bats and bugs and other creatures of the night. When the sounds continued without pause of alarm we'd take a few more wary steps. It took four hours to descend the two-hundred-yard wide strip of trees that hid the entrance to the Comanche camp.

At the edge of trees we mounted up. Quanah and I were in the center of our battle line, with ten or so Comanche braves to his right. The American contingent and a few more braves lined up to my left. Andy was beside me. Bass was next to him, and then the line continued on to Bigfoot bringing up our left flank. Pierpont was there, too. He was waiting back at the entrance to our sanctuary, ready to record the incident as it unfolded. The old woman waited with him, as did Isatai'i, who had somehow come up lame walking down the trail.

Below us, the lights of more than a dozen Higbee campfires stretched out across the mouth of the valley. As the blackness of night became the gray pre-dawn we could see a few of them up and about tending cooking fires and coffee pots. It was a brisk morning and there was a slight breeze ruffling the leaves as the sun rose higher in the east behind us. Spreading sunlight slowly revealed the valley while we remained in the shadow of the cliff and trees. Morning birds started chirping and a woodpecker was already hard at work just above our heads. The Higbee pickets hadn't spotted us yet, and didn't seem to be paying much attention.

"Ready?" I said to Quanah, the red and black paint fierce across his handsome face. Down the line to his right the young Comanche were poised and ready. So were those to my left. Still, the half mile of open grass we'd have to cross looked as wide as Kansas.

"Ready," said Quanah just as shouts and gunfire erupted from across the canyon floor. Britt and the two braves charged out of the brush near the horses, whooping and shrieking like banshees. Britt fired shots in the dust near the young horse tenders and the panicked boys raced off toward open grassland.

The Higbee men, ripped from sleep, leapt up in alarm at the unexpected attack from the rear. They fired a ragged barrage of hurried shots as Britt and the braves sprinted through the herd screeching and flapping blankets.

Quanah screamed like a panther and our line of Indian ponies burst out of the trees. Feathers and scalps and calico streamers whipped in the wind as we streaked over the grass. Beyond the ravine, Britt and the braves had leapt atop some saddled horses and were stampeding a hundred loose horses toward the Higbees' defensive position.

Bewildered Shizzites recoiled at the howling terrors roaring down on them from out of the sun. A few shot at us, and a few shot at Britt. Most took one look at the painted screeching devils coming for their lives and took off running. We hit their line and soared over the flimsy tree-limb parapet, blasting pistols at the scrambling Shizzites. Several fell to our guns and others scurried down the ravine, seeking cover behind rocks and sage brush. The stampeded horses thundered down into the ravine, kicking up a thick, choking cloud of red dust.

Dodging careening horses we chased the fleeing Higbees through the swirling red cloud. Warriors screamed their lobo wolf war cries as their agile Comanche ponies spun and darted to cut off the escaping Shizzites. I heard Bigfoot and the others blasting away behind me as the Comanche warriors leapt from their ponies and split Shizzite heads with sharpened stone war clubs. Thrashing tangles of arms and legs rolled past. It was knife work then, and it was bloody. The sharp blades of the Indians at my feet dug deep into the bellies of the Higbee men and sliced them open to the breastbone. I fired at shadowy targets as a charging horse crashed nose-first in the dust near me and threw its rider ten feet.

In the whirling dust and smoke I caught a glance of a dismounted Bigfoot hoist a screeching Shizzite high over his head and heave him into a sun-crisped brier patch. Bass galloped through on his big white stallion, reins in teeth and slinging lead with both hands.

Out of the corner of my right eye a young Comanche took a bullet and went wheeling off his horse. Another horse galloped past, and a Comanche clinging to the offside fired his pistol underneath his pony's neck at a mounted Higbee rising up to take a shot at me. The Comanche bullet caught the Shizzite square in the throat and he flipped backward in a spurt of bright red blood. Quanah galloped his big gray through the dust. A ferocious swing with his steel ax sliced off a man's shoulder. A second removed the man's head. Up on the bank I saw Clay and a cluster of Apache shooting pistols at each other from ten paces away. Twenty Higbees lay dead or dying and only a few still stood and tried to make a fight of it.

I hadn't seen Porter Higbee. It looked like we'd won this battle pretty handily but if Porter wasn't put down there would be many more. I knew I had to find him. I rode past the rock wall and onto the open grassland. Two hundred yards away a dry creek bed ran between two squat, flat topped buttes. I trotted my pony that way, stopping beside the ditch in a small mesquite patch to reload my Colts.

Just as I snapped the last cylinder closed a gang of Higbees galloped around the nearest butte, not a hundred feet away. Porter Higbee, in full armor, was in the lead. He charged straight at me on his giant black stallion. Porter's mane and beard swept over his shoulders and his cape of purple and gold flapped in the wind. His steel breastplate shined and he waved the gleaming, golden hilted sword high overhead.

I put spurs to my pony. The horse leapt ahead but his hoof came down in a sandy dip and he stumbled. He recovered quick, but the big war horse of Porter's was upon us. I ducked as the massive chest of the big black smashed into my mustang and Porter swung his sword mightily at my head. The sword missed but the impact of the crash blasted us off the edge of the steep ravine, sending me and my mustang air-borne and belly-rolling. I flopped down the embankment as Porter's big black soared over my head. My ribs slammed into a kettle sized rock and pain exploded through me. My right hand struck a sharp-edged limestone and knocked the gun from my hand. Porter's big horse skidded in the dust and he whipped around to face me.

In the blue fog of pain I saw Zach and Andy galloping toward me, but a barrage of shots from Porter's men caught them. Zach's arms flew up and he flipped out of his saddle. Andy cut his horse sharply and charged his attackers. He shot one from the saddle before his horse crashed to the ground and he went sliding face-first through the dust.

Porter had dismounted and was walking toward me, sword raised, smiling, eyes gleaming, ready to administer the death blow. I screamed with pain as I clawed at my left side pistol, pulling it up and dropping it with my shattered hand. I groped for my boot scabbard with my left hand and pulled out my bone handled Bowie knife. I got to one knee, coughing blood on the ground as Porter smirked. He towered over me, the deadly sword raised in both hands.

I heard running feet and a war cry. Quanah Parker was sailing through the air, long-bladed knife in hand. As he sailed past Porter his left arm hooked the big man's throat. Quanah yanked Porter to the ground with a loud, dusty thud. In a single motion, his Bowie knife swung down and through Porter's throat, pinning him to the ground. Blood spurted and Porter's legs kicked half a dozen times. Then he shuddered and fell limp. When Quanah walked toward me, his hands were empty. His last weapon, the bone handled knife, was sticking out of Porter Higbee's throat like a battlefield obelisk.

The group of Shizzites that had shot down Andy and Zach had turned toward the unarmed Quanah. Porter's sword was on the ground not far away, but that wouldn't save Quanah. Porter had a pistol belt on, but the gun was under his steel-clad bulk. Quanah grabbed the only weapon he could, a dead tree limb as the Higbees closed in. He stood tall and started his death chant as the Higbees got closer. Their guns and eyes were on the young Comanche chief and they didn't see Andy rise up out of the sage, aiming his Henry rifle. His first shot blasted a Higbee from the saddle. He jacked the lever and kept firing from the hip as he walked toward us, blood streaking his face, shirt ripped half off from his slide through the prickly pear. Two more Higbees flipped out of their saddles and the others raced toward the open grass.

The shooting had stopped and the Shizzites were dead or gone. I saw some movement from beyond Andy. Zach stood up shakily, bright red stains on his shirt. Andy put an arm around him and helped him walk. Bigfoot had joined them, putting Zach on his horse until they reached us. They had just plopped down next to me when a distant dust cloud appeared far down the canyon.

"Oh, what now, look over that way," Andy said, looking toward the horizon.

"It's Carleton, God Bless that murdering bastard," Bigfoot said, looking through binoculars. "He'll be tickled pink to find you've taken care of Porter Higbee for him, Quanah. That should buy you a fair piece of good will."

"Maybe," Quanah said. "But I cannot trust that to be true."

"No, I reckon not," said Bigfoot.

"I reckon you got that big medicine now, Quanah," I groaned through the pain. "You will make a fine leader of your people."

"Maybe," Quanah said. "And now we must get to our village."

"Yep, probably better get moving," I said. "We'll make sure Carleton don't send anybody after you."

"Are you coming with me?" Quanah said to Andy.

"Yes," Andy said, then asked me. "You going to be all right?"

"As long as the pony soldiers will drag me under some shade and let me lay still for a few days until these ribs heal, I'll be fine," I said.

"Good. I'll be riding on, to find Coralee, try to get that other camp to safety," Andy said.

"I wouldn't expect otherwise," I said, with a half-smile, half-grimace. "Best get going. Time to shine, Bravo-Too-Much."

"You are a brave man, Andy," said Quanah. "And a worthy man. If Sparrow wishes to go with you, she is free to go. I cannot deny her what I wish for my mother."

"Thank you," Andy said.

"You saved my life. For that, you are my brother," Quanah said.

The historical characters in Beyond the Goodnight Trail

## CHARLIE GOODNIGHT, CATTLE RANCHER

Charles Goodnight, later to become known as the "Father of the Texas Panhandle," first joined the Texas Rangers in 1857, at age 20.

In December 1860, he was the scout for Capt. Sul Ross's combined Ranger and U.S. Cavalry column that attacked Peta Nocona's Comanche camp on the Pease River. The raid resulted in the rescue of Cynthia Ann Parker, the daughter of a prominent white family. She had been kidnapped by the Comanche in 1836, at the age of 9. The return of "The White Squaw," after 24 years of Comanche captivity, became an international sensation.

During the Civil War, 1861-1865, Charlie served in the Texas Frontier Regiment guarding against the scourge of raids by guerrilla bands and Indians which flamed across Texas in the absence of the Army.

In 1866, Charlie and Oliver Loving drove their first herd of cattle northward along what would become known as the Goodnight-Loving Trail. The original trail extended 600 miles from Ft. Belknap, Texas to Ft. Sumner, New Mexico and the Bosque Redondo Navajo Reservation there. Eventually the trail stretched 2,000 miles through Colorado into northern Wyoming. Over the next couple of decades, the Goodnight Trail was one of the most heavily used cattle trails in the West.

For his initial drive, Charlie rebuilt an army surplus Studebaker wagon to meet the needs of his eighteen men for the two months on the trail. His creation was dubbed the "chuckwagon."

After many years as a successful cattleman Charlie founded the JA Ranch in the verdant Palo Duro Canyon, the first ranch established in the Texas Panhandle.

In 1876, Charlie realized the bison were on the verge of extinction due to the devastating Indian War policies of the U.S. Government. Charlie started a herd on his ranch, which, for many years, was the only surviving bison herd in America. Charlie's herd of bison continues to thrive today and probably saved the species.

## JOHN COFFEE "JACK" HAYS, TEXAS RANGER

"Cap'n Jack," "Devil Yack," "Colonel John C. Hays," "Bravo-Too-Much," "Sheriff Hays," "Surveyor General Hays."

John Coffee "Jack" Hays, the oldest of seven siblings, was only 15 years old when his parents died. To support his brothers and sisters he found work as a land surveyor, an occupation that he would pursue intermittently for many years.

Jack was the great-nephew of President Andrew Jackson.

After the fall of the Alamo in March 1836, Jack joined the Texas Rangers at the age of 19. He quickly rose to the rank of captain. Jack was also an officer of the Republic of Texas Army. He fought in the Comanche and Mexican wars from 1836 to 1848. During the Mexican-American War, Colonel Jack Hays served with General Zachary Taylor and commanded the legendary First Regiment of the Texas Mounted Rifle Volunteers. The Hays Regiment gained nationwide fame during this conflict.

Hays, who is called "the greatest Ranger chief in the history of the Lone Star State" and "the ideal Texas Ranger," was a brilliant tactician, known for his enormous courage and gallantry. He instituted a strict training regimen for his men, and formed them into a cohesive, disciplined and greatly feared fighting unit.

Hays was the first Ranger captain to use the Navy Colt Paterson five shot revolver. He outfitted each of his men with at least two Army surplus revolvers and extra, pre-loaded cylinders they could swap out quickly in battle.

At Walker's Creek, Texas, on June 8, 1844, Hays and his fourteen men were confronted by up to 200 Comanche warriors who had been raiding across Texas. Jack ordered a charge, surprising the Comanche who expected the Texans to be armed with their single shot weapons. The ferocity of the charge by the Rangers, and their overwhelming firepower, sent the shocked Comanche fleeing. The Rangers pursued, inflicting a devastating number of casualties while suffering very few. The battle at Walker's Creek marked a turning point in Ranger warfare. It was the first effective use of revolvers in close combat.

In 1849 Hays moved to San Francisco and was soon elected Sheriff. He built the city's first permanent jail, disbanded a murderous vigilante group called the Committee of Vigilance, and declared that all accused criminals had a right to a fair trial.

At the start of the Civil War, John "Jack" Coffee Hays declined offers of command by both the North and the South.

## BOSE IKARD, TRAIL SCOUT

Bose Ikard was born into slavery in Mississippi in the 1840s. His mother was the slave of Dr. Milton Ikard, who is believed to have been Bose's father. Dr. Ikard moved his family and slaves to Texas in 1852 and Bose became a skilled ranch hand, cowboy and Indian fighter.

Obtaining his freedom after the Civil War, Bose was a vital member of legendary West Texas cattleman Charlie Goodnight's first crew which blazed the Goodnight-Loving Trail. He stayed with the Goodnight herds through 1869.

"Bose surpassed any man I had in endurance and stamina," Goodnight said. "His behavior was very good in a fight and he was probably the most devoted man to me that I ever knew. I have trusted him farther than any man. He was my banker, my detective, and everything else in Colorado, New Mexico and the other wild country... He was the most skillful and trustworthy man that I had."

Charles Goodnight had this statement inscribed on Bose's gravestone: "Bose Ikard served with me four years on the Goodnight-Loving Trail, never shirked a duty or disobeyed an order, rode with me in many stampedes, participated in three engagements with Comanches, splendid behavior."

## BRITT JOHNSON, INDIAN FIGHTER

Britt was born a slave in Tennessee in 1840. He came to Texas as a child, with his master, Moses Johnson. Although legally slaves, the Johnson family was allowed to live as free people. As a young man, Britt was appointed foreman of the ranch in Young County where he raised his own horses and cattle.

During the Comanche and Kiowa Elm Creek Raid of 1864, Britt was away from his farm. When he arrived at his home he found the raiding Indians had killed his son and taken his wife, two daughters, and several white women and children as captives.

Moses Johnson gave Britt his manumission papers and a substantial amount of money so that he could search for, and ransom, his family and the other captives. The other ranchers and people in the area, including other slaves, also chipped in on the reward.

Britt made several trips into Indian Country and his search became legendary. He befriended several Comanche and lived amongst them for months. The Kiowa finally agreed to ransom his family and others in 1865.

After getting the captives safely home, Britt used his fame and respect to build a freight business in Weatherford, Texas, traveling between Forts Richardson, Belknap and Griffin.

On January 24, 1871, a band of Kiowas attacked his wagon train in Young County. When his body was found, there were 173 spent shell casings scattered around him.

## BASS REEVES, LAWMAN

Bass Reeves was born into slavery in Arkansas in 1838. Bass was eight years old when his owner, Arkansas state legislator William Steele Reeves, moved his family to Texas in 1846. William Steele Reeves's son, Colonel George R. Reeves, a sheriff and legislator in Texas, became Bass's enslaver after the move.

When the Civil War broke out, George Reeves enlisted as an officer in the Confederate Army. He took Bass Reeves along as his personal body servant. One night in a Confederate Army camp George and Bass got involved in a heated argument over a card game. The dispute led to Bass giving George a severe beating before escaping to freedom in the Oklahoma Indian Territory.

Bass initially lived with the Creek Tribe, but, after discovering they were slave owners, he joined the Black Seminole Reservation. He learned Indian customs and languages, as well as many tracking and man-hunting skills. Bass worked as a border guard for the Black Seminole and stayed in the Indian Territories until the War ended.

Free, Reeves returned to Arkansas, married Nellie Jennie from Texas, had 11 children, and became a successful rancher. He also often served as a scout and guide for U.S. Deputy Marshals which had jurisdiction over Indian Territory.

Isaac Parker was appointed federal judge for the Indian Territory in 1875, with a mandate to hire 200 deputy U.S. marshals and put an end to all the violence in the 75,000-square-mile Indian Territory. The Territory was then a safe haven for outlaws and was filled with criminals hiding from the law.

Parker heard of Bass's abilities and actively pursued him. Bass hired on as a deputy U.S. marshal for the Western District of Arkansas and was the first black deputy to serve west of the Mississippi River. Reeves worked for 32 years as a federal peace officer in the Indian Territory, and became one of Judge Parker's most valued deputies.

Legendary for his valor and determination, Bass captured more than 3000 outlaws, and killed 14, during his long career. Reeves brought in some of the most dangerous criminals of the time, but was never wounded, despite having his hat and belt shot off on separate occasions.

Bass was a master of disguise, and sometimes left a silver dollar as his calling card. Many argue Bass Reeves was the inspiration for the "The Lone Ranger."

When Oklahoma became a state in 1907, Bass Reeves, then 68, became an officer of the Muskogee Police Department. He served for two years before he became ill and retired.

Bass Reeves died January 12, 1910.

## WILLIAM A. A. "BIGFOOT" WALLACE,
## TEXAS FRONTIERSMAN

William Alexander Anderson "Bigfoot" Wallace was a legendary Texas frontiersman, soldier, Texas Ranger and scout.

Bigfoot was born in Lexington, Virginia in April 1817 and was a descendant of the Scottish Highlanders William Wallace and Robert Bruce.

After learning that his brother was killed in the Battle of Goliad during the Texas War of Independence with Mexico, 19-year-old Bigfoot went to Texas determined to "take pay of the Mexicans." Bigfoot fought in many battles and campaigns against the Mexican Army, including in the Mexican-American War.

In 1842, Bigfoot fought with the Texan Army to halt an invasion by the Mexican Army. He fought with distinction at the battles of Salado Creek and Hondo River. Later, he joined the Somervell and Mier expeditions into Mexico, which ended in disaster. Bigfoot, along with hundreds of others, was captured and spent two years in the notoriously brutal Perote Prison in Vera Cruz. Although many of the Texans managed to escaped, they were quickly recaptured, then forced to participate in the "Black Bean Incident." Black and white beans were placed in a crock at a ratio of ten black beans to one white bean. The prisoners drew from the crock. Any man who drew a black bean was executed on the spot. Wallace drew a white bean.

Following his release, in 1844, Bigfoot joined the Texas Rangers under Jack Hays, fighting border bandits and Comanches until the outbreak of the Mexican War.

During the Civil War Bigfoot was a Lieutenant in Capt. R. A. Gillespie's Company of Texas Mounted Volunteers. In his later years, in exchange for his loyal service, the state of Texas granted him land and he ran a small ranch on the Medina River.

## JOHN HORSE, BLACK SEMINOLE LEADER

Juan Caballo, John Caballo, John Cowaya, or Gopher John El Capitán Juan Caballo.

John Horse was the most successful black freedom fighter in U.S. history. He was the warrior leader of the Black Seminole against invading American forces in Florida in the Second Seminole War. He was the war chief, political leader and dominant personality of the Black Seminole people for half a century. As a diplomat, John argued for the freedom and permanent land for his people in the courts and political chambers of Washington, D.C. and Mexico City. He survived three wars, four attempts on his life, and the relentless pursuit of slave hunters.

The Black Seminole were associated with the Seminole Indian Tribe but lived and thrived as a separate, self-sufficient society. Nominally considered slaves of the Seminole in an arrangement set up for mutual defense, their bondage was closer to tenant farming, in which they paid a percentage of their harvest to the Seminole.

During the Second Seminole War (1835 – 1842), John Horse rose to become a feared and respected Black Seminole warrior. This Second Seminole War was fought after the Indian Removal Act of 1830 was enacted, forcing 100,000 Native-Americans from their lands in Georgia and Florida and onto reservations in the Oklahoma Indian Territory. This forced exodus was known as Trail of Tears, and thousands of Indians died along the way.

Rich plantation owners coveted the fertile Florida land, and considered all Black Seminoles as valuable property to be returned to them. Although some Black Seminole were escaped slaves, most were descendants of people who had escaped slavery 150 years prior. Some were legally freed. However, all were considered property.

For over two years, John led a ferocious guerrilla campaign against the overwhelming American invasion. He gained national fame as a war leader fighting alongside dynamic Seminole war chiefs Osceola and Wildcat.

By spring of 1838, John realized the fight against the Americans could not be won and negotiated the best terms for his people. He was given the promise of freedom for his band of fugitive slaves and free Black Seminole if they would surrender and agree to relocation to Oklahoma.

John agreed and the Black Seminole moved. However, that treaty was broken as soon as they arrived in Indian Territory. They had been given a reservation on land controlled by the Creeks, who were slave-owners themselves, and had the same slave codes as the American South. The Black Seminole settlements were frequently raided by Creek slavers, white slavers and Comanche kidnapping and enslaving blacks, freedmen or not. The Army refused to protect them.

Fearing that his family, and other Black Seminoles would be re-enslaved, in 1849 John Horse led hundreds of Black Seminoles on a frantic escape to Mexico, with Creek Indians, the U.S. Army, white slave hunters and Comanches hot on their trail. The group was granted land by the Mexican government in the state of Coahuila. In exchange, the Black Seminole agreed to fight against Apache and Comanche raiders.

## CLAY ALLISON, GUNFIGHTER

Clay Allison was a cowboy, cattle rancher and notorious gunfighter of the American Old West.

When the Civil War broke out, Clay immediately enlisted and fought for the Confederacy in the Tennessee Light Artillery. He was soon discharged, after threatening to shoot a superior officer who wasn't chasing fleeing Union troops as vigorously as Clay thought he should. The reason given on Clay's medical discharge was "Emotional or physical excitement...a paroxysmal of mixed character, partly epileptic and partly maniacal." Clay's Army records state that the outbursts could have been the result of a head wound he suffered as a child.

Clay quickly reenlisted, this time with Gen. Nathan Bedford's 9th Tennessee Cavalry. He served with them until the end of the war, and became a scout and a spy. Legend says that at the end of the war, he was convicted of spying and sentenced to death by firing squad, but killed his guard and escaped.

Another says that after the war, back home in Tennessee, Yankee soldiers showed up to foreclose on the family farm. Clay shot and killed one of them. Once in Texas, Clay did settle down for a while, and learned ranching. He became an excellent cowhand, even signing on for Charlie Goodnight's first cattle drive on the Goodnight-Loving Trail.

However, before long, Clay was back to his wild ways and quickly gained a reputation as a greatly feared killer, gunfighter and vigilante. He survived dozens of knife and gun fights and was implicated in several vigilante jail break-ins and lynchings. Clay played a significant role in the Colfax County War that claimed some 200 lives.

In 1876, in response to a negative story in the local newspaper, he blew up the newspaper office with black powder, and threw the printing press into a nearby river. Another impressive tale says that a highly intoxicated Clay once rode his horse through town wearing only his gun belt. When a deputy tried to arrest him, Clay overpowered the deputy then forced him to drink whiskey all night as Clay sat there naked. After an extremely painful tooth extraction in 1886, an angry Clay held the dentist at gunpoint and pulled several of his teeth.

In 1887, Clay Allison was killed when he fell off a wagon and it rolled over his head.

## JAMES HENRY CARLETON, U.S. ARMY COLONEL

James Henry Carleton was a U.S. Army officer and a Union general during the American Civil War. He spent most of his career as an Indian fighter in the southwestern United States.

In 1859 Carleton investigated the Mountain Meadows massacre in southern Utah. One hundred twenty Arkansas emigrants, men, women, and children, had been killed. Carleton concluded that Mormons, dressed as Paiute Indians, had committed the murders and plundered the wagon-train's possessions. However, the American Civil War soon had the full attention of the government and the perpetrators of the massacre were not brought to justice.

In October 1862, Carleton established Fort Sumner and the Bosque Redondo Reservation. He sent Col. Kit Carson and his Army into New

Mexico and Arizona with orders to kill all Navajo and Apache men who resisted coming to the reservation. Carleton was quoted as saying: "All Indian men of that tribe are to be killed whenever and wherever you can find them... If the Indians send in a flag of truce say to the bearer that you have been sent to punish them for their treachery and their crimes. That you have no power to make peace, that you are there to kill them wherever you can find them."

Carson and Carleton campaigned relentlessly, killing Indians, destroying their crops, and stealing their livestock. Over 8,000 Navajos and Apache were starved into submission and surrendered. The Bosque Redondo experiment ended in failure, however. The land and water were poor and the captured Indians faced constant death, disease, and hunger. Eventually, the high cost of maintaining Bosque Redondo persuaded the government to allow the Navajos to return to their homeland.

## QUANAH PARKER, WAR CHIEF

Quanah Parker was a leader of the Quahadi band of the Comanche Nation. He was the son of Comanche chief Peta Nocona and Cynthia Ann Parker. Quanah's paternal grandfather was the renowned chief Iron Jacket.

Quanah's mother, Cynthia Ann, was a member of the prominent Parker family that settled in east Texas in the 1830s. At age nine, in 1836, she was captured by Comanches during the Fort Parker massacre. Cynthia Ann fully assimilated into the tribe and later married Peta Nocona. In December 1860, during the Battle of Pease River, Cynthia Ann was unwillingly "rescued" by the Texas Rangers and forcibly returned to white society. She tried to return to her Comanche people many times and eventually was held as a prisoner by the Parker family.

Quanah rose to become the most powerful, and last, war chief of the Comanche. He led his people in many successful campaigns against the Cavalry and overwhelming odds. The starvation of his people after the destruction of the bison herds eventually forced his surrender during sthe Red River War of 1874.

242

After surrender, Quanah Parker led the Comanches successfully for a number of years. He built schools, created ranching operations and brought in agricultural technology. He established the first Comanche police force. He promoted self-sufficiency and self-reliance, and encouraged the tribe to function in contemporary society.

Quanah had many very prominent friends from white society, including President Theodore Roosevelt who often visited him to go on hunting trips.

## CYNTHIA ANN PARKER

Cynthia Ann Parker is the most famous Indian captive in American history. The daughter of a very prominent Texas family, she was nine in 1836 when she was kidnapped by the Comanche during infamous Fort Parker Massacre.

Cynthia Ann lived with the Comanche for the next twenty-four years, fully assimilating into the tribe. She married the powerful Comanche War Chief Peta Nocona, with whom she had three children. Her son Quanah would become the last great war chief of the Comanche.

In December 1860, Texas Rangers and U.S. Cavalry, led by Captain Sul Ross, with Charlie Goodnight scouting, attacked a Comanche hunting camp in what became known as the Battle of Pease River. They discovered Cynthia Ann and returned her to her white family, which she had not seen in a quarter-century.

She no longer remembered the Parkers. She was miserable and wanted to return to the Comanche, who she now considered her people. She tried to escape many times, and was kept as a prisoner. Heartbroken, she stopped eating and died in 1871.

Alan Lemay's novel entitled "The Searchers," and later the movie of the same name starring John Wayne, were based on Cynthia Ann's story.

## MOUNTAIN MEADOW MASSACRE

The Mountain Meadow Massacre was a horrific, brutal and bizarre slaughter committed by Mormon militiamen on Sept. 11, 1857, in southern Utah. The Mormons, dressed as Paiute Indians, and joined by a few actual Paiutes, murdered 120 members of the Fancher Party, a peaceful wagon train comprised of a dozen large and prosperous families, making their way to California.

At the time of the massacre, Utah and the United States were on the brink of war. Utah was ruled by the Church of Jesus Christ of Latter-day Saints and its President Brigham Young. The U.S. Government saw Young as a religious dictator and his power made them nervous. The Mormons of Utah were convinced the U.S. was preparing to invade them.

Oblivious to the rising passions, the Fancher train crossed the territory, stopping in the Mountain Meadow to rest for a few days. The Mormons viewed the wagon train as unwelcome intruders, and church leaders spread rumors the people in the train had previously engaged in religious persecutions of Mormons. The militia whipped up a frenzy of hate and paranoia.

The painted militiamen first attacked on Sept. 7, and the siege continued for five days, by which time the Fancher party ran completely out of water. On the 11th, a small party of militiamen scrubbed off their war paint, and approached the wagons with a white flag. They told the desperate travelers they had negotiated a truce with the Paiutes, who they claimed were behind the attack. They persuaded the Fancher party to let them escort them out of the territory.

The forlorn Fancher Party agreed. After handing over their weapons, the travelers were escorted away from their wagons. On a given signal, the militiamen attacked and killed all the adults and older children in the group, sparing only seventeen very young children. These children, deemed "innocent blood" by Mormon doctrine, were adopted by church members.

Members of the militia were sworn to secrecy. A plan was set to blame the massacre on the Native Americans. and the truth would be concealed throughout the church hierarchy. Brigham Young himself would play a part. The massacre is called "the most hideous example of the human cost exacted by religious fanaticism in American history until 9/11."

Few of the culprits were ever brought to justice, and that didn't happen until decades later. One man, John Lee, was executed for the massacre in 1877.

## BLACK SEMINOLES

The Black Seminoles are black Indians associated with the Seminole tribe in Florida and Oklahoma. Also called Seminole Maroons, Seminole Freedmen, Estelusti, or Black Muscogulgesa, historically they were a society of free blacks and runaway slaves living in Florida from the late 1600s to the early 1800s. Allies of the Seminole, the Black Seminole lived and thrived as a separate self-sufficient society.

In an arrangement set up for mutual defense, the Maroons were considered slaves of the Seminole. However, their bondage was closer to tenant farming. They paid a percentage of their harvest to the Seminole, were allowed to own weapons, and had control over their labor. Seminoles refused to sell them or turn them over to slave hunters, and protected them fiercely. Many Black Seminole rose to become esteemed war leaders, negotiators, and interpreters for the Seminole chiefs.

The Maroons lived in separate communities next to the Seminoles, with their own leaders and political systems. The two groups sometimes intermarried. Black Seminole culture and religion were a mix of Seminole, African, and European customs and rituals. The Black Seminoles were relatively prosperous and amassed significant wealth. Many knew English, Spanish and the numerous Indian dialects. The language of the Black Seminole was an English Creole similar to Gullah.

In the 1830s wealthy planters and investors wanted the fertile Florida land already cultivated by the Seminoles and Black Seminoles. The planters also demanded the return of their hundreds of slaves that had escaped the plantation and found refuge with the Seminoles. Those same Southern slaveholders lived in constant fear of the hundreds of armed Seminole Freedmen. Raids on plantations to burn crops and entice slaves to escape were common.

The federal government enacted the Indian Removal Act in 1830, which stated the government's intent to move the Seminoles from Florida to what is now Oklahoma. This mass removal also included 100,000 Cherokee, Creek, Chickasaw, Choctaw, and Seminole. 15,000 died during the horrific exodus called the Trail of Tears.

Some Seminole bands resisted ferociously. By 1835, large scale battles were being fought in the Second Seminole War. The Black Seminoles joined the Seminole Indians in fighting a vicious guerrilla war against the U.S. Army. They took the lead in a slave rebellion, raiding hundreds of plantations. They recruited many slaves to join the fight against the rich planters and their militias and armies. Black Seminoles were recognized by friend and foe for their bravery and ferocity in battle and their excellent strategic minds, most notably John Horse.

By 1838, the leader of the Black Seminole, John Horse, realized the war against the massive U.S. Army was unwinnable. He had been promised freedom for himself and all Black Seminoles if they would surrender and move west. John Horse agreed to those terms and took his people west.

However, the Army never honored their promise of freedom. In Oklahoma, the Black Seminole were placed on a reservation controlled by the Creek Indian Government, longtime enemies of the Seminole and Seminole Maroons. The Creeks practice chattel slavery, just as brutal, or worse, as the ante bellum South. The Black Seminole were subjected to the Creek slave codes, and were banned from owning weapons and property. Creek, Cherokee and Comanches raided the Black Seminole communities, capturing free blacks and selling them into slavery. The Army offered little protection.

In 1849, John Horse led hundreds of Black Seminoles on a frantic escape to Mexico, with Creek Indians, the U.S. Army, white slave hunters and Comanches hot on their trail. The Black Seminole established a prosperous community in Nacimiento, Coahuila that continues today.

## NOTES:

Charlie Goodnight
https://www.legendsofamerica.com/we-charlesgoodnight/
https://www.tshaonline.org/handbook/entries/goodnight-charles

John Coffee Hays
https://www.tshaonline.org/handbook/entries/hays-john-coffee
https://www.texasranger.org/texas-ranger-museum/hall-of-fame/john-coffee-jack-hays/
https://www.legendsofamerica.com/law-johnhays/

Bose Ikard
https://www.tshaonline.org/handbook/entries/ikard-bose
https://blackcowboys.com/black-cowboys/bose-ikard/

Britt Johnson
https://truewestmagazine.com/britt-johnson/
https://www.tshaonline.org/handbook/entries/johnson-britton

Bass Reeves
https://www.bass-reeves.com/
https://www.washingtonpost.com/history/2019/12/14/fiercest-federal-lawman-you-never-knew-he-was-african-american/

Bigfoot Wallace
https://www.history.com/this-day-in-history/texas-ranger-big-foot-wallace-born
https://www.legendsofamerica.com/we-bigfootwallace/
John Horse
http://www.johnhorse.com/black-seminoles/faq-black-seminoles.htm
https://www.archbalt.org/story-of-john-horse-a-black-seminole-warrior/
https://www.questia.com/library/journal/1G1-13689004/john-horse-forgotten-african-american-leader-of-the

Clay Allison
https://www.history.com/this-day-in-history/gunfighter-clay-allison-killed
https://www.legendsofamerica.com/we-clayallison/

James Henry Carleton
http://www.drumbarracks.org/index.php/en/key-figures/117-james-henry-carleton
http://militarymuseum.org/Carleton.html

Quanah Parker
https://www.tshaonline.org/handbook/entries/parker-quanah
https://www.legendsofamerica.com/na-quanahparker/

Cynthia Ann Parker
https://www.tshaonline.org/handbook/entries/parker-cynthia-ann
https://www.history.com/this-day-in-history/cynthia-ann-parker-is-kidnapped
Mountain Meadow Massacre
https://www.historynet.com/mountain-meadows-massacre
https://historytogo.utah.gov/mountain-meadows-massacre/

Black Seminoles
https://www.thoughtco.com/black-seminoles-4154463
https://texoso66.com/2020/02/27/black-seminoles-of-texas/
http://howcanamandiebetter.com/black-seminoles/

Made in the USA
Monee, IL
27 June 2021